Lindsay.
WJAC's news is n[...]
moved up! I miss
coming into my livingroom everyday!
J.T. Baroni

CW01024169

The Legend of Rachel Petersen
(Revised Edition)

J.T. Baroni

Published by Sky Publishing, 2023.

The Legend of Rachel Petersen
By J.T. Baroni
Cover Art by: Dawne Dominique
Original Version Edited by : April Duncan
Revised Edition Edited by: Skyler Baroni
Copyright 2023 J.T. Baroni

I would like to dedicate this book to my lovely, loving wife, Rebecca. Without her words of inspiration, my words never would have been.

To my son, Skyler, thank you for doing a great job editing these words.

The Legend of Rachel Petersen

— By JT Baroni —

Chapter One

Christian Kane, on this particularly important night, knew better than to recline back in his much too comfortable, overly plush Lazy Boy while waiting for his wife as she prettied herself for their evening out.

The man dared not prop his feet up; rather, he sat erect. From lessons learnt in the past, he knew if he went horizontal while she got ready, he would definitely end up dozing off.

He was not allowing himself to make that mistake tonight, not a snowball's chance in Hell!

His antique Wall Hugger should have been tossed out years ago during Spring Cleanup, but the beat-up chair had become molded perfectly to his buttocks; Christian deemed it too damn comfortable and couldn't pitch the old recliner. It has been his friend since college, an inanimate one, but one whose sanctuary he could rely upon at any time.

Over the years, due to his nodding off and not gently reminding her of the time, husband and wife ended up being late for numerous appointments. It did not matter if the scheduled event were a casual dinner date with friends, or a crucial business meeting such as the very decisive function slated for tonight at the downtown Pittsburgh Sheraton; but try as he may, he could never seem to rush his wife.

Hoping she'd take the hint to *get her ass in gear*, he's nervously been jangling his car keys for the past twenty minutes while staying upright in his recliner, trying like Hell to stay awake and *not* yawn; it seemed his eyes would automatically go closed if he did. However, they would not always re-open!

Meanwhile, his incredibly attractive wife has been sitting in front of her makeup mirror, *fussing with every single blond hair on her head.* He so desperately wanted to be early, or at the least, be on time.

Especially tonight, of all nights, God!

Too bad for him, he let the RSVP invitation lay on the table last week and she knows what time tonight's gala event starts, or he would have told her it began thirty minutes earlier than the actual time. This little trick he frequently employed worked in the past for the couple to be where they were supposed to be on time, or at the least, arrive only ten minutes late.

For several of the more important occasions, he had to drive like Batman, but he got them there on time!

Even though it was days-old news, ESPN, as it has been every day for the past eighteen years, played on the TV at a low volume. Having already heard this regurgitated drivel, the bored man was no longer able to ward off Mr. Sandman; he succumbed to a huge yawn that clamped his eyes tightly shut!

Albeit he put up a respectable fight, his resistance was all in vain, for the man drifted off to Dreamland while waiting for his wife once again!

Now sound asleep, he still clutched his keys; but snoring had replaced jangling.

Upon subconsciously hearing the sports announcer say, "That's all the news we have from the dugout, let's go now to the ice rink where Sidney Crosby has just signed a new three-year contract with the Penguins," Christian sprang to his feet and bitched at himself, "I can't believe I did it again! Damnit!"

The man knew ESPN's time slots; therefore, he knew it was a quarter past six. He guessed he slept for only five minutes before the announcer's statement caused that ice cold sense of being late to descend over him and he jumped up.

Uncannily, this was one of his ways to keep track of time, for he never wore a watch. To Christian Kane, a wristwatch was just one more electronic gadget requiring batteries, and the man absolutely hated any *hi-tech crap*, especially when it either took batteries, or needed plugged into a charging port. He had no idea what a USB was, or how to program co-ordinates into a GPS; the only reason he carried a cellphone was because his boss insisted upon it; however, he hardly ever used it.

Christian was definitely *not* the stereotyped husband who hogged the remote control; but as previously stated, ESPN seemed to be on the tube constantly, so rarely did the 24/7 sports channel ever change; also, that station was the only one programmed into his car radio.

This man devoted his life to sports, and the woman he married, but not in that order.

After another big yawn escaped him, Christian frowned as he once again headed back to the bedroom; this would be his *second attempt* at hurrying his wife along; according to his schedule, they were already thirteen minutes late leaving for the annual awards banquet.

More so than any other day of their lives since their wedding, tonight could possibly turn out to be the most significant life-altering event for both of them, mainly him. The man just could not believe that his wife would be lollygagging this long!

He tried reassuring himself, "Perhaps I'm just anxious about tonight; I still have time. If the red lights co-operate, I can make it to the Sheraton in less than twenty minutes."

Upon entering the room, his tone held a hint of patient urgency when he asked his wife, "Shelby, Honey... Are you *about* ready?"

"Relax, Baby, it's only fifteen past six. The dinner doesn't start for another forty-five minutes," she said with a casual stroke of her hand.

"Let me touch up my hair and pick out a necklace, then I'll be all set."

She twisted a curling brush through her already perfectly combed bangs, applied another little spritz of hairspray, then reached over and pulled a necklace from her jewelry box.

"How's this angel pendant look?" she asked while holding her favorite piece of jewelry to her neck, a sterling silver necklace he gave her for a Christmas present a year before they exchanged wedding vows.

"It looks great because I picked that one from the display case myself many Christmases ago," he razzed her, then said, "But it's a tossup between that one..." he pulled a long and skinny black box from the pocket of his rented tux, handed it to her, and finished his statement, "... and this one!"

She gave him her, "*You shouldn't have look*," then asked, "What's this?" She opened the box, then gasped ever so lightly when laying eyes on the beautiful string of pearls nestled in the black velvet liner.

"Oh, Christian! These are absolutely gorgeous, but can we really afford something this extravagant?" she asked while holding them with deep approval against her black evening gown. Shelby realized her husband had purchased a rather expensive string of genuine pearls, not cheap cultured ones.

He rested his chin on her bare shoulder and addressed her image in the mirror, "You are looking at the new *Chief Sports Journalist of the Pittsburgh Post Gazette.*"

Then, in an overly snobbish British accent, he confidently added, "Of course we can afford them, My Lady. Your husband's annual salary shall be increased by... Oh! I must say, at the minimum... Twenty grand!"

For extra theatrical effects, he looked down his nose and said, "Allow me, Madam," as he did the clasp around her neck.

"Oh my God! They are really stunning; I'm glad I decided on this dress for tonight," she exclaimed while staring at her reflection; then a frown shot across her face, "But what am I going to wear for earrings now? Everything I have will clash."

Then her eyes widened, "I know! My snowflake pair will work. Tis the season, right?"

Sounding like Sean Connery again, Christian said, "Somehow My Dear, I predicted you were going to be up against that dilemma."

He pulled a second, smaller box out of his pocket which also had the golden DeRoys logo embossed on the lid.

Her jaw about hit the floor, "Oh, for Christ's sake! You are just full of surprises tonight!"

"Hey! The prettiest woman at this party has to be all decked out. The old bags will be eyeing your pearls with envy while their husbands are admiring your sweet little ass. I'll have you know I caught The Old Geezer staring at your tooshie more than once. I think the only reason McKelvey hired me eighteen years ago was so he could get an occasional peek at your cute little caboose."

He continued teasing, "Wait till he gets an eyeful of these buns tonight! They are definitely nicer now than they were back then."

He reached down, gave her butt a tiny, affectionate pinch and smiled; he then chuckled deviously while commenting, "They're much firmer!"

"*Ow*!" She squeaked in feigned pain, then told her husband, "Quit talking about my derriere like that. Mr. McKelvey does not look at my butt! You always say that just to make me blush."

A devilish smile of her own crept across her lips. She secretly relished the fact her husband not only still notices she kept her girlish figure, but he still can't keep his fingers off of it. All those times she resisted chocolate-covered temptations and opted for a piece of fruit or celery sticks instead, had paid off. They both turned forty-three this year, the time of life when shedding extra pounds becomes harder.

Weekly, Shelby exerts one hundred percent in the gym.

However! On a, *bi-weekly*, basis, she gives one hundred and ten percent in the bedroom!

She does this to keep her man at home. And satisfied!

Christian Kane was a good catch; one that any woman would be delighted to reel in. Standing six two, and weighing one-hundred and eighty-five pounds with a thirty-three-inch waist, he was lean and toned, but not skinny. Good looking, but not dashingly handsome like Mathew McConaughey; he resembled a taller, more athletic version of Michael J. Fox.

Her husband was the clichéd clean-cut All-American boy who attended the University of Pittsburgh on a football scholarship; all four years playing Safety. Although a decent player, he didn't impress any NFL scouts. Not even his hometown Steelers; but at least he gets paid to write about the Black and Gold, and interview the players, which he enjoys.

Turning her head from left to right and back again, she marveled at her reflection wearing the new earrings. Teasingly, she imitated Mae West and cooed seductively, "Later on, when we get back from the Sheraton, I'm going to wear these pearls and... *Nothing else*... Just for you, Big Boy! I'll have you... Come on up, and we'll celebrate your big promotion."

Christian mouthed the words, "Oh yeah!"

One of the highlights planned for tonight's banquet was honoring Max Reynolds for his forty-two years of being a sportswriter at The Post Gazette, the last twelve of which he had held the prestigious position of Chief Editor of the Sports Department. His ailing wife was the only reason he had decided to retire; if not for her battle with lung cancer, Reynolds would have probably worked at the Gazette until paramedics carried him out in a body bag. More importantly scheduled for tonight's banquet was the Senior Editor of the Paper, Robert McKelvey, announcing publicly who would be promoted into the retiring man's vacated position.

Again sounding like Ian Fleming's famous British spy, Agent 007, "Now? My Sweet Lady? Are we ready to depart for tonight's festivities, and the anointing of Sir Christian Kane to knighthood?"

Shelby smiled, glanced in the mirror at her pearls, gave her hair one final minute adjustment, and told him, "I'm ready. Let's go, Chief Sports Journalist of The Pittsburgh Post Gazette!"

Christian thanked God his beloved Steelers played on Sundays now instead of Fridays; if they had been playing tonight, cars and semis would have been backed up for miles. He made excellent time driving to the waterfront; the traffic was unbelievably light, especially on a Friday night with Christmas two weeks away, and the much warmer than seasonal December weather.

Shelby couldn't believe she only needed her white, lace-pattern shawl!

"Just think, now we'll finally be able to move out of our tiny townhouse and buy that dream home in the suburbs we've always talked about," he confidently told his wife as he down shifted and flipped on the turn signal.

While stroking her pearl necklace, she dreamily said, "Boy, I hope so. I especially liked that A-frame we rode past out in Derry Township when we took the scenic route to Elmer's Aquariums two years ago, and I bought that Fighting Beta for my niece Valerie's birthday present. Remember? The countryside is so beautiful out there; I'd love to have a home like that where I'd be able to plant flowers."

"Yes! I do remember that place. It had those two long flower beds leading from the front door to the driveway, where that beautiful 1960 Thunderbird was parked," he said as he wheeled his BMW into the Sheraton parking lot, with *a whole six minutes to spare*!

"Yes! That's the one!"

"I recall you particularly pointed out how you liked all those different colored flowers, and how they outlined the sidewalks."

"Wow! I figured you'd only remember the T-bird, especially since it was a ragtop, and not the house. Sometimes, you really surprise me!"

The happy couple walked hand in hand to the entrance while the city's lights shimmered atop the wake trailing The Gateway Princess as she slowly moseyed up the river; apparently, Pittsburgh's beloved paddle-wheel boat had once again been chartered for the night by a wedding party.

A squawking clarinet and deep base notes booming from a tuba in a Bavarian version of the Chicken Dance Polka blared up and down The Monongahela River while a man could be seen throwing up Fuzzy Navels overboard.

Turns out, the gent was the best man! And he claimed he was not drunk, just seasick from doing a shot, then puffing on a cigar with the groom after swinging the bride, his sister, around during the bridal dance.

Chapter Two

Over the din of the crowd, they found their reserved seats in the huge, packed banquet hall; Mr. and Mrs. Kane were to sit with Campbell, Rogerson, and their wives. Dave Campbell, not as tall as Christian and sporting a beer gut, stood when Christian and Shelby walked to the table.

The two men shook hands, Campbell said, "Good God, Christian, I was beginning to wonder if you were going to show up for your big night."

Christian nonchalantly nudged his wife as Campbell informed him, "I called your phone, but as usual, I got your voicemail and knew there was no sense in leaving a message."

Christian shrugged his shoulders implying, "Oh well!"

His co-worker then flattered Christian, "I like the tux. Nice touch."

Campbell then addressed Shelby before Christian had a chance to respond, "Whoa! You are looking *extra* good tonight, Mrs. Kane. What is it? A new hairdo?"

She gave Campbell a weak smile, "Thank you. Nope, same old cut."

Another flirtatious compliment, "I know what it must be — you've dropped a few pounds!"

"Thanks for reminding me, Dave! I actually gained a pound and a half since last year's banquet," she sarcastically scolded the man while watching his wife, Debbie, in her peripheral vision. The woman was rather plain-looking and obviously fighting a losing battle of the bulge; she looked as though she gained *thirty* pounds since last year. Debbie gave Shelby's slinky figure a quick once over from her blond curls all the way down to her black high heels. Then, as she looked her way back up, her eyes widened when she spotted the pearl necklace; then they really bulged when she noticed the *matching earrings. Bitch!*

To get Campbell's eyes off his wife, Christian interrupted, "We're late because traffic was heavy on the Parkway, there must've been an accident in the tubes again and we were detoured to Smithfield Street."

Then, while pulling a chair out for his wife, he asked, "Did we miss anything?"

"You did not miss a damn thing. It's actually been boring as shit so far; you know how stuffy these Old Farts are. But at least the drinks are free, and the appetizers are good."

"Yeah! They're freakin' excellent," Debbie interrupted in her nasal tone, then popped a whole mushroom stuffed with crabmeat into her mouth.

Through a muffled mouthful, she said, "Try one, Girl, I saved these for you." She pushed the plate towards Shelby. Only three were left; moreover, they were ice cold, sitting in coagulated butter.

"No thanks, maybe later. My stomach's been acting up; I'm probably just nervous about tonight."

"Well, uh yeah! You two are like George and Weezy, ya know!"

Debbie then butchered the famous Jefferson's jingle while flailing her arms in the air and swaying her big ass, "He's movin' on up... to the deluxe apartment in the sky... eye. Christian got a piece of the pie... eye."

A hint of jealousy was just a bit too evident in her voice, as was the fact she downed four Captain Morgan Spiced Rum and Cokes in under thirty minutes to chase down a plate and a half of the tasty shrooms.

Shelby and Christian didn't know what to make of her exhibition, so they forced a chuckle. Her embarrassed husband chortled along with them, but then shot a disgusted warning glance at his wife.

A high-pitched squeal blasted from the ceiling speakers when McKelvey turned on the microphone and began emceeing the party, "Good evening, everybody."

All the guests cringed as his voice sent an even louder and higher pitched squeal through the air. He then tapped the mic three times, which only added thumping noises to the cacophony. Finally, he realized he was too close to the mic and backed his mouth away. To the delight of the partygoers, the shrieking stopped.

McKelvey, a balding, rotund man with a large round face sitting on extremely broad, rounded shoulders, began perspiring. His furry eyebrows, thick glasses, and bulbous nose, sometimes made people look twice to make certain he wasn't wearing a pair of those funny gag glasses. His suit coat buttons were stretched to their limit. Even his hands were large with fat fingers resembling over-cooked hotdogs.

In an attempt to make light of the matter, he said, "Now that I have gotten everybody's attention! Good evening. Thank you all for being here tonight at The Pittsburgh Post Gazette's annual dinner and awards banquet. On behalf of the stockholders, I am pleased to announce that 2022 was a banner year. Exceptional co-operation between the Printing Department and the..."

Christian paid only half attention to McKelvey's rambling, monotone spiel about how well the Paper did last year, how the Internet boosted advertising sales, how the circulation department boasted an increase of seven percent due to the presses finally becoming computerized, and blah, blah, blah... For thirty-five minutes, the Senior Editor listened to himself talk.

However, Christian's ears perked up real quick when he heard The Old Geezer say, "It is with mixed emotions that I tell you one of our beloved co-workers, one of my dearest friends, has decided to hang it up after forty-two years of continuous and dedicated service. Please join me in giving a really big round of applause to... Max... Reynolds!"

The audience clapped; some whistled; others cheered. The retiree, a very well-liked gentleman and a true icon in the sports world, would be greatly missed.

"Max," McKelvey spoke into the mic once the crowd settled down, "Please come on up here to the podium."

A short and heavy-set bald man himself, but with a giant handlebar moustache, Max stood and went front and center; this man could have easily passed for McKelvey's little brother.

"Maxwell, my good friend," McKelvey said as they shook hands, "I am advising everybody here tonight to dump their stock in the Gazette since you won't be working here anymore!"

Once the dinner guests finished laughing, McKelvey continued, "Forty-two years! Forty-two... *Fine*, years. Gosh! How fast it goes, huh, buddy? Here's a little token of the Paper's appreciation."

McKelvey handed the retiring gentleman a small giftbox.

Mr. Reynolds, one of those forever-cheery people who always had a compliment or made people laugh with his quick one-liners, pulled the mic down to his level, held the box to his ear and lightly shook it, but nothing rattled. With an overly dramatic, surprised look, he told McKelvey, "Geesh! This is it? Nothing more than a tiny box? I could have sworn I just heard you say we had a banner year!"

The man then really lampooned the Senior Editor, "After forty-two years, I was expecting at the least a new car! I was hoping for one of those electric Teslas, but I don't hear any keys in here, Robert!"

The audience roared from that one. Once the laughs tapered off, he continued with the witty remarks, "I really hope this is not a gold watch, because I already have two, but, uh, now that I said that... I think one doesn't work, and I'm pretty sure the other one's broken!"

Again, the crowd had a small bout of laughter while Max nervously fumbled as he opened the present. He pulled two cruise tickets to the Bahamas, along with a check for five thousand dollars from the box.

The reality of retiring finally smacked him in the face. A tear sprang from the old man's eye as he held the tickets and check high in the air; he ribbed McKelvey again, "Thank you, Bob. I didn't get a really close look at the tickets. They *are*... Round-trip, right?"

Again, the audience laughed; Debbie pointed to the mushrooms and asked Shelby, "You sure you don't want them?"

"Positive. They are all yours."

Dave Campbell frowned at his wife's piggish behavior.

Max continued, "To everyone here tonight, I thank you from the bottom of my heart. I am going to miss all you guys dearly. This was one of those jobs, ya know, where you didn't hate getting up in the morning and going to work. You all..." he sniffled a bit, "... are a great bunch of people to be around. Thank you, all."

He turned to McKelvey and hugged him before walking back to his table; Max then bent over and kissed his bride of forty-six years before taking his seat. Mrs. Reynolds too, had tears running down her cheeks; she needed to move the tubing from the oxygen bottle to wipe her eyes with the tissue she held constantly clutched in her hand.

The Senior Editor had to wait for the applause to die down before resuming his speech, "The Post has selected a fine young man to fill some pretty big shoes left by you, Max."

McKelvey stopped talking, looked at Reynolds and asked, "They're a size sixteen, aren't they?"

This witty remark evoked another small stint of laughter from the crowd; Christian felt himself tensing up from the anticipation of McKelvey announcing his name very shortly.

The Chief Editor continued, "Yes, we are going to miss you, too. But the Post has selected a very qualified, young, aggressive writer to lead the sports team into the new year. He has been with us for quite some time now. Ladies and gentlemen, let's have another big round of applause, but this time... for the new Chief Sports Journalist of *The Pittsburgh Post Gazette*..."

Christian got himself poised, ready to stand while Debbie popped the last stuffed mushroom into her mouth.

"Mister... *David... Campbell*!"

Applause echoed from the hall once again. Christian and Campbell looked at each other in sheer amazement. Both men were purely bewildered. However, Christian's face also held anger mixed in with his look of total disbelief.

So taken back by surprise, Debbie gasped inwardly and began choking on the last appetizer when it got lodged in her windpipe. Rogerson repeatedly smacked her back; on the fourth whack, the woman coughed it up and out. At what looked to be sixty miles an hour, the mushroom bounced off Shelby's forehead and left specks of crabmeat in her eyebrow as evidence before ricocheting into her water glass!

Campbell, in his cheap brown wrinkled suit, slowly rose to his feet as his gaping mouth quickly transformed into a smile from ear to ear; he turned and waved to everybody in the audience, then bowed to McKelvey.

Christian glared hatefully at The Old Geezer and thought, "*You lousy bastard!*"

When their eyes finally locked, Christian pretended he had something in the corner of his eye and used the middle finger on his right hand to rub it out. Then he flicked his finger from his eye towards McKelvey with all the rigor of a Marine's snappy salute while mouthing the appropriate two words. The Senior Editor's bushy eyebrows rose up from behind his thick glasses.

Still smiling, Campbell slowly sat; Rogerson started to congratulate him when Christian sprang to his feet. Pissed off, he told Shelby in a disgusted, loud enough voice for all to hear, "I'm feeling sick all of a sudden, Honey. Let's get out of here before I *puke*."

He melodramatically offered his elbow to his wife; she stood without looking at anybody and took her husband's arm. As they hurried for the exit, he held his head high while she stared at the floor and felt her face redden.

One of Shelby's few bad habits was not wearing a seatbelt; she had issues over wrinkled clothing.

Nevertheless, the woman quickly put it on after the little black BMW coupe laid rubber the entire length of the Sheraton's parking lot before fish tailing onto Station Square Drive.

Then she must have heard her husband exclaim a hundred times on the ride home, "I can't believe it. I just... can't... fucking... believe it! What a... *lousy bastard*."

However, he must *not* have heard her pleading over and over in a frightened voice as she dug her fingers into the dash, "Please slow down, Christian! C'mon Baby, slow it down! You're scaring me!"

On the contrary, he did hear when the cruiser came up behind him and hit the siren; then he saw the lights. "Shit! This is all I fuckin' need right now!" Christian bitched as he slapped both hands off the steering wheel, then pull over to the curb.

Officer Fitzpatrick walked up to the driver's door. "License and registration, Speed Racer," the cop, sounding like a Drill Instructor, ordered Christian; he spoke out of the right side of his mouth through clenched teeth.

Christian pulled out his wallet and handed them over.

Then he just sat in his seat, closed his eyes, and steamed while keeping his temper in check.

"Any particular reason why you were doing ninety-five in a forty-five zone?" The cop asked, but then quickly added, "Tell me one I haven't heard yet in my twenty-four years of pulling speeders over, and I won't write you up."

Shelby spoke up before her husband spouted off some pissy remark that was not going to help the situation any, "It's all my fault, Officer. I felt like I was going to throw up, so I asked my husband to hurry. I must have eaten a bad mushroom back at the Sheraton. Sorry."

Fitzpatrick bent down to get a better look at the passenger. Shelby, holding both arms around her stomach, batted her large, seductive brown eyes at the middle-aged patrolman and gave him a weak smile.

He smiled right back, "Sorry, Cutie, but puking is in the top ten, right after, 'Officer, if I don't get home real soon, I'm going to shit my pants!' You should have told me a UFO was chasing you, I have yet to hear that one! But the bad mushroom? I liked that! That's really good. Now that's original!"

He stood erect, looked at Christian's license and said, "Kane!"

The cop then scrunched his face and asked, "Are you Christian Kane, the sportswriter?"

"Yes, Sir," Christian replied quietly and politely, spoken as though he respected authority.

"Well, I'll tell you what I'm going to do for you, Kane," the cop stated, still speaking out the corner of his mouth, which looked really odd, peculiar, "Your winning picks in last week's Gazette won me, Officer Michael Fitzpatrick, Steel Town's Finest, three hundred smackaroos in a football poll we have going on down at the precinct. To show my appreciation, I'm going to write you a warning and we'll call it even. How's that grab ya, Kane? Right by the hairy old nut sack, don't it? I never would've picked the Cowboys to beat the Patriots. Not in a hundred years. I don't know how you choose 'em, Boy."

Then the cop literally stuck his face deep inside the BMW and admired Shelby until she felt uncomfortable. She glanced at him; he winked at her and said, "Stay away from those Sheraton Shrooms, Cutie; they might be psylocibin."

After telling her that, the cop put his face a mere two inches from Christian's, he told him, "Now you get your pretty wifey home before she, haha, hurls... in your fancy little import. But do the speed limit for your safety. Her safety. And for the safety of all our fellow Pittsburghers."

Fitzpatrick smiled right in Christian's face; the sportswriter smelled coffee on the man's hot breath; the cop barked out, "Drive carefully!"

"Yes, Sir, I'll do that. Thank you. Dallas again this Sunday, Officer, by uh, two touchdowns," Christian said nervously while pushing his head backwards, deep into the headrest.

Fitzpatrick stared into Christian's eyes. Then he finally stood, handed the license and registration back, started to walk to his cruiser but hesitated momentarily, turned to face Christian and asked with those distorted lips, "You actually think the Cowboys can beat the Jets?"

He scrunched his face even more as he reached under his wide-brimmed patrolman hat; scratching his head, he asked,

"Really? The Jets are undefeated this year; they kicked some serious ass when playing the Eagles last week. Wow! I guess I'll have to change my scorecard now. Thanks for the tip. One more thing, Kane... You take a tip from Cutie there, and... *Buckle up*!"

MUCH TO SHELBY'S RELIEF, Christian did the speed limit the rest of the way home. Still fuming as they pulled into the driveway, he got out, slammed the door, and took the six steps leading up to the front door in two strides. Normally he would wait for Shelby, and they would walk into the townhouse apartment together, but tonight he was already inside before she got to the first step. He took off his dinner jacket and flung it across the living room.

"Bastard! What a lousy bastard. I just can't believe it," she heard him mumbling as she came inside. She walked over and picked his coat off the lampshade, folded it neatly, and laid it across the back of the sofa.

Christian sat down in his chair but bounced right back out of it and went to the kitchen. He took the bottle of Asti Spumante, which was bought specially for tonight, from the refrigerator, set it on the countertop, then retrieved a tumbler from the cupboard. When Shelby entered the kitchen, Christian was furiously fumbling with the corkscrew atop the bottle, swearing under his breath. She got herself a glass, filled it with crushed ice from the dispenser in the refrigerator door and set it beside his.

Shelby jumped from the familiar *pop*, when her husband finally concentrated long enough and pulled the cork out. He filled both glasses, raised his in the air and made a toast, "Here's to you, Campbell. You're a complete idiot. Have fun running the Post into the ground."

After chugging the entire glass in four gulps, he told Shelby, "The Old Geezer got one thing right tonight; everybody had better dump their stock."

He refilled his glass, then downed that one just as quickly.

"Christian, getting drunk won't help matters."

"It will if it makes me forget tonight ever happened. Besides, there's only one bottle. The mood I'm in, it would take a case."

After taking another small sip, Shelby told him, "Here, you can have mine; I don't think this is going to do my headache any good."

He slugged hers down.

Yesterday, on her way home from work, Shelby had picked up the sparkling bubbly which was for their own private celebration after tonight's banquet and the announcement of Christian's promotion. They very rarely drank, especially champagne, so she was unsure what to buy, her boss had advised her to try the Spumante. Neither she nor Christian had ever drunk it before.

She also picked up a new outfit for his and her celebration — a pair of assless chaps and a Stetson cowboy hat!

To keep the sparks flying in the bedroom over the years, Shelby would occasionally don a costume and become a different woman for her man to seduce. His wife was well aware how the human male thrives on fantasies, and that sex is just as much psychological as it is physical for a man, if not more. Oh, but how she greatly benefited from it too! Christian would become so intensely aroused and hard, then make love to her as if it was their first time.

Occasionally, Shelby made their love making sessions have all the exciting, lust filled elements of a secret affair, a tryst, if you may.

Oh, yes! The irresistible Forbidden Fruit! The ruin of many marriages, and a cause for expulsion from The Garden of Paradise.

His favorite costume had to be her cheerleader outfit. She would come out of the bathroom with her hair in pigtails, stand by the bed and cheer, "Yay, Christian! He's my man! He makes me scream like no man can!" Then she'd turn around, bend over, and wiggle her bare bottom three inches from his face.

Ironically, none of her outfits came with panties, not even her dominatrix get up. Of course, that black leather costume and whip only came out of the box for special occasions such as his birthday or their anniversary. This couple enjoyed a healthy and satisfying, sometimes erotically wild, sex life.

But just like Vegas, what went on behind closed bedroom doors, stayed there!

Nevertheless, these soulmates did love each other very deeply and supported each other's dreams and ambitions. Although Shelby would act like an expensive but shameless call girl, she was always a classy lady in public.

While pouring another glassful, he said, "I still can't believe it; Campbell doesn't know his ass from a hole in the ground. His picks are an embarrassing thirty-three percent; mine are ninety-two."

There wasn't enough champagne to fill another glass, so he polished off the little that was left and tossed the empty bottle in the trash.

Full glass in hand, he headed for his Lazy Boy, saying, "I'm lucky that weird cop didn't use Campbell's picks; I'd have gotten a ticket for sure."

Christian sat, his wife instinctively stood behind him and massaged his neck.

With her reassuring voice, she told him, "It will blow over, Baby. In a few months, McKelvey will realize he made a huge blunder and he'll be begging you to be the Chief Writer!"

"The Old Geezer can shove his newspaper where the Sun doesn't shine. Monday morning, I'm going to clean out my desk and hand in my resignation. I've had it with him and his Paper."

She immediately stopped rubbing his neck; that was one remark she was not expecting. A look of total incomprehension plastered her face as she took two steps forward to face him. She asked in an unbelievable tone, "Wait! What? You can't just up and quit your job!"

"I'm probably fired anyways, after whipping the fat, old bastard the finger tonight." He then let out a deep belly laugh remembering how he whipped McKelvey the bird. He exclaimed, "Fuck, him!"

"Christian! Please stop swearing; it's not you."

"Sorry, Honey. I just can't remember a single time in my life when I was this mad. You know, I actually saw McKelvey through a red haze, *I* deserved that promotion, not Campbell! I'm done with McKelvey, Campbell, and everything else connected to the Gazette."

"Calm down and think rationally. You can't just quit."

He took a swallow and continued, "Oh! Yes I can! I, *am,* quitting! I'm done with sports. I'll flip burgers or work at a carwash before I write another column for that rag sheet. If I were to stay there, I'd end up doing the Chief's job for my current salary while Campbell takes all the credit. *That,* is not going to happen."

"You're just upset right now; things will cool down and return to normal."

"And another thing, I am *not* going to let McKelvey shatter our dreams. We *will* get that house in the country! I'm sick and tired of the rat race in this filthy city anyways."

She resumed rubbing his neck for a few more minutes, then yawned while saying, "I'm exhausted, let's go to bed." She did have a slight headache from the night's fiasco at the party, and she felt there was no use in talking to him with his current mindset. Maybe tomorrow, hopefully after sleeping on it, he would return to his senses.

Christian chugged the rest of his Asti Spumante as Shelby turned off the Christmas tree lights, then the couple turned in for the night.

THE SPARKLING WINE caused Christian to sleep till noon. Shelby, wearing her robe, was sitting in the warm sunshine on their enclosed Sun porch sipping her morning cup of java when Christian came in, slowly sipping his. She had only been up for half an hour before he finally stirred. He kissed her good morning, then sat; the bright sunshine hurt his eyes, causing him to squint.

They looked at each other in silence for a few moments before she spoke, "Except for those two little sips I had last night, you drank that entire bottle of Spumante!"

After a slight chuckle, she commented, "Hangovers are a pain, aren't they?"

He gave her a crappy smile, "Aren't you the comedienne this morning?"

Then he calmly added, "I still can't believe it. David Campbell... Ha! Chief Journalist. What a freakin' joke!"

"Just give it time, Christian. Let it go. Please? Don't let it spoil the rest of our weekend, okay?" she asked, giving him her puppy eyes, causing him to appreciate her.

He smiled, and nodded, "Okay. God are you beautiful. That's what has me so torqued; I want to be successful for you."

"You *are*, Baby. You keep me very happy. It is true what they say, money isn't everything. We have enough to pay our bills and live comfortably. And we have each other; that's all I need."

"But I feel you deserve so much more. You're a very special woman, and I'm so lucky to have you."

He took a couple swallows of coffee, trying to wake up. "Know what? You were the prettiest woman at the banquet last night, as usual."

"I love you too, but last night's competition wasn't that tough!"

"Yeah, really. That Debbie is such a... slob, to be polite."

Shelby laughed and shook her head, "I couldn't believe it when she coughed up that mushroom and it hit my head. She damn near took my eye out! I have to agree with you; she is not much of a lady."

Christian took a big gulp, chortled, and said, "Ha! Campbell deserves her. They were made for each other."

She rose from her chair, "No more on that topic. Ready for your second cup?"

"Please, and make it as strong as possible."

He downed the grounds before handing the empty mug to her, then stretched his long lanky body backwards over his chair while yawning. His tee shirt rode up his belly, exposing his flat tummy and small, but defined abs.

When she returned with both cups, a brand-new Stetson adorned her head; while the pearl necklace and earrings made for a sexy, stunning contrast!

Christian looked at her, puzzled; her husband had never seen this hat before. His eyebrows flickered briefly in approval as the corners of his mouth turned up. "I like it!"

But then she let her robe fall to the ground, revealing her assless chaps and black leather brassiere! "I'm liking it more and more!"

Shelby exclaimed, "Yee haw!"

"*She's right,*" he figured, "*Why let assholes like Campbell and McKelvey spoil their weekend!*"

The man whinnied like Silver, The Lone Ranger's stallion, and said, "Ride 'em Cowboy!"

And she did, with all the fury of a professional bronco buster!

Chapter Three

E ight thirty. Monday morning.

Husband and wife headed out the door.

He wore a polo shirt, Docker cargo shorts, and sneakers. No socks. That was one of the perks that came with his job — he could dress casually, or formally when the need arose.

"Aren't you cold?" She asked.

"Not at the least!"

His wife, on the other hand, wore a drab two-piece light-gray business suit, but still looked sexy as Hell in it. As a secretary for one of the larger law firms on Grant Street in downtown Pittsburgh, she had to dress formally every day.

"Promise me you'll engage your brain before putting your mouth in gear," she said as he opened her car door for her.

His wife further warned him as she gracefully slid in behind the wheel of her tiny Mazda Miata, "You might want to think twice before you burn any bridges."

"Oh, I can assure you I won't burn any bridges, Honey."

She felt a little better until he added, "I'm going to blow them out of the water, sky high!" He threw his arms into the air, visually describing how a bomb goes off. "Kaboom!"

He had a frighteningly determined look on his face when he gave her a wink and a nod, "My mind's made up. Don't you worry any. I have it all figured out!"

"That's what scares the crap out of me. I really wish you would rethink this."

He closed her car door. "You have a good day at work Honey. I know... *I* will!"

Shelby drove off, shaking her head.

Christian found three empty boxes in the garage and threw them in his trunk.

Walking down the hall to his cubbyhole took him past Reynolds's office. He stopped when he heard the old fellow call out his name, then took two steps backwards, and went in. A surprised Christian didn't expect to see Max this early today. Apparently, the retiree had come in to clean out his desk, too. Boxes were scattered about, and the walls were bare; lighter spots revealed where pictures once hung.

Max immediately shot his hand out; they shook. "Christian, how in the hell are you doing, Lad?"

"Never been better, Max," Christian answered sarcastically, but politely. He respected his immediate supervisor; especially since Max had taken the twenty-five-year-old journal grad, Christian Kane, under his wing eighteen years ago and shared a lot of his knowledge and insight with the, *young lad*. Max had taken an immediate liking to him; he enjoyed Christian's enthusiasm, intelligence, and wit.

"I'm awfully sorry, Christian. I tried talking to McKelvey till I was blue in the face. He told me a week ago that Campbell was going to replace me, and I told him he's making a big mistake. I almost told you a couple of times, but I couldn't do it."

He looked around, made certain no one could hear, and lowered his voice, "Campbell's nothing but a pecker headed geek. And The Old Geezer's a dumb shit. My Elizabeth can't even walk from the bedroom to the bathroom without my help, and McKelvey thought she could go on a cruise to the Bahamas because that's where we honeymooned? Ha! What a joke! It was a nice gesture on his part indeed, but as usual, he didn't think it through; just like giving the promotion to Campbell, not you. I gave those tickets to my boy; he and his wife'll enjoy Nassau."

"Why, Max? Why did McKelvey pick Campbell over me?"

"I'll let the old shmuck tell you himself. I'm sure he's expecting you, and I'm even more certain you want to chat with him." Max shook his head, "You are not going to believe his logic!"

"You're damn right I want a chat with him. Good luck in your retirement. Take care of yourself and Elizabeth. Maybe I'll see you around; I'll try to keep in touch."

"You do that, Lad." They shook hands again.

Max spotted the empty boxes. "Don't tell me you're cleaning out your desk too?"

"I'm quitting, I've had it."

The flabbergasted old-timer's brow raised, "Don't you think that's a bit extreme? What will you do for an income?"

Very confidently, Christian replied, "I am going to be an author. I'm going to concentrate on science fiction, romance, or thrillers."

"You are an excellent writer, no doubt about that, much better than Campbell. I think you'll do just fine, if those genres don't pan out, you could always write non-fictional sports."

Christian shook his head, "No! If I wanted to stay in sports, I'd just go to a different paper."

They both heard when McKelvey's big mouth hit the floor, "Sharon! Any calls? Get my coffee," he bellowed at his personal secretary, as he routinely does *every* single morning on his way to his office.

"Looks like it's kickoff time!" Christian told Max, then stormed straight into McKelvey's office.

The man had just hung his hat and coat on his antique clothes tree, then turned to sit when Sharon, with her boss's personalized coffee mug in hand, followed Christian in, then placed the steaming mug on its matching coaster on McKelvey's desk. However, before the Senior Editor could reach for it, Christian picked up the coffee and dramatically slurped it loud and long; he then addressed the secretary, "Damn, Sharon! You sure do make a *mighty* damn fine cup of coffee! But I bet nobody ever told you that. *Have they?*" he asked the older, but perky woman while glaring at McKelvey.

"No. Nobody ever told me that I make a mighty damn fine cup of coffee; not a single time that I can recall," she replied, then glanced at her boss.

Christian's voice grew louder as his rant continued, "Some people just don't appreciate what they have, or even... *Know*, what they have! What do *you* think, Sharon?"

"I could not agree with you more, Christian," she said before scurrying out of the office and pulling the door behind her. She knew what fireworks Christian was about to throw a match to; she witnessed his anger Friday night.

McKelvey had yet to say a word; he watched Christian raise the mug to his lips, take another long slurp, then say, "Sharon does make a damn fine cup of coffee. Don't you agree? All high and mighty, *King Decision Maker*!"

His supervisor still did not respond; he was allowing Christian all the rope he needed to hang himself. McKelvey, a *ridiculously* tolerant man, thought, "*He is a good writer, but how much more of this bullshit till I shitcan him?*"

Christian slammed the mug onto the desk, not the coaster; coffee splashed out and onto important papers lying about McKelvey's desktop. "Answer me one question!" Christian demanded. "One, simple, fucking, question. Why? Just tell me why! Why Campbell, not me?"

Looking Christian square in the eye, McKelvey replied, "Simple. Campbell is a nerd and you're not! This planet, and this paper, are in the Electronic Age. Zoom, Skype, Facebook, Twitter, TikTok; the list is endless and it's always changing. But you remain in the Dark Ages and refuse to come out of your cave; you never stood erect and walked into the twenty-first century. You still use a word processor to write. I've never seen you text a single message. You very rarely even *talk* on your cellphone. Look how Campbell has his cubicle wired. He's always *texting*. He has Bluetooth in his ear all day long. iPods and any other new electronic gadget that hits the market, he runs out and buys, and then he masters the damn thing. Campbell writes his columns on his phone and then emails it directly to the printers. *Quick, efficient*. Look how I had to kiss your ass to get you to carry your cellphone, which by the way, *takes pictures*, too. You're way behind the times, Kane. You're a caveman!"

"At least I can *write* a column!" Christian shouted.

Then he got louder, "One that does not come back with typos and wrong facts. Campbell is not even sure how many *innings* are in a *basketball* game for Christ's sakes, and he's going to lead your paper into the new year?"

Christian then laughed very loudly, "Haha! With Dave Campbell heading up your sports department, your precious paper won't even be worth wiping your ass with, McKelvey. I hope you took your own advice and 'dumped your stock' like you joked. It too, like the Gazette, is going to be absolutely fucking worthless. I, for one, am not going to be on board when this ship goes down. He may be good with technology, but he doesn't know shit about sports!"

Christian began to see McKelvey in a red haze; when he felt his right hand wanting to ball into a fist, he decided it best for him to get out of there before he loses all control and regrettably takes a swing at the fool.

He turned to leave, but spun back around and said, "Here! Take your precious cellphone and shove it up your ass!"

He held the little flip phone six inches above McKelvey's coffee cup and let it drop. More coffee splashed out on to the papers; a few drops even splattered onto McKelvey's white shirt. Feeling much better now, Christian stormed to the door.

Just as his hand touched the knob, McKelvey spoke, "I can understand why you're upset, but I need to know for sure if you're going to stand behind me and my decision of Campbell replacing Max."

Christian turned to face the man; a look of total disbelief etched on his face.

Then McKelvey stated, while wiping coffee from his shirt, "Maybe after you cool down, Dave could teach you how to use a computer. Today's apps are user friendly, and the Internet is a great tool."

"You just don't get it! Do you? Dave Campbell? My supervisor? Haha! What a joke! Both of you can kiss my ass! I thought I made that point clear to you at the banquet, but apparently not! I'll try again!"

Christian whipped the bird to the Post's Chief Editor, who uncannily resembled a heavy-set Groucho Marx. Then, while holding his hand at arm's length, Christian marched briskly towards the man with his erect middle finger leading the charge, aimed at McKelvey's big, fat, round face!

He came to an abrupt stop when his finger was a mere two inches from that bulbous nose; McKelvey's bushy eyebrows rose high above his glasses as he stared down at Christian's finger.

The man appeared to be cross-eyed as Christian hollered at him, "I effing... *Quit*! Capiche?"

On his way to his car, carrying three boxes that now held eighteen years of memories, Christian popped his head into Sharon's office.

He told her goodbye, then thanked the woman kindly for the mighty damn fine cup of coffee!

Chapter Four

Christian, using a toothbrush and a Brillo pad to meticulously clean the wire-spoked rims on his BMW, looked up when Shelby pulled into the driveway. She got out of her coupe with a bag of takeout, walked over to her husband, and apologized, "The office was extra busy today, it seems Mondays are so stressful anymore. Hope you don't mind sandwiches for supper. Sorry, I didn't feel like cooking tonight, I just want to kick back and relax."

"Wow. It's five thirty already? Sure, Honey, sammies will be fine. Now that I think about it, I didn't eat all day. I'm starving."

He glanced at the sack, "Are they from Primanti's?"

"Of course. So? How did your day go?" she optimistically asked while half a dozen possible replies ran through her head that he might give her; hoping, "I quit," would not be his answer.

His car, she noticed, had already been washed and waxed; now he was detailing the wheels. The hose, a bucket, and a chamois were scattered about his BMW. She thought, "*He must have spent all day on his car!*"

"I need a break," her hubby said while getting up; he gave her a quick kiss, then stretched, "I'll tell you all about it over supper."

The anticipation was killing her. Although her intuition told her why he was home, apparently for the majority of the day, she could not figure out why he was so calm if he did quit like she sensed. Perhaps, she hoped and prayed, *"He just took the day off to cool down and come to his senses."*

Christian sat at the table with a knife and cutting board; he sliced the sandwiches in halves while Shelby, still in her business attire, grabbed paper plates from the microwave stand and two Diet Cokes from the fridge; she placed them on the table, sat, and asked, "Well? How long are you going to keep me in suspense?"

With a mouthful of Philly Cheesesteak, he answered, "McKelvey told me I did not get the position because I am not as technologically inclined as Campbell. And I told The Old Geezer I was not going to be around when Campbell ran the Gazette into the ground."

He chuckled as a faint smile appeared briefly on his face when telling her, "I even turned in my company cellphone."

"Does this mean that... *You up and quit*?" she asked in an unbelievable tone.

He took another big bite of his sub and calmly muttered, "Yes, it does!"

"That's just great. Fantastic! And just how are we going to pay our bills now? My paycheck alone won't cover all our expenses. I told you I was happy with the way things were."

Her hands shook as she opened the Coke, she criticized her husband, "I really didn't think you would just up and quit. You didn't think this through. Christ, Christian!"

"Calm down, Shell. I did think it through, things are going to work out just fine. I need you to stand behind me *now* more than you ever did in the past."

"Work out how, Christian? Are you going to try and get a position with The Tribune Review?"

He shook his head no.

"Do you know somebody at The Pittsburgh Press?"

Christian finished his soda and then flattened the aluminum can with his hands, "I do, but I'd be wasting my time applying for a journalist position with *any* paper, especially in this town. I'm quite confident McKelvey has me blackballed; he certainly is not going to give me a letter of recommendation!"

"Where are you going to find a job that paid as well as the one that you just up and quit? You know how bad the economy is out there. Goldberg's law firm is swamped with bankruptcies and foreclosures. He even hired a temp to help file papers; you met her, Nancy. It's a good thing I work there, Louis might give us a discount when *we* file Chapter Thirteen."

"Thanks for the shot of encouragement, Shell. I *need* you to stand behind me on this. We *will* eventually get that house in the country. Trust me. My plan starts with selling my Bimmer."

"Wow! We can buy two houses then; a summer home here, and a winter retreat in Florida," she stated extremely sarcastically, rolling her eyes.

At this point, Christian was becoming upset with her attitude, his voice rose a few decibels as he explained, "Selling the car and buying a cheap pickup truck is only the first step! That will be one less payment and give us some capital; these cars hold their value. Step two is moving out of this townhouse and *buying* a house that we can build equity in. For eleven years, we've been throwing money away every month on rent that we'll never see again. I don't even want to figure out that amount! I'll tap my 401k for a down payment."

He rose from his chair to snag another Coke, but kept rambling, "I've been looking at real estate ads in the paper for the past two months now. There's a couple of places I had hoped we could have checked out after I got my promotion. I remembered you saying you liked that A-frame outside of Delmont when we drove past it, so I had a real estate agent keeping me current with a list of properties in that area in our price range. I was going to surprise you with it. We'd be out looking at them. Right now! Tonight! But shit happened. Okay? To be more precise, *McKelvey* happened! But we will get our own house."

Shelby calmed down after she saw how mad he was getting, and his comment about the realtor floored her. In a more composed tone, she said, "That's all well and good, Christian, but how can we afford to keep the place after we spend everything we own to get it? You need a source of income. Creditors aren't going to be happy with you not working. How will we get a loan now? Did you consider that?"

"Yes. At the present time, we can't afford any of the properties on *that* list. I called my realtor earlier and told him to focus mainly on rent-option-to-buy properties, and foreclosures. Cheapies. With a large down payment from my 401k plan, you alone could qualify for a mortgage if we need one. I'm hoping we won't, but a mortgage payment will still be cheaper than rent!"

She interrupted, "I deal with foreclosures every day; most of the houses are really beat. And if you own a house, you can't simply call the landlord when something breaks like we do now. You'll have to either pay someone, or learn how to fix things on your own."

He nodded while answering, "I'm aware of the pros and cons of owning a house. Once we get situated out in the boonies, I will use the peace and quiet to write. I'm not going to start my book till we're moved in. Until then, I'll find a job, and we're going to be thrifty."

Shelby watched in disbelief when her famished husband took such a huge bite of sub, he had to use his fingers to keep it from falling out of his mouth while chewing; he continued with his muffled explanation, "I went to school for writing, and that's what I want to concentrate on. Only, I don't want to write sports shit anymore. I'm going to be an author and write... fiction!"

That revelation shocked her; she had no response other than, "I'm putting on sweats and hitting the gym. I need to think this through."

CHRISTIAN KEPT HIS word, within three days, he found work at Dunham's Sporting Goods, where, with his sports knowledge and gift of gab, he fit right in and turned out to be an excellent salesman.

However, nearing the last week of March, he informed his boss, "Clifford, April First will be my last day, I'll be closing on a house, and it needs a lot of work."

Clifford said, "I'm hoping this is an early April Fool's Day joke. Right?"

"Sorry, no."

"Oh well, I'm going to hate to see you go, but good luck. My cousin flips houses, he's doing pretty good. I think you will, too."

On the second day of April, the Kanes found themselves seated at Goldberg's massive mahogany table, signing the deed to a house which sat on a two-acre parcel situated thirty-five miles east of Pittsburgh on the distant outskirts of Latrobe. An agreed upon purchase price of seventy grand wiped out three quarters of his retirement savings; the bank had listed the property for eighty-five; Christian played hardball and made them drop their price. The foreclosed, four-bedroom fixer-upper was surrounded by cornfields, dairy farms, and potato farms; he called it rustic; she called it dilapidated. Christian said he loved the clean, fresh country air; Shelby said she hated the smell of cow shit and referred to the place as, "Green Acres."

Her husband knew it was not the type of house she had been hoping for; during the final walk-through inspection, he assured her, "This is only our starter home. We will eventually move on."

Shelby then asked him a question, but she teasingly sang it, nasally like Debbie had sung it, but swinging her derriere much better, "Are we movin' on up? To that deluxe apartment in the sky... eye? Will Christian get a piece of the pie... eye?"

With a roll of his eyes, he told her, "Oh please. I'm trying to forget that night."

That evening when Shelby went to the gym, she had done an awful lot of thinking and soul searching while pounding out eight miles on the treadmill. She concluded that her husband was a proud and stubborn man; in addition, any goal he set, he achieved it. Also, he was a damn good journalist. There was no argument on that point; he could write. Twice, Christian won the city's *Young Journalist* award early in his career. Several times in the past he had mentioned how he would like to compile a book on the all-time best homerun hitters or the most winning football coaches.

"*He just might make this work,*" she tried convincing herself.

However, she also had stipulations he had to agree to before she would stand one hundred percent behind her man. One, they were not tapping into her retirement account.

Two, they were not to touch his life insurance; she needed that cushion knowing money would be available if something were to happen to him.

Three, he had one year to prove he could earn what he gave up to be an author; at which time, he would either ask McKelvey for his old job back, or find suitable employment at another paper.

She told him, "After one year, you will find a job where the pay is comparable to what you were pulling down at the Paper. Then, if you want to keep on writing, it will have to be more like a hobby than treating it like a job that has no paycheck to show for it, only expenses."

There was just one part of his scheme she did not understand and agree with. During one of their many discussions concerning his new career, she had asked him, "Are you going to write about athletes, or sports personalities that you either idolize or are familiar with? You interviewed almost every Steeler; you could write a book called, "The History of the Black and Gold," you could include your pictures and interviews. I bet that would sell; it would make a great Coffee Table Book."

He replied, vehemently insisting, "I told you I'm done with athletes and sports figures in general! No more football, baseball, or golf; I'm going to pen a fictional story. Maybe I'll write about werewolves. Better yet, vampires. The public can't get enough of those kinds of thrillers."

She responded, "You'd better hope that the market hasn't been sucked dry. Pun intended."

For that smartassed quip, she had received his crappy smile, but he did agree to her terms.

CHRISTIAN'S EXPECTATIONS of moving in and immediately hammering out chapters to his novel were shattered the very first day when he turned on the water main. Many of the pipes had burst due to the fact the vacant place had not been winterized. Water gushed from the upstairs bathroom plumbing, then leaked through the kitchen ceiling. Their already damp and musty cellar had the appearance of having overhead sprinklers from the gallons of water spraying out of all the broken pipes.

Not being very mechanically inclined, and owning but basic tools, it took the man a week and a half to repair or replace the split copper tubing and busted S traps under both sinks. Pipes buried in the ceiling rafters proved nearly impossible to get at and replace; then he discovered a crack in the hot water tank and the only toilet, rendering them both useless.

Two more items for Spring Cleanup, however, his recliner stayed.

He actually hooked up the new toilet, and an electric hot water tank all by himself! His rusted truck proved to be a required, valuable asset when going to Home Depot.

Finally, with all the water woes repaired, and their lease expiring in three days, the proud new homeowner proclaimed the house as livable. The Kanes packed the rented U-Haul truck, said their goodbyes to the neighbors on the cul-de-sac, then moved into the old farmhouse.

Christian set up the smallest bedroom as his den, whereas Shelby temporarily hung murals and pictures to cover the more noticeable cracks that seemed to be on every plastered wall throughout the entire house.

Later on, once their clothes and belongings were somewhat organized in their new home, she took her time while scouring, then painting and decorating the old-fashioned farmhouse's bathroom; she spent two days alone on the huge, original clawfoot tub.

Once finished, the room resembled a picture from a magazine in the waiting room at work that she had thumbed through during lunch one day; you would swear Bob Vila and his team of professionals had come in and done the makeover; she removed six layers of different colored paint from the wainscoting before returning it to natural wood, then staining it light oak. The woman found her hidden talent.

Her next project? The kitchen! That too, turned out amazing; her husband commended her, "You wield that paintbrush and roller like a pro! You're really raising the equity in this old house. With you standing behind me, our plan can't fail."

"I'm just keeping busy; trying to brighten our home and make it pretty while you're fixing the plumbing; but isn't it amazing what stain, paint, and spit polish can do, though?"

Late on a Tuesday evening, a thunderstorm threatened in the distance as he excitedly sat down behind his *antiquated* word processor. He had just enjoyed his first, long hot shower in the new residence; he felt pumped, chomping at the bit to write his first novel.

Brilliant streaks of lightning zigzagged across the pitch-black sky, briefly turning night into day outside his window, as the April rains lashed at the old glass panes. "*Excellent!*" he thought, "*The perfect ambience for writing a best-selling thriller. I'll show you, McKelvey!*"

All the words and ideas that had been flooding his head for the past few months were now finally going to become reality. Ecstatic, he cracked his knuckles and rubbed his hands together.

The new author then began typing, "*The Vampire's Feast*", by Christian Kane.

"Chapter One... Count Igor Wazleski awoke. The Sun went down, and the vampire was hungry and required blood. He climbed out of his coffin and went out into the dark night, scouting for victims. He was six foot six and weighed in at two-forty. Lightning flashed. Thunder boomed. His fangs were sharp and long too. He spotted a young girl and ran very fast like a wide receiver at her. Thunder boomed again. He tackled her to the ground and sunk his fangs into her neck. She screamed and kicked trying to break loose. He drained six pints of red blood from her body..."

Christian's glee quickly turned to disappointment when a drop of rainwater splashed off his head; a second later, another one. Then another. Apparently, the roof required his attention, also.

Before he could react, a blinding, jagged lightning bolt streaked through the skies overhead, briefly turning night into day, followed by a long roll of thunder which rumbled and echoed up and down the valley.

Throughout the house, each loose glass pane in the seriously aged, wooden frames rattled from the thunder's bass. Several of the windows were beyond help with just new glazing alone. (Glazing — special window caulk used to help secure the panes in the frames.)

As could be expected, the tiny desk lamp went out at the same time his word processor whirled to a stop. The Chinese water torture only worsened as he sat in total darkness shaking his head in utter disgust. Within a few moments, his lamp flickered a few times and then came back on. However, with no battery backup, the monitor remained black, so he hit the *on* button. While waiting for the machine to boot up, he moved his chair and positioned his small trashcan so it would catch the dripping rainwater.

When his processor finally booted back up to full speed, all his beautiful words were gone. With no data recovery ability, Count Igor Wazleski was not to rise from the ashes, run like a linebacker, and suck anymore *red* blood from his tackled victims tonight.

He bitterly mused, "Perhaps McKelvey was correct; *I do live in the Dark Ages.*"

Ironically, he no sooner said that, and another brilliant flash knocked the lights back out; he sat in total darkness as the thunder rolled, sounding as though traveling through a gigantic, ten-mile-long barrel. This time, the power stayed off for half an hour!

SINCE SHELBY NOW HAD a rather lengthy forty-five-minute commute to Grant Street instead of her once twenty-minute ride from their townhouse, eight AM found Christian saying goodbye in the graveled driveway.

"Drive carefully, Honey, and thanks for letting me go get a laptop today. I need to pick up some roofing tar, too."

"You be careful on the roof; I'd feel better if you called a roofer."

"Believe me! I will be very careful up there. A fall would absolutely ruin my day!"

With stern eyes, she warned him, "It would ruin mine, too! You be careful! Love ya!"

After their goodbye kiss, he closed her door.

At Best Buy, the laptop that Christian had picked was the cheapest one in the store, with limited features. Young, pimple-faced Heather, the electronics clerk, was more than happy to spend an hour showing her handsome customer how to operate it; she quickly volunteered to give him a quick tutorial on Microsoft Word. Shoppers were sparse that early in the morning, allowing her the time. Apparently she also had an attraction to men with beards. Seeing as where Christian had not shaved or went for a haircut since quitting the paper over three months ago, he was rather downright scruffy, much to his wife's dislike. However, his appearance did match perfectly with the nineteen seventy-four rusted and dented Toyota pickup truck he was now driving; he'd pass as a construction worker when behind the wheel, hauling two by fours and drywall.

Satisfied with the roof-patching job, he washed the sticky globs of the shingle cement from his hands and the borrowed ladder from his father-in-law; he changed out of his filthy jeans and Pitt sweatshirt, made a cheese sandwich, then got comfortable in front of his brand-new laptop.

With renewed excitement, he started Chapter One again. Christian amazed himself on how much he remembered from last night.

His words were nearly identical to his first draft.

Minutes before Shelby's tires crunched through the gravel, he had just put the finishing touches to the first chapter of his *masterpiece*, then excitedly printed out Chapter One of "*The Vampire's Feast.*"

He had nine pages of Igor the Count *tackling* his victims to the ground like a Defensive Guard, then suck them dry of their 'red blood'; leaving a trail of lifeless bodies in Igor's wake.

And with the push of a button, those words were saved! Hallelujah!

The excited new author ran the pages downstairs and placed them on the table at his wife's spot.

"Oh boy!" he said while vigorously rubbing his hands together when he spotted the takeout Chinese that Shelby carried into the kitchen.

Christian placed a can of off brand diet cola on the table for both of them; their new penny-pinching budget did not allow for name-brand soda, and takeout food had now become a rare treat. His wife sat; her eyebrows raised when she spotted the printed pages.

But before Shelby could comment, Christian interjected, "It was only forty-nine dollars on sale, and I figured I needed one to print out manuscripts for the publishing houses. I knew you would understand, Honey."

With little boy eyes, he gave her a peck on the cheek.

"You knew that, huh?" she unenthusiastically asked, then pointed out, "Hopefully, all the publishers haven't gone green, and some still accept paper. Everything is on the cloud these days. I use it every day at work. It's quick, efficient!"

Her husband thought, "*Wow! Déjà vu,*" but told her, "Now I want you to read Chapter One, but I also need you to be my worst critic. Don't tell me it's excellent just because you love me. If it stinks, tell me. Pretend like you don't even know me."

She chuckled and told him, "Haha! That'll be easy enough. I *don't* recognize you anymore with that mange on your face. When *are* you going to shave and cut that mop?"

He finger-raked his lengthy locks off his forehead while saying, "All successful authors have long hair and beards. It's only natural once we turn into recluses, typing day in and day out, tucked away in secluded cabins deep in the mountains. After my novel gets published, I'll shave. I promise."

"At least if you were to trim it like Kenny Rogers's hair and beard, maybe you wouldn't look so much like a scraggly hippie at Woodstock. You could join a hair band right now."

"I always wanted to tour with Motley Crue, but enough said about my facial hair for one night," he said, then dumped half the Chow Mein noodles onto his plate, gave her the rest of them, then snatched an egg roll from the tiny plastic bag. "Go on and delight yourself in the first chapter, but remember, be honest with your critique."

He used his teeth to tear open the tiny bag of hot mustard, then squeezed some onto his eggroll, took a bite and professed, "Whoa! That'll open your sinuses!"

After taking a bite of a Crab Rangoon and wiping her fingers on a napkin, she picked up page one. He watched intensely as her eyes scanned back and forth across the page. Every so often, her eyes would widen. "*She likes that part*," he figured, "*Igor must be tackling the jogger in the park.*"

Ten minutes was all the longer it took her to consume his work, and for him to consume his General Tso's Chicken, Chinese noodles, and two eggrolls garnished with hot mustard.

She stacked the papers back together neatly and reached for her soda.

"Well?" he impatiently asked. "What do you think?"

"The title's not bad, but the rest? It is pure crap. Look at what you wrote. It's not the beginning chapter of a novel; you have no plot. It's what you did for eighteen years; all you have accomplished was writing a nine-page sports column. And your quarterback is a vampire named Igor Wazleski?"

She could not hold her chuckle any longer, his wife laughed while finishing her critique, "Haha! He sounds more like a Polish truck driver with a severe hunchback than a blood sucking vampire. Sorry for laughing, but I thought your vampire story was supposed to be a comedy!"

Christian's chin fell to his chest; he pouted while saying, "Boy! You sure *are* a tough critic."

"Hey! You asked for honesty, and I gave you my opinion without sugar coating it. Sorry if I hurt your feelings. You're going to have to learn how to accept rejection in the book-writing business."

Christian rose from his chair, in a depressed tone of voice, muttered, "No, you didn't hurt my feelings; you may have bruised my ego a little, though. I need some fresh air; I'm going for a walk."

His head remained hanging low as he started for the door.

"Well, if you wait until I finish my supper, and if I'm allowed, I'll join you."

He slumped back into his chair and stared at the floor. "Okay," he mumbled.

Attempting to lighten his spirits and possibly redeem herself, she asked, "Aren't you *reclusive* writers that live *deep in the mountains* also supposed to have a tough shell for rejection under that hair and beard?"

Shelby reached over and placed her hand under his chin, raised his head, and gazed deeply into his eyes. She then gave him an encouraging smile while putting her other hand atop his. "All you need to do is change your style, wipe those old formats from your cute little head, and learn how to write fiction."

She chuckled very lightly, "Ha! You even gave Igor a ninety-three percent success ratio in his tackling abilities. Your protagonist is not a vampire, he's a freaking linebacker with fangs and a thirst for, '*red*, blood'!"

Christian smiled weakly; he shook his head lightly in agreement, "You're right, it sucks the big one! I'll never be able to write like Anne Rice, or Stephen King."

She disagreed, assuring him, "Why not? What's stopping you? They are no smarter than you. If you're going to write a make-believe story, you have to quit writing from your head. Throw away all those facts and figures. You must do what those writers do..."

She pointed to her ribcage and said, "You need to learn how to... *Write from your heart, Christian*!"

Oh, but how his woman's simple words and gentle touch had the uncanny ability to soothe and heal his tortured, battered soul. However! Not until later, when he fully understands her value, and the merit of her spoken words, will he be delivered from his personal Hell.

He smiled contentedly and said, "That's the kind of 'shot of encouragement' I need, I'll try to do that. Thanks, this is why I love you."

"Love you back, more!"

After she ate, they stepped outside; Christian pulled the door behind him.

Walking hand in hand and engaging in small talk, mostly about the law firm and deciding on a better name for Christian's protagonist, the Kanes walked the perimeter of their two-acre parcel. Christian liked referring to their run-down property as — "The Kane Estate."

After coming up with several names, Shelby conjured up the moniker, *Draven Blackstone*, for Christian's night-stalking blood sucker. "I like that!" he enthusiastically agreed, "That's great! I'll use it."

An old logging trail ran along the boundary line of their back yard, they mindlessly wandered on to it. As far back as the Eighteen-thirties, horses carved these tram roads when pulling downed trees from the forest. The sapling riddled path started out four-feet wide, then funneled down to a deer trail, which took them to a small creek. (Pronounced, 'crick', in The Appalachian Mountains.)

Christian took Shelby's hand and helped her across the slippery rocks as they continued their nature hike. Walking up a small incline, she pointed to a patch of black and yellow wildflowers, "Look, Christian. I guess April showers do bring May flowers!"

He had to chuckle at her *little girly* remark.

As he admired the blooming Black-Eyed Susans, he saw an odd rock protruding from the ground, he exclaimed, "Look, Shell! Is that a... *Tombstone,* over there? Under that snapped-off branch?"

They walked to the flat-faced, rounded-on-top stone sticking two feet out of the ground, being careful not to walk on the grave itself. After Christian tossed the pine limb, Shelby bent over and squinted to read the badly weathered inscription, she spoke slowly while deciphering the words and numbers, "Rachel, Petersen. Born, Eighteen, Fifty-One. Died. Eighteen, Sixty-Three."

Then she added, "This girl was only twelve years old! She died so young. That's sad."

"I wonder how she died. That's right around The Civil War era, right?" he asked.

Goose bumps ran up and down Shelby's arms. "Yeah, I think so. This is too spooky for me. Let's go back home." She took his hand and tried to walk away, but he remained standing, staring at the crudely chiseled flat rock.

His fascination with the stone and refusing to budge stopped her in her tracks; he told her, with glazed over wide eyes, "Hunchbacked Igor Wazleski just backed his truck over Draven Blackstone."

He nodded with determination, and confidently said, "I'm going to write this young girl's story!"

"That's nice, Christian. Can we go home?" she nervously asked, tugging his hand to hurry him.

"What's the matter? Don't tell me you're scared."

"A little. I feel like someone is watching us."

She quickly glanced all about. "Come on, Christian! Please?"

He tried absorbing everything about the tombstone into his memory in two quick seconds, while thoughtlessly saying, "Sure, Honey. Whatever you say."

Wishing he had a camera, McKelvey's caveman comments smacked him upside his head, *"These phones, by the way, also take pictures!"*

Shelby straightened up the kitchen while Christian pounded away at his laptop. He read aloud the few pages he had typed. "Rachel's Story by Christian Kane. Chapter One... Rachel Petersen was born in 1851 on a cold December morning. She was seven pounds, two ounces and nineteen inches long. She had brown hair. Her mother's name was

Matilda. She was happy to give birth to Rachel. The pain was not that intense. Mr. Petersen was a proud father, too, because Rachel was their first girl; the Petersens already had four boys..."

Then Christian hit the delete button and mumbled, "I have to get these damned basketball players and statistics out of my head. No more sports columns!"

He went back downstairs, grabbed a bottle of water from the fridge, then plopped his butt into his Lazy Boy.

"*As usual*," he thought, "*There's nothing worthwhile watching on the tube.*" He's felt this way ever since he vowed never to watch anything sports-related ever again.

"May as well catch the weather and the news, then turn in," he told Shelby, who was curled up under an afghan in her corner of the sofa, already half asleep.

"Okay, Baby," she muttered back.

AS ALWAYS, CHRISTIAN walked his wife to her Mazda after their breakfast of coffee and English muffins; this time topped with homemade strawberry jam they bought at the local Mennonite store.

However, this morning he forewarned her, "Last night when you were sawing logs on the couch, Channel Four said we might get a freak snowstorm this morning. You drive extra careful today, Honey."

"You always say I snore! I know I don't! Quit telling everybody that!"

She glanced at the sky and said, "Oh! It does look a little threatening. Darn it! I just got the studs taken off Saturday.

Don't worry about me, I'll take my time, you start writing that best-seller. Think about what I told you. Love you."

He gave his usual response, "But I loved you first." Then he kissed her goodbye.

After she drove off, Christian went back inside, grabbed a folding stadium chair and his laptop. Briskly, he walked to Rachel Petersen's grave, hoping she could give him inspiration.

Once he had the tiny collapsible chair propped up against the base of a nearby pine tree, he opened his laptop. Quickly he typed, *Rachel's Story, by Christian Kane, Chapter One...*

And nothing more. His mind went totally blank.

He looked at the tombstone and asked aloud, "What's your story, Rachel?" He listened for half a minute. Nothing but silence answered the man.

"Talk to me little girl. Why did you die at such a tender age?" He waited as if expecting to hear words to be spoken from the twelve-year old girl who died one hundred and sixty years ago.

Again, no response, "But my biggest question is, why are you buried out here in the middle of the woods? Were you murdered and not supposed to be found? Or did you die from a very contagious disease, and they buried you way out here to prevent it from spreading?"

Christian looked all around when he heard leaves rustling; apprehensively, he asked, "Rachel? Is that you? Shelby felt your presence! I know you can hear me! Rachel?"

Of course, nobody replied, then he began to mentally erode, admitting to himself out loud, as if confessing to his wife, "God! Who in the Hell am I trying to kid? I'll never write fiction. I'll never be Stephen King. I'm a sportswriter, and now I'm trying to communicate with the dead. You're losing it, Man!"

Thoughts of him on his knees, kissing McKelvey's big fat ass flooded his mind as he stared out from under the evergreen's branches into the eeriness of the silent forest; into nowhere, except for the abyss of his own psyche. "How could I have been so stupid? Egotistical! Why didn't I just let Campbell prove to McKelvey he would fail? I totally disrupted Shelby's life. I moved us from our beautiful little townhouse into a shack! I sold my BMW for a piece of shit truck."

He shook his head in total self-disgust while reprimanding himself, "And then I even squandered my life savings. What a fool I am! An *unemployed*, blundering... Fool!"

"Christ, man. You got your head up your ass," he further lectured himself.

A beautiful, light tan colored doe and her two white-spotted fawns rustled more dry leaves as they tried to sneak past him; all three stopped and stared at the man.

"How could I have been so stupid?" he asked the deer, causing the doe to snort, sound the silent alarm, then run off with her fawns following her raised white tail.

Moreover, to make the whole situation worse, a fine, light powdery snow began falling; the kind that makes driving treacherous within minutes. He prayed his beautiful, loving, supportive wife made it safely to work, to earn a living and provide for *both* of them. Something he felt *he* should be doing! Not her! Guilt, humility, and self-loathing began gnawing away at his soul.

Christian stared at his laptop's screen for two seconds, then frowned as he deleted the little he had typed. He put his hand on the lid and slammed it shut. "I am so sorry, Shelby. You are one in a million, I don't deserve you."

He closed his eyes, forcing out the few tears that had pooled; he then reflected on his wife's natural beauty, her gentle touch, how her unique contagious laugh caused others to join in, and especially her soothing voice, just like last night when she tried comforting him by gently saying, *"Write from your heart, Christian."*

Precisely at that moment...

The wind picked up a bit and carried dry leaves off in a small whirlwind that danced around the tombstone. Then, the miniscule tornado lingered as it crisscrossed back and forth over the grave.

Immediately, thoughts of this dead girl and her life so many years ago swirled throughout Christian's mind. It was as though Rachel Petersen herself stepped from her grave, sat down with the man under that pine tree's boughs deep in the middle of the woods outside the small town of Jonesboro, Pennsylvania, and graciously unraveled her life story for him to write, and for the entire world to read and be told why she was out here, all alone.

Tiny snowflakes fell as his words flowed effortlessly, flawlessly, magically falling perfectly into place, one following the next, as he penned the dead girl's story which begins in the year 1950.

Eighty-seven years after she was buried!

Chapter Five

"The Legend of Rachel Petersen"
by Christian Kane
Chapter One

Gigantic snowflakes, bigger around than silver dollars, began floating lazily down from gray skies over the southwestern corner of Pennsylvania. They blocked the first of the Sun's rays as the orange ball began its early morning ascent over the Appalachian Mountain Range, welcoming the much-anticipated opening day of deer hunting season. In fact, so many snowflakes were falling, that a hazy gloom had settled in over the landscape which made the time of day look more like dusk, not dawn.

With no wind whatsoever, the few dried up brown leaves that defiantly disobeyed Mother Nature by stubbornly clinging to the trees, did not rustle. In the eerie, roaring silence of the woods and harvested cornfields, these enormous snowflakes pirouetted straight to the Earth, making their own little wispy sounds upon landing. The frozen precipitation quickly transformed the entire terrain and every bit of vegetation into a solid white, surrealistic world.

"Perhaps there is a God after all," fifteen-year-old Thaddeus Yoder jokingly whispered very quietly to his thirteen-year-old brother Seth. The two young hunters were hunkered down in the eerie pre-dawn darkness underneath a huge, century old hemlock tree a half mile deep in the woods. "Last night I prayed for snow today. Now we'll be able to track Bocephus; that is if we are lucky enough to kick him out. Remember, don't shoot at any does, or even at any small bucks; we don't wanna scare Ol' Bo off. We can always pop a doe or a spike later if need be."

Seth nodded that he understood.

The enormous whitetail buck that had successfully dodged the Yoder brothers for the past two hunting seasons was known to be sporting a twenty-two-point rack this year. Thaddeus affectionately nicknamed their elusive quarry, *Bocephus*, after hearing the name on The Grand Ole Opry show one evening on the radio. In addition, the two young brothers were more determined now, than ever, to bag this monstrous trophy buck.

Especially Seth. For he did manage to squeeze off a round at the deer last year, but missed.

"Given a chance, I ain't gonna miss that big sonna bitch this year," the younger brother whispered matter-of-factly, then spit a mouthful of tobacco juice on the freshly fallen snow. His hot, brown saliva, peppered with tobacco grains, immediately melted through the snow, resembling a necrotic wound devouring its way through flawless, pale skin.

"I'm hopin' to get that big bastard in *my* sights," the older, taller brother said. "One shot with my Ol' Henry here, an' Ol' Bo's goin' down, I tell ya. I ain't gonna miss like you did when you had your chance of baggin' him last year."

"You oughta try shootin' sometime with glasses on, Thaddy. It ain't that easy," near sighted Seth made an excuse to his brother, who was blessed with twenty-twenty vision.

The truth of the matter was that Seth missed the big deer due to an acute case of *Buck Fever*, not his glasses, as he had himself convinced. Bocephus was standing broadside at a mere forty-five yards from the youngster, offering him a perfect kill shot. However, Seth was shaking so badly when he *jerked* the trigger, the fifty-caliber led ball whizzed twelve inches safely over the deer's back. With no snow on the ground, tracking was impossible; they never spotted him for the rest of the year. The smart old buck holed up in thick cover only to venture out at night, returning once again to his nocturnal feeding habits.

This year, the Yoder boys were in the woods one half hour before daybreak in the exact spot where Seth missed last year. They were hoping to ambush Bocephus when the deer made his way back to his bedding area after a nighttime feeding in the harvested cornfields. With an occasional shiver, they waited in the frigid twenty-degree morning air for daybreak. Per Thaddeus's prayer, the huge flakes had piled up deep enough for excellent tracking.

When the Sun had finally climbed halfway over the ridge, Thaddeus spoke quietly, "We musta missed him. You stay put here, an' I'll sneak on down to the pine grove, then circle on back up from...."

The muffled sound of a twig snapping cut him short. Both boys instinctively froze; they used their eyes only to scan the area from where the noise came. Seth's heartbeat quickened when he spotted a white tail's ear twitching in his peripheral vision, roughly forty yards away in a group of saplings. Squinting overtop his glasses and through the falling snow, he saw it was a big old doe. "*Damn.*"

For the next two minutes, the doe and the brothers were locked in a stalemate; neither the boys, nor the antlerless deer would move. She had winded them and knew they were close by, but she could not see them. Finally, sensing danger was near, the doe let out a long, loud snort; then her tail went up. She snorted one more time and bolted. Behind her were two younger, smaller does, which also took flight.

And behind them, in all his grandeur! Stood Bocephus!

The dominant buck also snorted and took off in graceful leaps and bounds, crashing through the oak saplings, following his does. Both boys raised their guns; the quicker Thaddeus fired. Click. Sha-boom! Unfortunately, he missed.

"Damn it!" he shouted, then ordered his brother, "C'mon Seth. Shoot that sonna bitch!"

Shaking even worse than last year, the younger boy held his breath and *squeezed* the trigger; he didn't jerk like the last time he had Bocephus in his sights. Click. Sha-boom! Through a cloud of black powder smoke, Seth watched the led ball tear through hide, flesh, and bone, causing the twenty-two-point behemoth to stumble and go down. "Yeah!" he excitedly hollered. "Yeah! I got him, Thaddy! I got that big sonna bitch this time! Wa Hoo!"

However, Seth's victory celebration was short lived. Much to his dismay, he watched as Bocephus struggled to his feet, then take off running before either one had a chance to reload their antiquated firearms for a second shot. "God damn it," Seth swore, "Shit." All they could do was watch as the huge set of antlers gradually disappeared deep into the forest. Gone!

Both boys stared in the direction the wounded deer ran, long after he had vanished completely.

Thaddeus eventually spoke, "I didn't even see him till he started to run. I know I had that big bastard dead in my sights, though. Musta hit a sapling; I tell ya."

"Wonder how bad he's hurt?" Seth pondered.

"He went down, didn't he? Let's reload an' wait a half hour, then we'll start trackin'. Betcha Ol' Bocephus is gonna lie down somewhere an' bleed out," Thaddeus suggested, as if he were a guide leading a hunt on a game preserve.

"I suppose," Seth, still trembling from the excitement of actually seeing Bocephus and handed a chance to redeem himself, agreed while pulling a thermos of hot tea from his oversized hunting coat. Just like the *smoke guns*, their clothing and thermoses were old, battered or stitched; all of which were handed down through the generations of the Yoder clans. Nevertheless, Seth and Thaddeus did not mind; the guns fired accurately, the patched coats were warm, and the tea was hot and sweet.

Actually, Seth was rather extremely proud of wearing his dead uncle's Woolrich coat. Clyde Keselyak, the happy-go-lucky man who married their father's sister, held a reputation for being the best shot ever in the tri-county area. Sixty pairs of antlers mounted on his barn testified to that fact. Uncle Clyde's coat was four sizes too big for his small stature; but even being too large and having a half dozen patches hand sewn on it did not keep that old red and black plaid coat from being one of the boy's most cherished Christmas presents, ever.

Thirty minutes later, with a couple of swallows of hot tea warming their bellies and fresh powder and ammo in their flintlocks, the brothers walked to where Bocephus went down. "Holy shit!" Thaddeus exclaimed, "Look at all the blood an' hair. He ain't goin' far, I tell ya. A blind man could follow this blood trail. We'll find him easy. I doubt if he'll make a hundred yards." As usual, he led the way.

The weather changed as the young hunters tracked their wounded prey; the snow fizzled out as the clouds drifted by. The Sun now shined brightly down from a beautiful sapphire sky, sparkling off the pristine white snow like millions of tiny prisms. However, the mercury rose only five degrees; little puffs of steam escaped their mouths when they breathed or talked. "Christ, Thaddy. We been trackin' that sonna bitch for over a half mile now, an' he still hasn't gone down. How much blood's he got?"

"Not too much more I hope. You musta either gut shot him or put one in his ass," Thaddeus replied as he stopped by a downed tree; he used his foot to wipe a patch of snow from the old oak, sat, and leaned his rifle against the log. From the pocket of one of three flannel shirts he had layered under his coat, the youngster pulled out the *fixin's* for a cigarette and proceeded to twist one up.

Seth spit out his tired side chew, took another swig of tea, and told his brother, "No, I didn't put one in his gut; I'm sure I hit him high in the shoulder."

"I figger we might as well give him another chance to lie down," the older boy said, then fired up his hand rolled smoke with a wooden kitchen match he struck against his metal thermos. Tobacco was just one more crop, like tomatoes, beans, and cucumbers, which their father grew in the huge family garden that provided enough vegetables lasting from season to season. Extra produce was grown strictly for canning, to get them through the winter.

Their father, Ralph Yoder, had nailed, "Posted! Private Property!" signs on the trees outlining his three hundred acres of woods, fields, hills, and streams that made up his potato farm which had been passed down to him, which his boys were now hunting on. Thaddeus and Seth did not need a hunting license; for the most part, they did not care what was in season, or what season it was. Meat was meat. Their mother, Mary Yoder, could spice up a venison hindquarter or a ground hog, slow cook either in a pressure cooker, and convince her dinner guests they were eating pulled pork.

The potato farmer appreciated it when his boys took one more *whistle pig* from the fields. The damned woodchucks were excellent diggers; and holes in a potato field made it rough on the machinery, and costly for the farmer. Besides, using a 22-caliber rifle with open sights to shoot the varmints was fun target practice for the brothers, they made it more challenging by aiming for the critters' heads.

"The blood is gettin' less an' less. Ol' Bocephus should be droppin' soon, I tell ya," Thaddeus informed Seth, still speaking as if he was an experienced hunting guide; he took another long draw on the cigarette and passed it to his little brother. Seth removed a glove and finished what little bit his brother had saved for him, which was only three tokes. Then he packed his cheek with fresh side chew to curb his nicotine pangs.

"Make sure there's powder in your pan before we start out," Thaddeus instructed Seth.

Both boys made certain there was an adequate powder charge in the ignition pans. Without that small amount of gunpowder, the flint would spark, but the gun would not discharge. Many deer, and numerous men in fact, were fortunate to live another day because there was no, '*flash in the pan*', which ignites the main powder charge in the barrel, which in turn fires the rifle. These *ball and patch* rifles the two boys were toting actually witnessed and partook in the bloodshed on the killing fields at Gettysburg. Their primitive weapons were indeed guilty of laying two dozen or so Confederate soldiers into an early grave. Thaddeus's old Henry rifle had nineteen tally marks carved into the stock. However, nobody knew for certain who put them there and if the count was for slain deer or fallen soldiers.

Thaddeus liked to believe the notches were for the latter, and his great, great grandfather, Elijah Yoder, was a superior Union sharpshooter.

Again, the boys set out on Bocephus's blood trail; as always, Thaddeus took the lead and Seth followed.

After two hours, the wounded deer had led them a mile and a half through the woods; he took them across the picked potato fields, down the span of six utility poles on the never-ending power line before jumping off into a thick pine grove which was full of fresh deer beds, droppings, and spots of yellow snow; from both male and female deer.

"Well, we know where they bedded down last night," Thaddeus said, then pointed out a fact that his father had taught him, "Look how the does leave one nice, little hole in the snow, but the bucks are pissing everywhere because they're trying to pee on their scent glands."

Then the buck circled up over the ridge, across the barren cornrows, and back into the forest once more, but now, he was heading straight for Old Man Woodley's apple orchards, one quarter of a mile away. The brothers saw where the buck had stopped and undoubtedly watched for his pursuers, then run off. An occasional small blood clot melting a hole through the snow, or a patch of hair, gave the boys hope that the buck was soon to die from blood loss. The deer probably did see them or hear them approaching, but the boys never caught a glimpse of him.

The brothers still spoke quietly as they stopped for a breather just inside the tree line which encircled the vast field; Thaddeus scanned the woods and the field for any sight of their prey while saying, "Hope nobody took a stand in the orchard; it'd be a real bitch to chase Bocephus to some hunter that's been sittin' on his ass all morning."

"Yeah, I've been thinkin' that too," Seth agreed, also watching for any movement in every direction. "You know somebody always takes a post in there. Woodley's orchard was Uncle Clyde's favorite spot, an' he got his deer every year. I can remember him sayin', 'Sooner or later, that buck will get hungry from chasing his lady friends, an' he'll come in here for an apple; an' that's when I shoot 'em!' Then he'd laugh. I miss Clyde, but I really like his coat."

Thaddeus pulled out his pocket watch. "Yeah, I liked him, too. It's ten thirty; whatta ya say we grab a bite, then have a smoke an' get back on his trail before somebody else picks him up?"

He leaned his rifle against a tree then wiped the snow from a log and sat.

"Sounds good to me, Thaddy. I am a bit hungered." Seth propped his flintlock beside his brother's gun, kicked a spot clean on the log, then sat to enjoy his smoked ham on homemade rye bread.

Halfway through their sandwiches and... Boom! A gunshot rang out from the orchard and echoed through the valley. "Damn it!" Thaddeus exclaimed through a mouthful of sandwich.

Boom! Another shot roared. Then another, and another. Thaddeus laughed, "Haha. He missed him. Ol Bo's runnin'! Keep your eyes peeled Seth. He just might come back up this way. If *I* would've had that semi-automatic this morning that he was shootin' just now, Ol' Bocephus would be hangin' in the barn right now, I tell ya. I still say I hit a sapling."

Both boys were on their feet now, scanning the forest, watching the cornfield, and wolfing down the rest of their sandwiches.

"That sounded like a thirty-thirty lever action," Seth, with his mouth stuffed full of sandwich, pointed out.

"No way. Those shots were too loud. Sounded more like Clyde's thirty ought six. Betcha that was Amos," Thaddeus corrected his younger brother.

Amos, Clyde's twenty-two-year-old son, was too large to fit into his dead father's Woolrich coat, hence the reason it being passed down to Seth. However, Amos did keep his father's rifle.

"There he goes!" Seth hollered so excitedly that bits of his sandwich flew from his mouth. He pointed to the cornfield, holding the last bite of his sandwich in the same hand. Thaddeus turned just in time to see Bocephus, fifty yards away, cut through the far corner of the field, and flee back into the woods. The big buck was running on three legs now; his front left leg was mangled and flopping about.

"Hurry up! Let's go! Whoever just blew his knee apart is gonna be hot on his trail," the older brother stated. They shoved the last of their sandwiches in their mouths, pocketed their thermoses, grabbed their guns, then took off on a steady jog through the harvested corn stalks.

Within minutes, they found the deer's tracks, which led them back down in the hollow towards the pines and eventually onto an old tram road leading back up to the ridge, back onto their property. The brothers followed the blood trail and hoof prints on the old logging trail, which zigzagged for a quarter mile.

The tram road eventually went around a sharp bend and then straightened out, where they came upon Bocephus, only twenty yards in front of them, standing in the middle of the tram road offering a perfect side-shot as if he were a live practice target! The once magnificent and glorious, but now twice wounded and dogged Alpha Male in this part of the county, was now huffing and puffing like a coal-fired locomotive. Blood covered his entire side, steam rose from his back, and his front left leg was nauseatingly twisted under his body.

Seth's fifty caliber ball had ripped the buck's shoulder apart, whereas Amos's thirty ought six took out the deer's knee on the same leg.

The trophy buck turned his head and looked directly at his pursuers; sunlight reflected off his massive rack, which he lowered, as if preparing to charge.

Just as both boys raised their guns, the buck leapt off the trail into dense Mountain Laurel and once again disappeared.

"Shit!" Both brothers swore simultaneously.

They hurried over and resumed tracking through ten feet of Laurel, and then into a giant briar patch. "How can a deer with horns like that go through this shit?" Seth asked, using his arms to shield his face as he plowed through the jaggers behind his brother. The thorns ripped at their clothing, hands, and faces.

Twice, Seth's hat got yanked from his head and swung in the jaggers.

"I haven't a clue," Thaddeus replied as he emerged into a tiny clearing in the middle of the briars.

"Look!" The older brother hollered out in amazement. On the other side of the small clearing, lay Bocephus, motionless. Finally! The monstrous buck was lifeless, and their never-ending quest was over.

"Wow!" Seth exclaimed slowly as he walked up to the dead deer. "Look at that rack!"

"Later. Put one in his heart. Hurry up!" Thaddeus instructed.

"Why, Thaddy? He's dead. He ain't gonna run no more," Seth questioned that order.

"I can see he's dead; just do as I say, Little Brother," Thaddeus commanded, a hint of arrogant dominance in his voice.

With the flintlock pointed at the buck's ribcage, the smaller brother pulled back the flint, then squeezed the trigger. Click. Sparks flew, but no ignition, therefore, no discharge.

"We musta lost all the pan powder when we were high tailin' it through the corn field. Hurry up, get some powder in there an' shoot him."

Seth pulled a tiny vial from his coat pocket and poured a small amount of powder into the pan. He took aim at the heart again and pulled the trigger. Click. Sha-boom! Blood oozed from the puncture hole.

"It's shame we had to waste his heart. Mom could've made it taste like calf liver, but now, he's your deer for sure, Seth!" Thaddeus exclaimed.

Then he said, "Let's have our long overdue smoke."

The older brother propped his gun against a large flat rock that hadn't been completely covered in snow; oddly, the *fieldstone* had a rounded top.

Seth, while looking at the antlers, absentmindedly propped his gun against the same rock.

Smiling intensely, he passionately admired the buck while his older brother rolled two cigarettes.

"Twenty-two points, Thaddy. Look at the size of them tines. Christ! Even Uncle Clyde ain't got a rack this big on his barn," the proud young hunter said as he ran his bare hands admiringly over the dead buck's antlers.

"I ain't never seen a rack like this'n before, I tell ya. It sure is a beaut," Thaddeus congratulated his brother and handed him a cigarette. "Too bad we ain't got the money to get the whole head mounted. I know Pa would never spring for that."

"Yeah, I know," the younger boy sadly agreed as he struck a kitchen match off his old Stanley thermos; he extended his arm to light his brother's smoke before lighting his own.

"Maybe I'll do a skull mount. You know, let the bugs an' ants eat the brain and all the flesh off his head, but make sure to keep the antlers secured."

Thaddeus took a drag, then spoke as he exhaled, "Yeah, I guess that would be neat. It'd be like them Texas Longhorn skulls you'd find in the desert. Just keep the mice away; they like to eat antlers."

"Yeah they do. But boy, though, I sure would like to get the whole head done by a..."

Both boys turned to the thrashing sounds and swearing coming through the briars as Seth finished his statement, "... taxidermist."

Amos Keselyak came into view, then eventually into the small clearing. His normally red cheeks were even more flushed from the short hike, and his face was bleeding from the briars. As cold as it was, sweat dripped from his nose.

"Alright!" The six-foot one-inch heavyset boy exclaimed while walking toward Bocephus, "You boys found my buck for me!"

Seth now understood his brother's motive for shooting an already dead deer!

"No! We didn't find your buck! We found *Seth's* buck, Amos!" Thaddeus sternly stated to his cousin.

Amos raised a finger to silence Thaddeus, then talked down to him, "I shot this buck down in the orchard, in my dad's stand. Then I tracked him to here. I let four smaller bucks go by, waiting for this big bastard. Now help me gut him and drag him out of this thorn grove."

"Look here, Amos. Seth shot this buck at sunrise, I tell ya, up at the Big Hemlock, an' we been trackin' him ever since. Then we heard when you emptied your ought six at him down in the orchard. Tell me you ain't seen the blood trail leadin' up to when you blew his leg off," Thaddeus stated and folded his arms, waiting for a rebuttal.

"That's right, Amos, I shot him first. Didn't ya see the blood trail?" Seth backed up his brother's testimony, then folded his arms like Thaddeus did, the hand rolled cigarette hanging from his mouth.

"The only blood I seen was from when I shot him in the leg, and, in his heart," Amos insisted, using his rifle to point to the deer's shattered ribcage.

Their cousin then said, "He was broadside. I had his kill-zone in my crosshairs."

"He woulda dropped on the spot if you were the one that put a bullet in his heart with that ought six, and you know it. But he woulda survived with that busted leg though, until the coyotes got him. Seth plugged him here where he fell, I tell ya. That's the gospel truth, tell me different, Amos," Thaddeus pleaded his case.

"Yeah, Amos," Seth added. "Like Thaddeus told ya, I shot him first in the shoulder up at The Big Hemlock, then in the heart as he stood right here."

Amos looked down at Seth, pointed a finger in his face, got loud, and ordered him, "Shut up you little pip squeak! You're not even old enough to be smoking. My dad would be rolling over in his grave if he knew a *Yoder* was wearing his coat."

After resting his dad's powerful Remington rifle against a small sapling, he pulled out his Buck knife, then addressed Thaddeus as if he were a child, "I have a deer to gut. Now I strongly advise you to take your baby brother, and your old smoke guns, which couldn't kill a chipmunk let alone this monster, and get on home!"

Amos puffed up his chest, pointed his knife at them and shouted a warning, "Or I'm going to open up an extra big can of whoop ass on the both of you! Now git!"

A startled Seth jumped back. Thaddeus took the last drag from his cigarette, flicked it away, and calmly picked up his rifle as Amos dropped to one knee beside the deer.

Thaddeus then aimed the barrel directly at Amos's chest! In a low growling voice, through clenched teeth, he threatened his much bigger cousin, "You touch one hair on Seth's buck, Amos, an' there's gonna be another unfortunate hunting accident on the openin' day of deer season in Pennsylvania; just like there always is."

The fiery look in Thaddeus's eyes told Amos that the Yoder boy was serious about keeping Seth's trophy buck.

Amos told his smaller cousin, "Every one of you God damned Yoders are insane. You're all inbreds!" He then stood and sheathed his knife.

Thaddeus pulled the flint back into the firing position, "I should plug you for that remark alone, I tell ya. Get your fancy rifle an' get on out of here before I do just that an' show you what this, 'old smoke gun', will do. If your daddy's turnin' over in his grave, it's because he's embarrassed that he had you for a son. Clyde woulda downed this buck with one shot. He was a good shot an' a good man. Not like you, ya fat ass."

The Yoder boy then hollered at Amos, "Now, *you* git!"

"Yeah, Amos! *Get* on out of here," Seth, now much bolder, spoke up, "You're trespassin' anyways."

Amos picked up his rifle and turned to leave. Thaddeus kept his muzzleloader pointed at him and said, "An' for your information, *Asshole*... Your mother? Did ya forget that she's a Yoder?"

The bigger, defeated boy simply grunted an inaudible swear word and plowed his way back through the ring of jaggers. Seth looked at his brother after Amos was back out on the tram road and said, "I thought for sure you were gonna plug that sonna bitch."

"Couldn't have even if I wanted to. I was bluffin', an' he fell for it."

Thaddeus chuckled before continuing, "Did your gun fire the first time? No. Which means mine won't either."

Then, to prove his point, Thaddeus took aim at a stump ten yards away in the thicket and squeezed. Click. Sha-boom! The stump blew apart. Both boys stared at each other with wide-open eyes, then laughed.

"That coulda been really ugly, I tell ya," Thaddeus said while laughing, relieved that he didn't mistakenly shoot, and possibly kill, his cousin.

"Anyways, here's the plan, Seth. You stay here an' gut Bocephus, an' I'll take both guns home an' put a yoke on Dolly. Then I'll bring her back up here to drag this big boy home."

Thaddeus referred to an old mule Ralph Yoder kept on the farm for no good reason other than to occasionally pull a small manure wagon from the barn; Dolly was more of a family pet than a work animal.

"Good idea, Thaddy. We could never drag this big bastard by ourselves," Seth agreed.

The older brother reached for Seth's rifle but froze. "Whoa! Seth... Take a look at this!"

The rock their guns were leaning against was not just an ordinary rock, but a crudely chiseled gravestone!

"Wow! All these years an' we never knew there was a cemetery on our property," Seth exclaimed.

Looking around, Thaddeus commented, "Ain't no cemetery... just this one, lone, grave."

He wiped the snow off. "Can't make out the name or the date though; it's too weathered."

Seth pulled out his black-powder horn and poured some powder in his gloved hand. Then he wiped his glove over the front of the stone. The powder blackened the surface, but not the engraving, making the inscription somewhat legible.

"Rachel Petersen... Born 1851... Died 1863," Seth read the engraved words slowly.

"Holy Hell, Seth. We just found Rachel Petersen's grave! This proves that all of them stories about her *are* for real, and she's *not* just a legend, I tell ya!" Thaddeus exclaimed.

"And she's buried on our farm!" he added.

Seth's eyes widened to the size of moon pies; his jaw dropped open causing his cigarette to fall from between his lips. An icy shiver started between his shoulder blades and ran the entire length down his spine. Then it ran the whole way back up, tingling his scalp.

While shivering, thirteen-year-old Seth exclaimed, "Well... I'll be one dirty little sonna bitch!"

Chapter Six

Although Christian never hunted, or even shot any guns, the man described the hunt, and the muzzle loaders perfectly! Not giving those facts any thought, he furthered the little girl's tale...

Chapter Two

The young hunters knew transferring the huge deer from the woods to the barn would be quite an achievement, even with the old mule's unwilling assistance. Moreover, once Seth had found out the deer was lying on top of a grave, especially the infamous Petersen girl's final resting place, he begged Thaddeus to stay and gut the deer while he went for Dolly. Visions of a half-rotted corpse springing from the grave filled the youngster's head; not surprisingly, with her knife in hand.

"C'mon Thaddy; I'll go get Dolly. I can carry both our guns. Besides, you're a way better butcher than me; ten times better. An' what if Amos comes back? He's not scared of me like he is you," Seth hoped plea bargaining along with flattery would convince his brother to stay and gut the buck.

Thaddeus knew what was going on inside his little brother's head, he teased him, "I'll tell ya what, Seth. Let's drag him out of the jaggers to the tram road. You'll be safe there, *an' Rachel won't reach out of her grave and slice you up*!" Thaddeus laughed, then made haunting sounds.

"Ain't funny, Thaddeus. You heard all those stories. You know how evil that crazy girl was."

"You know the rule — "You shoot 'em, you gut 'em." Wanna gut him on the tram, or on top of Rachel's grave?" Again, Thaddeus teased, making additional ghost sounds.

"Knock it off, Thaddy."

"Seth! The tram or the grave? I'm goin' for the mule. Now hurry and make up your mind," Thaddeus ordered his sibling, who knew this would be the older brother's final warning.

"Let's drag him out to the tram," Seth said in a beaten tone, accepting his demise.

Due to the volume of briars, the sheer size of this monstrous buck's antlers, and just his bulk alone, that task turned out to be nearly impossible. Once on the tram road, Thaddeus commented, "I ain't never seen jaggers this thick before! Them bastards hurt!"

Then he laughed and said, "Haha! You gotta go back in there an' get our rifles! See ya in a bit."

Two hours after the younger brother had a steaming gut pile next to the giant buck, Dolly had pulled the deer to the barn effortlessly and was back in her stall, happily, noisily, munching on oats.

The boys hanged Old Bocephus by his back legs from a rafter. A place where hundreds of his kind were skinned and butchered over the decades.

Compliments of US Steel, a homemade leg spreader which had been welded together from scraps of rebar, was hooked into the deer's tendons of the lower back legs and tied to a block and tackle pulley system. Hoisting deer, pigs, and beef cows, up to a secure and workable height, made butchering them safer, and the task much easier.

"Wonder what Mom has simmerin' on the stove today?" Thaddeus pondered out loud as they pulled the barn door shut; once securely latched, the brothers headed for warmth and a hot meal.

The delicious aroma of vegetable beef soup greeted the boys as they entered the farmhouse, making them even hungrier. "Smells great!" Seth said, his stomach growling in agreement.

They kicked off their hunting boots, and after removing the black powder from the pockets, laid their coats on the big, warm radiator in the mudroom before entering the kitchen.

Their mother, with her long brown hair braided into a ponytail, had on her usual apron; she stirred the huge kettle of soup which sat on top of an old wood stove while instructing her sons, "Wash up before sitting down, you two."

She asked, "Either of you see any deer?"

"Yeah Mom, we did! Guess what?" Seth excitedly asked of his mother, while scrubbing the deer blood off his hands.

However, before she had a chance to venture a guess, he blurted out, "I bagged Ol' Bocephus!"

"Wow! You did? That's wonderful!" she said, truly excited for her son. "I knew you wouldn't miss, like last year. Your father sure will be surprised and happy for you, too. He really wanted to be out there with you two this morning, but the livestock auction was scheduled for today."

"An' then," Seth continued as he and his brother took their seats, "Amos tried to say the deer was his, because he shot it, too, but he only shot it in the front leg, an' it ran off."

She sat two bowls of steaming soup on the table, then turned to get the bread and butter.

With his mother's back to him, Seth continued telling his story, "But Thaddy told him that on the first day of buck season in Pennsylvania..."

His brother kicked him under the table, held his index finger to pursed lips, and briefly shook his head. Seth took the hint and faked a cough, he continued, "... Uh, Thaddy told him how this always happens because there's so many hunters on the first day. Thaddy explained how *I* shot him first, an' we tracked him all morning, an' he only shot the deer in the leg, but that didn't kill it. He was as mad as a hornet at first, but he let us have the deer."

"That big bully let you have the deer?" she asked in awe. "Maybe he changed his ways since his father's accident."

Although Clyde Keselyak loved living in the country, and actually did buy a small farm and raised a beef steer every year, the man was not a farmer. Rather, he opted to earn his living at a Pittsburgh steel mill as a machinist, thirty miles away. Also, he did not mind the lengthy commute, which could sometimes be an hour or longer on snow-covered roads. Ultimately though, his career was the reason he was no longer walking among the living.

Sixteen years of being a finishing lathe operator gave Clyde the experience, seniority, and knowledge, he needed to bid on, and be granted, the prestigious position of Roll Shop Foreman.

Three years ago, on the very day management informed him of his promotion, his relief called in sick; Clyde ended up pulling a double shift before making his routine stop at Murphy's Pub on the way home for his usual shot of Four

Roses bourbon chased down with a Schlitz draft. However, after working three to eleven on top his scheduled daylight shift, the man found the tiny bar to be wall to wall with U.S. Steel employees on that hot August night. Adding to his fate, it was also payday, which meant money, liquor, and laughter, were flowing as if tomorrow had been canceled. All of Clyde's friends and co-workers congratulated him on his promotion with handshakes, pats on the back, and round after round of top shelf whiskey. The man consumed more than his usual draft and shot that Friday evening.

Way too much more, unfortunately!

While driving very slowly and being only three quarters a mile from home, Clyde nodded off and drove his brand new 1947 Power Wagon straight into a telephone pole, which knocked the transformer down onto the cab of his truck, which in turn, decapitated the man and left his wife and son without power until the Pennsylvania Electric Company replaced both the transformer and pole.

Forty-five minutes after he wrecked, the coroner arrived and pronounced Clyde dead at the scene. The man found no skid marks, or any evidence of Clyde swerving to avoid hitting a deer; he declared, "Judging from the strong odor of alcohol on the deceased, it is safe to presume Mr. Keselyak drank too much; and then, after working sixteen hours, he simply fell asleep on the way home and drove straight into that pole. His truck suffered only minimal damage; in my opinion, he more than likely would have survived the crash if that particular pole wouldn't have had a transformer on it."

Thaddeus continued, "Yeah, he argued at first, but then he said Seth could have it!"

He then quickly changed the subject by saying, "Guess what else, Mom? All those stories about Rachel Petersen? They *are* true!"

"Now don't go and believe anything Amos told you about her. Rachel Petersen is just a figment of somebody's wild imagination. She is just a tall tale somebody made up a long time ago, like the Boogey Man, so little children would be good, listen, and do their homework. My mother would scare the dickens out of us children when I was a little girl. She would say, 'I can hear Rachel sharpening her knife,' and we'd all run to our beds and hide under the covers until we fell asleep."

"No, it ain't a tall tale, Mom, she *was* for real. We found her grave!" Thaddeus said while spooning soup into his mouth. "So that proves she did go around an' hack people to death, I tell ya!"

Seth contributed his two cents, "We tracked Bocephus till he fell over dead on her grave! We read her tombstone; she died in 1863! The Legend of Rachel Petersen is true!"

"How did you two make it through all those... Briars?" she asked, realizing what she had said before finishing her question. As soon as the woman said that, she knew she stuck her foot in her mouth.

Up until that point, Thaddeus had been shoveling soup into his mouth like he was a machine, hardly chewing the diced vegetables; his mother's words caused him to stop immediately. He held a suspended spoonful of vegetable beef soup close to his wide-open mouth.

Seth, too, could not believe what his mother had just accidentally revealed.

Both boys stared at her as if she had been betraying them for all these years.

"You knew? You knew that Rachel Petersen was for real... an' that she was buried on our property... but never told us? An' then you even lied about it?" Seth asked in disbelief. "Why?"

"Your father and I were going to tell you both, when you were a little bit older," she admitted, somewhat ashamed. "We just didn't want you to be frightened, that's all."

"Yeah, Seth, just like earlier when you didn't wanna gut Bocephus by the tombstone. You shoulda seen him, Mom. I thought he was gonna drop a load in his pants, I tell ya."

"I did not. I just thought it wouldn't be a nice thing to do. Ya know, puttin' deer guts on somebody's grave."

"You were afraid she was gonna come out of her grave an' carve you up," Thaddeus teased, making slicing motions with his butter knife, adding slashing sound effects.

"Boys! Now you see why we wanted to wait until you were older, and more mature?"

Then Seth asked, "Since she was buried on our property, does that mean she grew up in this house, too?"

She nodded. "I am afraid so. But the story goes that she was not born here, rather she moved here from Ohio when she was about twelve-years old. When her mother died, her father sent her here for her aunt to raise. She never adapted, and became emotionally unstable."

"What's that mean? Are you sayin' she went nuts an' really did stab her aunt, her uncle, an' cousins? In this house?" Seth asked with a bewildered, nervous look on his face.

"Again, I am afraid so. That's why your great, great grandfather, Elijah, bought this place so cheap after The Civil

War. Nobody wanted to live here after four people were found dead, stabbed to death while they slept," their mother said, frowning.

"What happened to her then?" Seth asked, as he finished his soup without realizing he had resumed eating, the boy was focused intensely on his mother's words, "Did she get the electric chair?"

His mother smiled and replied, "No. Remember now, this all happened almost ninety years ago; they didn't have electricity yet."

Seth wrinkled his forehead and asked, "Well then, what did happen to her?"

"The story goes that she hanged herself."

Before the inquisitive youngster could ask where, what, and why, his mother explained, "In the barn. Then, after they buried her, people would come from all over just to see her grave. Elijah got tired of city folk walking on his property, so he planted all those briars around it to keep the nuts away."

"Well, this is just great," Seth said sarcastically. "We are living in a house where a twelve-year-old girl went cuckoo, killed her family, an' then hanged herself in our barn."

"And she probably slept in *your* bedroom," Thaddeus said, along with his ghost sounds. "Listen, Seth," he cupped his ear with his hand, "Hear her sharpening her knife?"

"It ain't funny, Thaddeus," Seth hollered, just as they heard footsteps in the mudroom.

They all froze and watched as the doorknob turned. The door opened, and all three jumped. Their father came in and looked at them; he asked, "What's the matter? You all look like you seen a ghost."

"We thought you were Rachel Petersen," Thaddeus said.

Ralph Yoder, tall and lanky, with crystal blue eyes, and a sense of humor, asked, "Why? Were you expecting her? I haven't seen her around here for a couple of weeks now."

Seth's eyes widened, "You've seen... Rachel Petersen?" he asked, then looked around the room as those familiar shivers crept up and down his spine.

"Sure, lots of times. Usually at night when you're asleep and I'm..."

"Ralph!" his wife interrupted while filling a soup bowl for her husband, "This ain't a time for your nonsense. The boys stumbled upon her grave today while hunting. Didn't you notice how scratched up they are? So, I thought now was as good a time as any to tell them the truth about her."

In her mind, Mary Yoder did tell her boys the truth, simply because that's how it was told to her. The Legend of Rachel Petersen was passed down from generation to generation. Consequently, the boys' mother, along with countless others, believed that was exactly what had happened eighty-seven years ago in their quiet and peaceful hometown of Jonesboro, Pennsylvania, a small town where everybody knew everybody, and nobody locked their doors at night.

An incident of this horrible magnitude spread like wildfire back in 1863. Rachel Petersen slaying her family was talked about more than Abraham Lincoln freeing the slaves.

Even the War Between the States took second billing when town folk gathered.

Chapter Seven

C hristian's words continued to flow beautifully. He took his story even further back in time...

Chapter Three

Springtime in Ohio, 1863.

In and around Prosser's Hollow, Mother Nature once again painted the forests and fields various shades of green, as multi-colored wildflowers began blooming everywhere. The meadows and woods came alive with mating calls from the flocks of migratory birds returning from their southern sabbatical.

In front of the Petersen's farmhouse, a rather elegant and stylish, one-horse carriage, was tethered to the hitching post.

Doc Ferguson finished examining Rose Petersen as the woman lie comatose with shallow, but labored, breathing; the elderly gentleman then informed the dying woman's husband, "I'm afraid Rose's condition has taken a severe turn for the worst, Ishmael. She is not going to get better."

The Petersen's daughter, Rachel, sat by her mother's side as the doctor delivered the rest of his dire prognosis, "Other than making her last days comfortable, there's nothing anybody can do for her at this point. Here, this morphine will help ease her pain."

The doctor handed a small vial containing tiny white pills to Ishmael, then advised him, "With the war going on, this is a very precious commodity. Go sparingly with it. Chances are, though, Rose may not even regain consciousness and ask for any. I give her two weeks tops. Sorry."

The usually very shy and timid twelve-year-old girl tugged at the good doctor's suitcoat. With tear filled eyes, she frantically begged, "Please Doctor Ferguson, make Momma better. You can't let her die! Please wake her up! You have to!"

The very kind and caring doctor choked up from the desperate little girl's pleas, but he managed to maintain composure and hold back his own tears as he bent down to her level; he spoke the gentlest words he could find, "I am so, so, sorry, Rachel. I have done everything I can for your momma. Jesus wants her to be an angel and sing in Heaven's Choir."

Her mother did have an angelic voice; Rose sang in the church choir every Sunday as long as Rachel could remember, until bladder cancer weakened and ravaged her body.

Before becoming deathly ill, the woman would hum the hymns constantly while patiently teaching Rachel how to bake, sew, or can vegetables.

Her father walked the doctor to his buggy, "Sorry to be the bearer of bad news, Ishmael, but like I said, it won't be long, now. There's no charge for the pills, or today's visit."

Other than an occasional dash to the outhouse, or an infrequent meal, the faithful daughter would not venture far from her dying mother's side, continually saying things to her such as, "Wake up, Momma!" or, "Are you thirsty, I brought you water." and, "Look, Momma! Aaron's here!"

Then, sadly, exactly two weeks to the day after the doctor's dismal diagnosis, the frail Rachel placed her handpicked bouquet of wildflowers on her mother's casket as family and friends had gathered at the tiny church cemetery in Prosser's Hollow to pay their last respects to the late Rose Petersen.

Reverend Nolan, with outstretched arms and his eyes to the heavens, was bringing the funeral ceremony to its end. In a booming voice, he proclaimed, "Lord, your daughter Rose has suffered too long, and her hardships were numerous in this life. We know now, Father, Rose is finally free of her earthly bonds. Her heavy burdens have been lifted, and she is in your ever-loving hands. Happy is she, for she has been called to join you at your table. Amen."

In unison, the handful of mourners repeated, "Amen."

Then the extremely tall preacher addressed the two dozen or so people who were mostly all dressed in black, "This concludes our graveside service for Rose. Thank you all for being in attendance today. May the good Lord bless each and every one of you. Go in peace now, to love and to serve the Lord."

Slowly, everyone filed past the casket, then stopped to offer a covered dish, along with their condolences and kind words, to Ishmael and Rose's two children; then they continued to their awaiting carriages, a few choir women continued sobbing.

Clara Tremont, sister to Rose, attended not only to say goodbye to her older sibling, but also to take Rachel back to Jonesboro, Pennsylvania. There, the little girl would start a new life with family members she knew of, but could not remember ever meeting.

"No! I don't want to go!" Rachel cried out when her father took her by the hand and tried leading her to Clara's buggy. The tiny girl firmly planted her feet and frantically tugged in the opposite direction, leaving her father no alternative other than picking up the tiny girl and carrying her to the carriage.

"No! Please don't make me go, Papa! I want to stay here with you and Aaron," Rachel desperately pleaded, her spindly arms wrapped around his neck; with all her might, she held onto him and buried her face against his shoulder.

"Now child! You know you must go and live with your Aunt Clara! I don't have the means, or the knowhow, to raise a girl here on the farm," Ishmael, a stubbornly stern man, stated while forcibly setting Rachel on the seat between her Uncle Josef and Aunt Clara. The two of them had to help pry Rachel from Ishmael's neck while her older brother, Aaron, placed her bag in the rear of the buggy.

"I sure does appreciate you looking after Rachel for me, Clara. I know this is what Rose wanted," Ishmael told his sister-in-law. "I'll be sending money from time to time."

Clara hugged the sobbing little girl, not only for solace, but to prevent her from bolting; she told Rachel's father, "We are going to get along just fine, Ishmael. Don't you worry none. Rachel will be the daughter I've never had, but always wanted," she said with a forced smile.

Then she looked down at Rachel, who was watching solemnly as the undertaker began lowering her mother's casket into the ground; Rachel's Black-Eyed Susans lie on top of it. The little girl closed her eyes as tears raced down her cheeks, she cried out, "Oh, Momma, no! Momma!"

"Be careful gettin' home now, Josef," Ishmael warned his brother-in-law. "Keep your eyes open for any of them Southern rebel bastards."

"Will do, Ishmael. My boys are bringing up the rear; we brought every shooting iron we own. I hear the Southern Army hasn't made it past the Mason Dixon Line yet."

Josef was correct in his assumption of the Confederate Army's northerly advance. Being the first day of May in 1863, most of the war's battles were mainly fought in the South. It would not be for another two months yet, on the very first day of July, when General Robert E. Lee would lead his Confederate forces into one of the bloodiest battles men ever fought — The Battle of Gettysburg, Pennsylvania.

They said their goodbyes, shook hands, and Josef hollered, "Giddy up." The huge chestnut colored horse obediently lunged forward, jerking Rachel's head backwards as they began the fifty-mile trip that would take four hours, or longer, over the up and down twisting back roads. That is if their luck held out, and they had no broken wheels or encounters with Confederate soldiers.

Rachel turned and looked back. She saw her father climb into his carriage while Aaron stood by, wiping his eyes with one hand and waving goodbye with the other. The brother and sister were close, and Rose's only two children knew they would miss each other tremendously. Again, tears streamed from her red and puffy eyes.

During the long trip back to Pennsylvania, Clara tried several times talking to Rachel, but the distraught girl would not engage in any conversation. "That certainly is a pretty dress, Rachel." No response from the girl.

"We have a bedroom fixed up just for you." Again, no reaction; Rachel simply stared ahead of the horse; she felt numb, hollow, all cried out.

Finally, they turned onto a lane, bringing their exhausting, and fortunately, uneventful ride, to an end. The Tremont farm came into view. The large four-bedroom house had a wraparound porch where a swing and a pair of handmade rocking chairs welcomed guests. A huge red barn sat a hundred feet behind the main house; next to it were a chicken coop, a pigsty, and a small pond where a few white ducks were wading. To their left was row after row of thousands of tiny potato plants sprouting through the soil. On their right, four beef cows were grazing in the pasture alongside a dozen or so dairy cows.

As they were driving down the lane, a beautiful black stallion came charging through the pasture. His mane flowed elegantly, as did his tail, which he held upright. The majestic steed charged up to the fence, reared up on his back legs, and whinnied a loud greeting. "Well! Glad to see you too, Midnight," Josef said, speaking to the horse as if the animal were human.

Josef's two sons, Jacob and Jeremiah, tethered the horses to the hitching post and retrieved Rachel's bag. Her aunt suggested to Rachel they go see her room, but the little girl sat motionless.

"Now, come on, Rachel. I know how hard it must be for you, but life goes on."

She held her hand out for Rachel and pleaded, "Please? Rachel? You can't stay out here in the buckboard all night.

What do you say we go see your room; I dyed the curtains pink, just for you."

Reluctantly, the girl took her aunt's hand; Clara helped her step down from the carriage.

Clara led the way to Rachel's new bedroom. Upon entering, Rachel sat on the bed and stared at the floor. Her bag was already on the bed; her aunt pointed to a small dresser. "You can put your things in here; I'm going back downstairs to fix us a bite to eat. I will call you when it's ready. Do you like ham and sweet potatoes, Dear?"

Again, no response; her aunt shrugged her shoulders and left. Rachel simply sat on her bed and remembered her life back home, back to a time when she was happy, and her mother was not sick. It saddened her to think that Aaron would never chase her with a garter snake ever again.

Josef and his boys changed out of their Sunday clothes; then they took care of the horses, parked the buggy, and fed the livestock while Clara tended to supper. Rachel, oblivious to any noises, allowed her memories to carry her far away to more favorable times. In her mind, she was back in Prosser's Hollow using a cookie cutter, helping her mother bake; her mother was saying, "I think these sugar cookies are Aaron's favorite. Don't you think so, too, Rachel?... *Rachel?*"

For a brief moment, the little girl imagined she heard her mother speak her name. But all too sudden, the wretched reality of where she actually was, descended upon her like a heavy cloak of gloom when her aunt, who sounded similar to the girl's recently departed mother, called up the stairs for the third time, *"Rachel!* Come on down. Please? Supper is on the table."

Five minutes later, Clara was standing by Rachel's door. "Supper is ready and it's getting cold, Rachel; you must eat." Her niece was in the same position when her aunt first showed her the room, and her bag was never opened.

Clara's words brought no response; the woman's heart was breaking; she sat on the bed beside the distressed little girl and spoke in a soothing, caring voice, "Rachel, Honey, I know this is all so sudden for you, and you're going through a very rough time in your life, but we are all trying to help you. I also realize I could never take the place of your mother, and I would never try to do that. But eventually, you will learn that you are better off here with us, than you would have been back in Prosser's Hollow with your father. He has got to be the meanest man I ever met!"

A tear rolled down Rachel's cheek, which her aunt tenderly wiped away, then she hugged the little girl and said, "Oh Rachel, I do feel so bad for you. I only want to be your friend and help you through this. Once the war is over, we'll go visit Aaron. I promise. Would you like that?"

Hardly noticeable, she nodded.

Clara began humming "Amazing Grace." Then she commenced rocking Rachel while tenderly stroking her hair. Slowly, Rachel put her arms around the compassionate woman and tightly hugged her back, then she began sobbing extremely hard. The two of them sat there, slowly swaying back and forth for a few minutes until Rachel finally ran out of tears.

Clara stopped humming; she told the girl, "You have the prettiest shade of red hair I've ever seen."

Then she stood and offered her hand to Rachel, "I don't know about you, but I am really hungry. What do you say we go down and get a bite to eat? Okay, Honey?"

Another barely noticeable nod.

Famished, Josef and his boys were sitting patiently at the table.

Staring at the steaming bowl of sweet potatoes, peas, and biscuits, combined with smelling the delicious aroma from the humongous ham, only intensified their hunger. On her way upstairs to retrieve Rachel, Clara had pointed a finger at Josef and warned him, "Don't any of you boys touch a morsel till I return with Rachel. Understand?" All three had nodded yes.

Timidly, Rachel entered the dining room; her aunt gently nudging from behind.

Clara helped her niece to a seat, sat beside her, then turned to her husband, "You may *now* say grace, Josef."

"Let us bow our heads and pray. Lord, we ask you to bless this bounty we are about to receive. We also thank you for the plentiful harvest. We ask you, Lord, to deliver peace between the States and to bring an end to the unnecessary bloodshed. Most importantly, Lord, we thank you for gracing our family with Rachel. Please watch over her and keep her safe. Amen."

Clara and her sons repeated, "Amen. Glory be to God."

Then Josef addressed his youngest boy, "Jacob, my son, would you please pass those sweet potaters?" Josef and his two boys then proceeded to eat like it was their last meal.

Eventually, after much gentle coaxing from her aunt, Rachel ate one bite of sweet potato, a small slice of ham, and two peas. Clara regarded this as a huge success and a giant leap forward in the relationship she so badly wanted to establish with her niece.

Time passed agonizingly slow for Rachel; she would either sit on her bed, or rock away the hours in one of the rocking chairs on the front porch. Never did a smile cross her face; memories of happier times filled her head, providing a comforting sanctuary where she could escape the brutal realities of why, and where, she now lived.

From her rocker, Rachel was able to watch the stallion as he raced through the pasture. At times, Midnight would either rear up on two legs, or buck and snort while running. The horse fascinated Rachel with his antics; he resembled a large dog having the zoomies.

TODAY, THREE WEEKS have been crossed off the calendar since Rachel's traumatic uprooting from Ohio...

And, she has yet to speak!

This gorgeous afternoon finds the despondent girl sitting in her favorite chair, idly rocking away the hours to another melancholy day by staring into the pasture, wondering why the horse was not outside. While Rachel daydreamed of Prosser's Hollow, her Aunt Clara sat close by in the other rocker, sewing patches on her boys' overalls. The patient woman constantly talked to her niece; however, it was always a one-sided conversation.

In the distance, the clip-clop of horses' hooves coming down the lane caught Rachel's attention. A buckboard with two riders came into view; they had a mare in tow.

As on all farms, every animal served a purpose, mainly for food, transportation, or working the fields. The reason why Josef's prized stallion, Midnight, resided at the Tremont Farm was for none of those reasons. However, the horse did provide an additional source of income. The magnificent Tennessee Walker stud demanded a pretty hefty fee for his service, and he got it.

Clara told her niece, "Here comes Mr. Woodley with Misty. Looks like Midnight will earn his keep today."

The Woodley Farm was only a mile away from the Tremonts, making them their closest neighbor.

Clara and Rachel watched as the buggy drew nearer, then pass by the house and head towards the barn where Josef stood waiting.

Midnight was already inside the barn, anxiously pacing in his stall; the stallion had detected Misty's pheromones in the breeze; also, he knew why he was inside on a sunny afternoon, not out grazing in the pasture. The excited studhorse neighed loudly, continually.

The driver was tall and thin, while the rider was a young boy with reddish blond hair protruding from under his straw hat. Rachel stopped rocking; she leaned forward and put both hands on the ends of the chair's arms. She stared intently at the boy.

The girl excitedly exclaimed in a long, low whisper, "Aaron!"

She then sprang from her rocking chair and raced down the porch steps to the buckboard.

The boy watched his father and Josef untie the fidgety mare, then lead her into the barn.

Unaware of the approaching girl, he had his back to her the entire time; oddly, he was clutching a small, wooden box.

Just as Josef pulled the door shut, Rachel stopped three feet from the boy and called out, "Aaron!"

Startled, the boy turned to face Rachel, whose jubilation quickly turned to dismay when she realized this boy was not her brother, rather, just another strange face.

Very easily, though, this boy could have passed as her brother's twin.

"You are not... Aaron!" the extremely disappointed Rachel stated.

"No. I'm Samuel Woodley!" he smiled while thinking, "*What pretty red hair!*"

"But I like everybody to just call me... Sam."

The boy's bright blue eyes were beaming, he asked, "What's your name?"

Short and barely audible, she answered, "Rachel."

"That's a pretty name. I never heard that before," the twelve-year-old Samuel Woodley quickly shot out, sensing her disappointment in confusing him with someone else.

"Want to see my pet toad?" he asked while opening the tiny box.

"I named him Shiloh, he's two years old and eats bugs; he catches them with his really long tongue." The boy then pulled a huge, wart-covered toad from its nest, just made with freshly pulled grass.

"No!" Rachel shrieked, "Keep it away from me! I hate toads and snakes."

She took off running with Samuel clutching his toad in hot pursuit.

"He's a friendly toad, Rachel. Just take one little peek at him."

"No!" she hollered while running as fast as she could.

Even with his arm stretched out, and holding Shiloh but mere inches from Rachel's head, Samuel had no problem keeping up with her, "Get that ugly thing away from me!" she demanded from her tormentor.

Clara, now smiling, sat up in her rocker as she watched Samuel chase Rachel down to the pond.

"Amen, Samuel," she praised the boy out loud, "You made that little girl finally speak."

Rachel sprinted around the pond's edge and leaped over a muskrat hole; however, she lost her footing on the way down and tumbled. Samuel also leapt over the hole, gracefully, but when forced to jump a second time over the rolling girl, he too lost his balance. Needing both hands to soften his blow to the ground, he instinctively dropped the toad and braced himself for impact. His momentum caused him to do a somersault on the ground, and he ended up in a sitting position.

When he reached back to grab the toad, it took two leaps, splashed into the pond, and dove under.

"Shiloh!" The boy cried out.

Rachel let out a small, victorious laugh, "Haha! Good! That's what you get for chasing me with that ugly thing when I told you not to."

"It's not funny," Samuel scolded Rachel. "He was my pet. My dad won't let me have a puppy."

He scanned the water's surface for any sight of his toad.

Rachel looked at the heartbroken boy. In her opinion, he even pouted just like Aaron. "I'm sorry your toad got away.

Maybe you can catch him when he comes up for air," she said in an attempt to lighten his spirits.

"I doubt that!" Samuel said while shaking his head.

He replaced his hat, which flew off in his tumble, then explained, "He can hold his breath for a long time, and he's a very good swimmer, I'll have you know."

A few moments passed; Shiloh's head and two beady eyes popped through the surface about four feet from the water's edge. "There he is!" Samuel, pointing, excitedly whispered to Rachel.

She looked to where his finger indicated, "I see him!"

However, the toad spotted them also; it did a one eighty, swam to the opposite shore, then hopped out of the water. In a feeble attempt to sneak up on the escaped amphibian, Samuel crawled on all fours. When he was within three feet of the toad, he took off his hat and leapt like a frog towards his prey with the intention of trapping the toad under his hat. The toad was too quick and dove back into his watery refuge. "Gosh darn it! I almost had him," Samuel proclaimed, as Rachel giggled at his silliness.

Intrigued by Rachel's interaction with Samuel, Clara had snuck up to the barn, staying out of the children's sight. She desperately wanted Josef to witness this too, but she would have to wait until the men exited the barn. Proper women and children would never be present when any animal husbandry activities were being conducted. She could hear the men inside ordering the horses about, and Misty's occasional whinny. She also heard their hooves shuffling on the dirt floor, along with muffled crashes when the mating horses collided into the stall rails.

When she heard Josef say, "Well, I think he got her, Eli," Clara knew the deed was done.

Josef opened the barn doors; when he saw his wife standing there, a puzzled look fell upon his face; she immediately put her index finger to her lips and motioned for him to follow. Clara led him to the side of the barn and pointed to Rachel and Samuel. The children were sitting at the far end of the pond... Engaging in conversation!

"Well, I'll be! Ain't that something?" Josef quietly exclaimed.

He and Clara watched for a few moments longer, then he told her, "I have to square up with Eli. Come along, you can say hello to him." They both walked over to Mr. Woodley.

After he and Clara exchanged greetings, the man addressed Josef, "I have the full stud fee, but it will break me. I'm hoping I can pay you half in cash, and the other half with a beef calf and two bushels of apples. I just got a fresh load of Macintoshes in this morning. Would that be acceptable, Josef?" Mr. Woodley asked while securing Misty to the rear of his buckboard.

Josef really did not need another steer or apples, but he knew all too well what it was like to be short on funds and having to ask for a favor. Besides that, Eli was a good-hearted man, a trusted friend, and a helping neighbor. "Sure thing, Eli, I can always use another head of cattle; and apple strudel pie for dessert sounds appetizing."

Smiling, he then looked at his wife, but told the man, "Maybe I can talk Clara into putting up some applesauce!"

"I'd be happy to; we're down to two quarts from last year."

"Great! Thanks, Josef. I will bring the apples and the little Angus over tomorrow afternoon."

"Could you bring Samuel along, too?" Clara interrupted.

"Good as done. But may I ask why, Clara?" Her odd request piqued Eli's curiosity.

Together, the Tremonts explained who Rachel was, and why she was now living with them. They also went into detail on the little girl's behavior.

"She is in such a severe state of depression. I don't think she will ever be the same," Clara explained, "I think she resents us for uprooting her from Ohio. She never once spoke or smiled since she's been here. That is till today, when she met your Samuel. She's a totally different girl right now, with him. Follow me."

She led Mr. Woodley to the corner of the barn and pointed to the conversing children, "Look at them! I think Samuel reminds Rachel of her brother and happier times. Like I said, she hasn't spoken a single word to any of us since she's been here, it's been about three weeks now!"

Just then, they watched, and heard, Rachel giggle at the funny face Sam made.

Eli, overwhelmed by the tragedy this pretty little girl was suffering, assured Clara, "You know you are more than welcome to have my son over as often as you like if you think it will help that little girl. I'll be sure to bring him along tomorrow."

Later that evening, as Clara placed a pork roast, mashed potatoes, *and applesauce*, on the supper table, she informed Rachel, "Mr. Woodley will be bringing apples and a calf over tomorrow; Samuel will be with him!"

Although she remained silent, the little girl's eyes smiled, but only momentarily.

Chapter Eight

C hristian gave Rachel's story that bit of background, but now he focuses on The Yoders again...

Chapter Four

Eighty-seven years after Clara Tremont had placed that pork roast on her supper table, Mary Yoder was placing a steaming bowl of vegetable soup on *her* supper table for her husband. As a matter of fact, it was the exact same table that Clara had served *her* meals on. Many useful items, mainly furniture and tools, remained with the property when Elijah Yoder bought the farm, which Ralph then eventually inherited.

"Oh! There's nothing like a bowl of hot soup on a cold winter day to warm the belly," Ralph said, after taking a deep nasal inhale of the steam wafting from his bowl.

He slurped a spoonful, then addressed his youngest son, "Being all wrapped up in Rachel Petersen, you didn't say if you boys seen any deer today, Seth."

Ralph then buttered a thick slice of homemade bread and dipped it in his soup.

Seth's eyes lit up and a huge smile shot across his face. "I bagged Ol' Bocephus today, Pa! He's hangin' in the barn," the youngster proudly stated.

"Yeah, Pa!" Thaddeus was quick to interrupt, "Seth blew his shoulder apart up by the Big Hemlock at daybreak, an' we tracked him for two miles. Then Amos blew his front knee apart when he went down in Old Man Woodley's orchard. He emptied Uncle Clyde's ought six at him, but lucky for us, he's a lousy shot and only hit Ol' Bo in his knee; then he ran back up past us, an' me an' Seth jumped back on his trail before Amos did. Then we found him lyin' dead on Rachel Petersen's grave, I tell ya."

"That's right, Pa," Seth took his turn to interrupt his brother and finish telling *his* story, "Then Amos followed the blood trail to us an' he tried laying claim to my buck."

Seth glanced at his brother, "But we set him straight on whose deer it was. Ain't that right, Thaddy?"

Thaddeus smiled. "Yeah. There's no way I was gonna let that big sonna bit, uh... sonna gun take Seth's buck. Especially after we tracked him all morning."

Seth smiled deviously, remembering how Thaddeus almost shot their cousin, while Mary Yoder gave her eldest son the *hairy eyeball* for damn near cussing.

"Even Uncle Clyde doesn't have a rack as big as Ol' Bo's on his barn," Thaddeus stated.

"That is one heck of a story. It sounds like you two had a very interesting morning. I wished I could have been out there with you two, but the clowns who run our state scheduled the auction on the opening day," Ralph said, then added, "We'll have to go out to the barn and inspect this trophy buck after supper."

Another bite of broth-drenched bread went into his mouth.

"I'm too cold to go back outside, Pa. You and Thaddy can go ahead and check him out. I'm staying inside to warm up," Seth informed his father.

"You're just a big ol' scaredy cat, Seth," Thaddeus teased his younger brother while picking up his butter knife, telling him, "You're afraid Rachel will swing down from the rafters."

He then made a slashing motion with the knife, saying, "An' slice your throat, *wide open*!"

Ralph almost choked on his mouthful of bread while holding back his chuckle. He knew where his smart-aleck boy got his twisted sense of humor.

Mary immediately reprimanded her oldest son, "Knock it off already, Thaddeus. I really wish you would quit picking on your little brother, especially at the supper table."

She addressed her husband next, "And you! Don't laugh and encourage him."

Then, to change the subject, she asked him, "How'd things go at the auction today?"

"Better than I expected! I got top dollar for those two big boars. Pork prices were actually up three cents a pound from last year," Ralph replied, as he brought his bowl to his lips and slurped down the last drops of broth and a lima bean that was stuck to the side of the bowl.

"That is great news, Pa. Do you think then maybe we could, uh, get my buck... mounted? That could be my Christmas and birthday present in one gift." Seth asked with a hopeful gleam in his eyes.

Ralph really hated disappointing his sons; neither one of them ever asked for much. "I am sorry, Son, but, no. We have too many other bills needing paid. But I promise you we will cut a nice piece of black walnut and make a plaque to mount the antlers on," Ralph said as he pushed his empty bowl to the center of the table and grabbed a freshly baked cinnamon roll from the pan. He enjoyed that with a cup of hot coffee; then using Tip Top rolling papers, he twisted a cigarette.

Both boys also wished they could enjoy a smoke after their supper, but they kept their nicotine habits hidden from their parents.

"Maybe I'll just dry the skull with the antlers still attached," Seth said with a lot less enthusiasm in his voice and a whole lot of disappointment on his face.

Mary nudged Ralph's foot with hers. He glanced her way. Her eyes quickly gave him her *see what you can do* look with a tiny nod of her head in Seth's direction, without either one of her sons noticing.

Ralph pushed his chair back from the table and stood. "Let's go take a look at this trophy buck. Shall we boys?" Thaddeus rose, but Seth remained seated as the other two headed for the mudroom and began donning their boots and heavy coats.

Mary whispered in Seth's ear, "Don't let your brother's remarks bother you. Go with them; prove to Thaddy you're not afraid. Nothing's going to get you, Seth. Your father will be out there with you. Hurry up, get."

He looked at his mother, she gave him a reassuring nod; he immediately sprang from his chair and also got dressed. Ralph waited for Seth to put his boots on, then all three headed to the barn as dusk consumed the last of the Sun's rays. Snow crunched under their feet as Thaddeus, of course, led the way. Seth was right behind his father.

Thaddeus pulled the barn door open, breaking down a small snowdrift that had already formed in front of it. Then all three entered the dark and eerie old barn. Glancing upwards at the thick, hand-hewn, rough-cut rafters, Seth felt those familiar shivers creeping down his spine. His father lit a kerosene lantern with a wooden match, then used that match to light his cigarette. He blew out the match, dropped it to the dirt floor then stepped on it. The glowing sulfur head sizzled from the snow stuck in the treads of his boot.

"What a monster! Holy smokes!" Ralph exclaimed once the lantern's dim light illuminated the giant buck.

"What'd I tell ya?" Thaddeus asked his father, "Ain't that the biggest rack you ever did see?"

Ralph grabbed the buck's huge brow tines and turned the upside-down deer's head upright. Two black lifeless eyes stared back at him while the buck's tongue protruded from a corner of his mouth.

Seth's father exclaimed, "Boy! I'll say! He might be a state record. Not only is that the biggest, *rack*, I've ever seen, but he's also the biggest, *deer*, I've ever seen!"

Then Ralph looked at Seth, "When you skin him out, make sure to leave enough of a cape for a wall mount. This big old boy has a perfect rack, and I'll see what I can do to get him mounted."

The youngster's face lit up brighter than a Christmas tree. "Wow! Thanks, Pa."

Just then, the resident barn owl fluttered from his high overhead perch to the opposite end of the barn, causing Seth and Thaddeus to cower. Even Ralph felt a twinge of apprehension when the wise old bird took flight. The older brother tried to cover up his cowardice and laughingly quipped, "I thought Rachel had you that time for sure, Seth."

"Ain't funny, Thaddy. Besides, you ducked, too."

"Did not."

"Did too."

"Did not."

"You two can stay out here in the cold and argue. I'm going back to the house where it's warm," their father said, then blew out the lantern.

The sudden lack of light caused the barn to appear much more ominous now and darker than before. A frightened Seth managed to position himself in between the other two for the brisk walk back to the house.

While helping his wife finish the supper dishes, Ralph told her how big the buck actually was. The boys readied their schoolbooks and any homework for tomorrow.

Mary called into the living room, "Thaddeus, I think you'd better use this time wisely and study for tomorrow's big history exam."

"Yes, Mother." Needless to say, his voice lacked enthusiasm.

Once done with the dishes, Ralph went down to the furnace room and banked the fire in the huge, old coal boiler for the night. Then the Yoder family relaxed in the parlor and listened to country music on the radio for an hour or so before turning in. Thaddeus had his nose in his book while his mother, very skilled with needle and thread, used this time to work on her needlepoint projects. Thanks to her hobby, nearly every lamp and candy dish in her house had a doily under it.

When Grandpa Jones announced the show was over and thanked his audience for tuning in to the Grand Ole Opry, Mary told her sons, "Time for bed, Boys. Get up them steps."

Of course, on the way up the stairs, Thaddeus had to tease his brother one more time by turning around and telling him, "You'd better check under your bed, and in the closet to make sure Rachel ain't hidin' in your room."

"Very funny, Thaddy," Seth sneered back. Nevertheless, the remark did cause him to run and jump into his bed. The boy crawled out of his jeans while under the covers and dropped them to the floor; he would be content sleeping in just his long johns and no pajamas tonight.

In an attempt to rid his mental image of Rachel Petersen hiding under his bed and clutching a knife, Seth concentrated on Bocephus. He especially remembered what his dad had promised out in the barn, *I'll see what I can do to get him mounted!*

He closed his eyes and pictured his deer professionally stuffed, hanging above the fireplace, looking larger than life. One by one, he counted the points, but on the fourteenth one, sleep ultimately carried the tired youngster off into Dreamland. Huge snowflakes began falling on the deer's antlers; the buck turned his head and stared directly at him, then it snorted, raised his tail and took off running to catch up to two does deeper in the forest. Seth dropped to one knee under the Big Hemlock; he calmly aimed down the barrel of his muzzleloader, pulled the flint into firing position, took a deep breath, and gently squeezed the trigger. Click. Sha-boom! The shot echoed across the valley.

Through a cloud of black powder smoke, the young hunter saw the sprinting deer's ribcage shatter and the humongous buck tumble immediately.

"Nice shot, I tell ya!" Thaddeus congratulated him. "No way I'd ever hit that sonna bitch. That bastard was delivering the mail!"

Seth led the way to the fallen buck. "Roll one up, Thaddy. I wanna enjoy a victory smoke before I gut this big boy."

"Sure thing, Seth. Whatever you want," his older brother said, then obediently began to twist a cigarette when they heard crashing noises coming through the saplings. Amos just entered his dream.

"Alright! You boys found my buck for me. I blasted this monster way down in Old Man Woodley's orchard." Amos rested his rifle against a tree, then pulled his knife from its sheath.

Seth calmly picked up his rifle, stuck it in his big cousin's face, and warned him, "You know God damned well this is my deer, you fat assed slob. Now you best turn around an' get the hell out of here before I get real mad an' squeeze this trigger. Unless you wanna be the hunter that got shot on this opening day? This flintlock may be old, but it'll blow your head off like you were a little chipmunk. You got to the count of three, you inbred sonna bitch!"

"One... Two..." He cocked the rifle.

Amos threw his arms up. "Don't shoot! My mistake. It is your deer, Seth. I'm sorry. It's your deer! I musta missed when I shot at it."

Using his flintlock, Seth motioned to Amos to get moving. The whipped bigger boy nodded that he understood, took two steps backwards, executed an about face, and hurriedly left.

"I was scared shitless when I saw Amos coming, Seth. But boy! Did you ever show him! I thought for sure he was gonna take your deer, I tell ya!" Thaddeus praised his brave little brother and handed him a cigarette.

Seth lit his smoke; while exhaling, he stated in a very matter of tone voice, "Thaddy! There ain't nobody gonna take this deer. I'm gettin' him professionally mounted, ya know."

Then he ordered his older brother, "Go get Dolly. She can drag this big bastard to the barn."

Thaddeus no sooner agreed to retrieve the old mule, and they had the disemboweled buck hanging in the barn.

He then informed Seth, "I'm cold. I'm goin' inside for a bowl of Mom's veggie soup."

"Go ahead, Thaddy. I'm gonna stay out here an' skin Ol' Bo. I have to be real careful to leave enough of a cape for a good mount," Seth told his brother.

Thaddeus left; Seth began skinning the deer. The dull knife left a jagged edge where he cut the hide, so he turned to the worktable behind him to hone the blade on a whetstone.

When he turned back around, the buck was gone!

However! In its place was Rachel Petersen! Hanging in a noose!

Blood smeared her petticoat and hands; a psychotic look had etched itself on her blood-splattered face. Fire burned in her eyes as she raised her arm, clutching a huge bloody butcher knife in her hand! She let out a loud, hysterical laugh as she viciously swung the knife at Seth's throat. He jumped back, but not quickly enough. The tip of the knife barely nicked his throat, causing him to stumble backwards and fall flat on his back.

He watched in an amazed state of terror as the little red-haired demon of a girl reached over her head with her empty hand and grab the rope. She then brought the other hand up and cut the rope in one swift motion, dropping herself lightly to the ground, ending up in a crouched position. An evil smile shot across her face once she tugged the noose from her neck. Raising the knife above her head, she howled another heinous, wicked laugh. She ran and jumped onto the fallen boy's chest before he had a chance to get up. He instinctively grabbed her wrist with both hands, preventing the knife from slashing across his throat. She pushed down on the knife; it was four inches from his jugular vein.

Seth's eyes were popping out of his head as he stared at the tip of her knife. She then put both hands on the handle. Grunting louder, she leaned forward, using her body weight to push the knife. Two inches closer! More animal-like grunting sounds came from the determined, bloodthirsty little killer. Then she pushed as hard as she could. Seth could not hold her weight back any longer; as the knife thrust downwards, he jerked his head to his right. The knife ended up sticking in the clay floor by his left ear.

Hissing an angry growl of defeat, Rachel gritted her teeth and jerked the knife backwards, pulling it out of the ground and breaking free of his hands.

Holding the shimmering knife high above her head with both hands, she now had a more crazed and even angrier look in her eyes. With a blood curdling cackle of victory, she thrust the knife downwards with all her might. Simultaneously, Seth forcefully jerked his knees upwards into her back, causing the knife to again stick in the ground only a mere fraction of an inch behind his head. Rachel flew over him, and the knife, onto her back.

Seth wasted no time in getting to his feet and bursting through the barn door, out into the dark. She wiggled the knife free from the clay floor and darted. Her footsteps and loud grunted breaths closed in behind him as he felt as if he was racing in slow motion to the house. He heard and felt his cherished Uncle Clyde's Woolrich coat being shredded from his back as Rachel madly sliced her deadly knife through the plaid material.

Seth disintegrated the porch door as he burst through it. He ripped open the kitchen door, flew inside, slammed it shut in Rachel's scowling face, and turned the dead bolt.

Thaddeus, sitting at the supper table enjoying his veggie soup, slowly looked up at his frazzled brother, revealing that his throat was sliced from ear to ear! Blood had soaked through his shirt, ran down his arm, and began pooling on the table.

The sound of glass shattering on the floor echoed throughout the kitchen as Rachel used the knife's handle to gain entry.

Thaddeus looked up and calmly told his brother, "She's gonna slice your throat too, I tell ya. She's pissed because you sleep in her bed, ya know."

The spoonful of soup he then swallowed poured out from the wide-open gash in his throat; pieces of cubed beef, peas, and carrots, trickled down his shirt.

Hearing a click, Seth looked over and saw Rachel's hand inside the broken window, turning the dead bolt. She smiled a wicked little smile through the remaining shards of glass.

He ran through the parlor but stopped when he heard his father holler his name. Above the fireplace, on a beautiful, black walnut plaque, was his father's mounted head! Ralph's eyes were no longer his sparkling blue eyes anymore. They had been replaced with brown glass marble eyes that taxidermists use when mounting deer heads. He informed his son, "Seth! Ain't no use in running. She's going to gut you, too!"

Seth heard the kitchen door fly open and bang off the wall, causing more glass to shatter, which meant Rachel was now in the house!

He took the steps two at a time going upstairs. Bocephus was lying at the top landing! Gutted. The buck raised his head but never took his eyes off of Seth as the wide-eyed boy cautiously crept by those dangerous antlers on his way to his mother's room. The boy kept his back tight to the wall; he jumped when the buck snorted.

Then in an extremely deep, raspy voice, sounding like the devil himself, the deer spoke, "Now you see why I led you to Rachel's grave? She's going to put you in yours! Run, Boy! She's going to track *you* down for the kill, like *you* did to *me*. Run! Run fast! Run till you can't run *no more*!"

Then the deer let go a low chuckle that slowly turned into deep laughter. The gutted buck laughed hard and loud until it became ear splitting. Even through the buck's insane laughter, Seth heard Rachel stomping up the stairs. Only now, she was giggling like an escaped mental asylum patient.

Seth ran down the hall, following a blood trail from the deer to his mother's doorway; he went in. His mother was sitting in front of a mirror with her sewing basket on her lap; she had her head tilted back, exposing the large gash in her throat. As easy as sewing torn jeans, his mother's hands were busy stitching the giant gash across her windpipe back together.

In her reassuring voice, she told him, "Don't worry, Seth, Thaddeus is next, but I will stitch you up too, after Rachel slices *your* throat!"

A reflection of Rachel standing in the doorway came into view in his mother's mirror. In a freakishly excited tone, she told her son, "Look, Seth! Here's Rachel now! Doesn't she just have the prettiest red hair you ever did see?"

An impish smile slowly appeared on Rachel's blood-streaked face when she realized she had Seth trapped. Screaming like a banshee on the warpath, she raised her knife high in the air. The psychotic twelve-year-old girl with demonic green eyes charged the boy at full tilt. Seth backed up and fell onto his mother's bed. Rachel leapt upon him and raised the knife high above her head!

As she thrust the knife toward him, he quickly rolled over and fell out of bed, which woke him.

In a heartbeat, he jumped back under the covers. While panting fast and deep, the only sound to be heard was his heart pounding in his ears.

A smile of embarrassment slowly formed on his face, he let out a small chuckle, then gave a gigantic sigh when he heard his father snore, realizing he had just experienced the worst nightmare ever of his thirteen years.

SEVEN HOURS OF BEING outside in the twenty-degree air combined with trudging over three miles up and down the hilly, snow-covered terrain of Western Pennsylvania had also taken a toll on Thaddeus. He barely had enough energy to kick off his jeans. His last thoughts of the day, when his head hit the pillow and moments before sleep whisked his mind into the fantasy world of dreams, focused on tomorrow's big test.

The boy needed a high score on this exam to pass History class and to get his mother off his back. Although he did find the content of this chapter fascinating, he had a hard time remembering names and dates. Over and over in his mind he recited, "*Howard Carter on November 4, 1922, unearthed the largest archaeological find ever, King Tutankhamun's Tomb, while excavating in The Valley of the Kings in Egypt.*"

His mental image of Carter leading a camel caravan loaded with tools and equipment, trekking over sand dunes with giant pyramids in the background, slowly transformed into Doctor Thaddeus Yoder leading Dolly laden with shovels and picks trudging through snowdrifts on their quest to discover the controversial, hidden Rachel Petersen Crypt. For years, scores of teams had scoured these hills surrounding Jonesboro in search of the famous tomb. However, absolutely no proof of her existence was ever unearthed. The experts in the archaeological world finally announced that her legend must be nonsense and that she was nothing more than just that — a legend. Carter himself was quoted as saying, "We will have more luck in finding the Boogey Man than discovering the mythical Tomb of Rachel Petersen."

However, the young Doctor Yoder knew better. Perhaps there was only one place where the treasure seekers before him dared not venture — through the perilous, mountainous, Ring of Briars.

Thaddeus labored madly, swinging his machete; with every swipe of his giant blade, huge clomps of intertwined jaggers fell. He chopped until he had successfully carved a tunnel through the briars, to the clearing in the middle, but it was an empty, snow covered clearing.

"What? It has to be here. It has to," he mumbled aloud in his sleep. He kicked at the snow with his boots, searching frantically until finally, he felt a rock under his foot. Thaddeus knelt and used an archaeologist's brush to whisk the snow from the rock's flat surface. It proved to be a small hand carved tombstone with gunpowder smeared on the front, rendering the weathered inscription legible. "*Rachel Petersen. Aha!*"

He began digging wildly in front of the tombstone. Within minutes, he was six feet down when his shovel struck something solid, causing a hollow thud to resonate throughout the ground. Brushing the dirt away revealed a partially deteriorated pine coffin. He pulled the lid open and found... sand! Nothing but sand. Once again, he dug like a mad man, flinging shovel loads of sand up and out of the grave onto the snow. Then he came across another rock, much bigger than the tombstone.

More digging exposed the entire rock, then another; Thaddeus realized what he had found — the top two steps of a chiseled-out stairwell.

He unearthed sixteen more steps, bringing him to a huge, oval-domed marble doorway which encased a gigantic teak door, split down the center; each half had an elaborately decorated solid gold dagger as a handle. He swept the sand and dust off from top to bottom of both doors, exposing hieroglyphics, which of course he deciphered, *"Behind these doors lie the remains of Rachel Petersen. Cursed will be all those who dare enter."*

"Ha!" Thaddeus scoffed at such a silly curse as he swung the huge heavy doors open, revealing a vast darkness. He struck a match on the door and held it over his head. On either side of him were cat-a-nine-tails in holders attached to the walls. Using the same match, he lit both torches, took one from its holder, then carefully held it high above his head. The cat-o-nine-tail's blazing flame roared from the downdraft, partially illuminating another stairwell which led him to a colossal underground cavern.

Thaddeus walked slowly past hundreds of chests, meticulously adorned with... Centipedes?

He paused at a chest that appeared to have been forcibly opened; he gazed in awe at the overflowing contents of gold and silver coins, pearl necklaces, diamonds, rubies, and bracelets made of solid turquoise, all which had overflowed onto a skeleton lying on the cavern floor; the human remains held onto a shovel as a swarm of the hundred leggers ran in and out of the eye sockets.

Unphased, the brave, young archaeologist followed a path between the stalactites, stalagmites, and chests, to the very end of the cavern where a small golden sarcophagus stood upright.

An exquisitely carved girl, having highly polished jade gemstones for eyes, adorned the golden lid; her arms were folded over her chest, and in her right hand, she held a *solid gold dagger*, identical to the ones on the doors.

He pulled on the lid's handle with all of the strength in his right arm until it finally creaked open. The flames of the torch shone inside the golden coffin, revealing a small body wrapped in strips of white cloth. "Rachel Petersen's mummy!" Thaddeus exclaimed. "I discovered her lost tomb! Wait till I tell the world about this!"

He closed the sarcophagus and hurried back through the myriad of treasure chests, through the domed archway, back up the stairway, then up into the small wooden coffin. Thaddeus then hoisted himself out of the grave.

Hundreds of flashbulbs going off in his face from the hordes of reporters snapping his picture startled him.

One member of the press asked him, "Doctor Yoder, what is the importance of this find?"

He scanned the crowd that had surrounded the weathered tombstone as he answered, "This find proves that Rachel Petersen is *not* just a legend, I tell ya. Her knife is down there in her tomb!"

The entire town turned out for this spectacular event. They all applauded and cheered at his revelation.

Thaddeus immediately recognized a handful of onlookers. Standing in the front row were Seth and his parents. Next to them stood his history teacher, Mrs. Mishler, overjoyed with pride for her star pupil. Even Amos, Uncle Clyde, and his wife were present for this historical event.

He recognized Old Man Woodley too, but not the man with his wife, their two sons, and a petite redheaded girl front and center. However, these people were not clapping, but rather, just standing; with solemn, blank stares on each of their faces.

Thaddeus had never seen these people before in his life. Never. Not even in a photograph.

Chapter Nine

Chapter Five

At breakfast the next morning, the brothers were unable to focus on their oatmeal as their thoughts kept revolving on the dreams they had last night. Seth could not think about anything except for how evil, blood thirsty, and vicious Rachel Petersen was. Thaddeus was wondering what Carter must have experienced when he unearthed the tomb of Egypt's most famous pharaoh, King Tutankhamen, the youngest ruler ever, also known as, which Thaddeus had just crammed into his brain last night, 'Egypt's Boy King'. "*All that fame, glory, and riches, must have really been something*", he imagined.

Both boys relived their entire dreams while mindlessly spooning in the hot cereal.

Seth shivered when he remembered how Rachel leapt onto him with her knife poised to deliver the deathblow. He then cast a fleeting glance at his brother to see if Thaddeus noticed. Luckily for him, he did not.

"Mom, do you think that guy who dug up King Tut's Tomb got rich?" Thaddeus asked his mother.

"I would like to think he got to keep some of the treasure, or else he got paid pretty well."

"Diggin' up tombs for a living sounds a lot more exciting than diggin' up potatoes, I tell ya," Thaddeus said, half seriously, as thoughts of grandeur flashed in his mind. Chests full of pearls, diamonds, silver coins. *And... A golden dagger!*

"I doubt if it is as glamorous as your history book makes it sound. I do hope you studied for that big test," his mother warned as she cleared the table.

"You two better get a move on. The bus will be here any minute now. Don't forget your lunches," she reminded her sons.

While standing at the end of the lane waiting for the school bus, both boys were sneaking their morning smoke. Thaddeus told Seth, "I bet they buried some kind of treasure with Rachel Petersen, ya know? Like maybe a ring or a necklace, which would be an antique by now. Come spring thaw, we oughta get up to the ridge an' excavate her tomb like they do in Egypt."

Seth looked at his brother in total disbelief, he asked with his face scrunched up, "*What*? Are you nuts? I'm stayin' as far away as possible from that psycho's grave."

Then he grunted a chuckle. "Ha! 'Excavate her tomb.' Really! Don't you mean... Dig up her skeleton?"

"Maybe they buried the knife with her. We could be rich an' famous like Carter, I tell ya," Thaddeus argued, an excited tone in his voice.

"Do you want somebody like her to haunt you for the rest of your life? You best get *this* lame brain idea out of your head, an' fast, Thaddy," Seth advised his big brother. He knew all too well how whimsical he could be. A crazy thought would take root in Thaddeus's brain, then fester, until he would ultimately act on impulse, from a fleeting thought. Then the boy would be driven by sheer stupidity or basic greed until he reached his goal, oblivious to the fact he was flirting with death while trying.

Like the time when he nearly blew his fingers off *minin' for gold*. Thaddeus fashioned three homemade sticks of dynamite from black powder and rolled up newspapers. Not anticipating the speed at which black powder burned, he tried jumping out of harm's way when the fuse went up in a split second. The *dynamite* erupted like a flare from the hole he had placed it in, burning the hand that held the match and all the hair from his arm.

Then there was the time when he had almost drowned himself while attempting to *explore the unchartered murky depths* of the farm pond, as he put it. The then wannabe scuba diver designed and built a diving helmet out of an old five-gallon fertilizer bucket and a dry rotted water hose connected to an air compressor. He turned on a flashlight, sealed it tightly in a mason jar, placed the bucket on his head and walked into the pond. His underwater exploration was going great, just as he had envisioned; the flashlight even illuminated the muddy bottom. He located his lost baseball with it. This escapade was so well planned out, he figured that it was fail proof. At least it seemed that way until he ventured into the deep end of the pond where the water pressure was greater, causing the brittle hose to collapse, which in turn cut off his fresh air supply; he came splashing to the surface, gasping for air and gulping in mouthfuls of stagnant pond water.

As usual, his little brother's advice was to be ignored, and the idea of excavating her tomb would not exit his brain. Rather, it defiantly remained embedded in the back of his mind, slowly gnawing away, torturing him; not only did treasure chests enter his dreams at night, but just a thought of a golden dagger would lure him into a *daydream*. Both mental pictures tempted and tantalized him till Spring Thaw, when he ultimately did act upon the mental imagery of the artifacts that continually popped into his mind.

Seth, grinning, changed the topic, "I'm really happy Pa said he'll get Bocephus professionally mounted for me. That surprised the heck out of me when he said that!"

Thaddeus looked up from his notes, "Yeah, I'll say! That surprised me, too. Ol Bo's goin' look great hanging above the mantle."

Seth agreed as he flicked his butt just as the bus's brakes squealed to a stop.

The younger brother kept an eye out for any deer, while Thaddeus poured over his notes for the entire ride to school; then, four hours later, he sweated through the test and managed to pull down a C plus, raising his grade average from an F, to a D, which thrilled not only him, but his mother more.

Those images of exhumed relics, such as the jewelry and golden knives, continually tormented the boy, causing the following months to pass excruciatingly slow for the young, up and coming archaeologist!

THEN FINALLY, ON AN unseasonably warm Ides of March morning, the ground had somewhat thawed, and Thaddeus found himself walking briskly past the Big Hemlock en route to the lone tombstone. He had nothing more than a shovel tossed over his shoulder and a scythe in hand as he rounded the sharp bend in the tram road where Bocephus had leapt into the Mountain Laurel.

High in the overhead branches of a Maple tree, a female robin — the proverbial harbinger of spring — heavily laden with eggs, incessantly squawked at her mate as the male robin put the finishing touches on their nest; apparently he was not much of a carpenter, for the poor sap was getting quite an earful from his missus.

From their lofty lookout, the birds watched as the boy waded through the dense Laurel and then swung his freshly sharpened scythe into the base of the jagger bushes. Thaddeus felt like he was leading an expedition through the Rainforest to Inca ruins as he blazed a crude trail through the briars leading to Rachel Petersen's Tomb.

A twinge of excitement shuddered through his body when he finally broke through the thorny vines and laid eyes once again on the crudely chiseled, weathered tombstone.

The rains and melting snow had washed away all evidence of there ever being three boys at this spot arguing over a dead deer. No footprints, blood, or even any grains of the black powder Seth had used on the stone's engraving were to be found. It was as though he was the first person ever to stand foot on these hallowed grounds after the secret burial ceremony. At least that's the way the young *Doctor Yoder* fantasized matters in his mind as he used the spade to outline where to dig.

With each shovel load of dirt tossed onto a pile beside the grave, the boy's heartbeat quickened; he would stop only momentarily to wipe the sweat from his brow and catch his breath.

The earthy smell of damp soil permeated his nose, while visions of awaiting treasures invaded his mind, fueling his madness.

After digging nonstop for two hours, the boy was at a depth of four feet when he felt the pointed tip of his shovel sink into rotten wood. "Yes!" he excitedly whispered. Taking much smaller scoops of dirt now, he tried not to damage the lid any further. His adrenalin rush caused a feeling of euphoria as he used his bare hand to wipe the loose soil and small stones from atop the homemade coffin. Finally, he exposed the entire lid of the small, deteriorating, pine box. There were no fancy engravings or golden handles, just earthworms, beetles, and centipedes crawling about.

He popped his head out of the hole and looked beyond the heaping piles of freshly dug dirt, making certain there were no intruders hiding in the bushes, waiting to rob him of his find. Satisfied there weren't any, he reached down and grabbed the lid. Rusted solid, the tiny hinges creaked loudly as he tugged. He yanked harder and harder until they snapped.

Then... Wooosh! A gigantic gale force wind blasted up and out from the coffin, violently ripping the lid from his hand. The plank door pinned his legs against the earthen side of the grave. Using his arms, he shielded his face as the tornado strength winds blew straight up past him. His hair was blown straight on end. The tree limbs above him thrashed and whipped wildly as the colossal, continuous gust of wind ripped through the leaves. Dust, dirt, and stones, tore at his arms and face as they were hurled from the hole. The rush of the air howled loudly with an eerie, awful sound, as though a thousand people were screaming at once. Thaddeus grimaced as the forceful wind would not allow him to catch his breath.

As fast as the howling wind had erupted from the coffin, it abruptly stopped. Then the lid slammed shut with a loud whack. The branches bounced and swayed to a peaceful rest as Thaddeus, trembling, cautiously began to wipe the dirt from his face and arms. He gazed at the top of the coffin and convinced himself that the blast must have been caused by all the gases built up within the decomposing body, and opening the coffin allowed them to escape, which was a logical and natural explanation, but only being minutely possible if the fact that the coffin was not airtight was left out of the equation. Which, of course, Thaddeus did.

Within a few moments, he regained his composure and surveyed the surrounding area again. With one arm protecting his face this time, he reached down and grabbed the lid once more. He heard his heart pounding madly. Being more cautious on his second attempt, he slowly lifted the lid while peeking over it through squinted eyes. No howling gust of wind greeted him as the mummified remains of the once very pretty and young Rachel Petersen, laid to rest in a plain floral print dress, came into view. A thin layer of dust covered her and everything else inside the tiny coffin.

But how could that be? After that violent windstorm, which just moments ago blasted forth from the coffin, no dust would have remained. That was just another curiosity that never crossed Thaddeus's mind.

Staring back at him were two large empty eye sockets in a tiny skull, which rested on a satin pillow. Her facial skin, once having a flawless peaches and cream complexion, was now brown, deeply gouged with wrinkles, and drawn tight, exposing her baby teeth. Her nose was reduced to two narrow slits. Red hair, parted in the middle, covered her forehead before coming to rest in curls on her shoulders.

The bones and joints in her hands and arms were clearly visible. Her skin-tight hands lay folded on her chest, clutching a rosary. An artifact!

"*She looks like a dried-out prune with red hair,*" Thaddeus thought to himself. Then his pulse pounded faster and louder in his ears when he spotted the holy prayer beads.

He stared wide-eyed at the white beaded rosary that had a tiny silver crucifix attached, then the corners of his lips curled into a sly smile as he congratulated himself on the find, "I knew there would be something of value buried with her."

Slowly he reached down for the *treasure*. "One more inch and it's mine."

Then he quickly jerked his hand back when Seth's warning echoed through his mind, "*Do you want someone like her to haunt you for the rest of your life?*"

"Nonsense," he reasoned to himself with a chuckle. "Ha! What does Seth know?"

Then his subconscious haunted him, "*What about your dream? The curse in hieroglyphics?*"

He answered himself out loud! "That's nonsense too! Take the treasure and cover her back up!"

Nervously, he wiped the beads of sweat running down his brow; again he reached for the holy rosary very slowly while staring at her ghastly, withered face. And those two empty eye sockets staring back! He was expecting her to move, or worse yet, holler, "*Grave robber,*" and grab at him with her boney hands. Nevertheless, he desired that rosary so badly, he was willing to take that risk.

Thaddeus delicately grasped the tiny cross. Firmly, but with a gentle touch, the young archaeologist raised it two inches until all the slack was out of the chain. Now taut, it would not come away from the corpse any further; the remaining beads of the rosary had been intertwined around those hideous looking hands.

Keeping a vigilant watch on her hollow eyes, he tugged a bit harder on the rosary. He did not see when the army of huge, dark orange centipedes scurried out from under her hands. Quickly, one after another, thousands of the ugly bugs crawled out from their hiding spot and ran up the chain. They raced across his hand and up his arm. "Oh!" Thaddeus hollered as he let go of the cross and flung his hand back.

Thousands more continued to pour out from their hiding spot, climbing over his shoes, up his pants, up his legs, under his shirt. "Oh! Oh! Oh!"

Moreover, they stunk. Like battery acid mixed with used motor oil and ammonia.

A part of his dream flashed through his mind, *"Within these walls lie the remains of Rachel Petersen. Cursed will be all those who dare enter."*

In one bound, he jumped the four feet out of the grave. The hideous bugs poured out of the hole and chased him down. Chills ran the entire length of his spine as he danced about, flailing his arms, trying to shake the repulsive insects off as more and more covered him.

He ripped his shirt off and used it to swat the creepy crawlers off his back, chest, shoulders, and stomach. They were in his hair; he shook his head. One was halfway in his ear when he pulled it out. He kicked his feet into the air while grabbing and shaking his pant legs; he stomped on the vile and relentless *hunnerd leggers* that did fall to the ground. The ones he missed, turned and came after him again.

For ten awfully long minutes, they kept up their never-ending assault.

If he wanted to escape, he'd have to run bare-chested through five feet of briars in any direction. He knew even the crudely chopped trail he blazed through them would rip and tear his bare skin, leaving embedded thorns; the boy was trapped in the circle of vicious jaggers — the infamous, '*Ring of Briars.*'

And he was becoming exhausted!

While jumping up and down, he tripped over the shovel's handle and fell face first over the freshly dug dirt pile back into the grave, landing three inches from Rachel's mummified face; he swore he saw Rachel smile at him!

He jumped back out and continued his swatting dance.

Then, suddenly and as unnatural as could be, the legion of centipedes began their retreat as if they were trained soldiers obeying a silent bugle call only they could hear. Even the ones that covered him, crawled off to join the multitude on the ground sprinting back to the grave.

What happened next was even more bizarre — Thaddeus watched in sheer amazement as the countless tiny drops of blood and guts, broken legs, and severed heads from the centipedes that he had decimated, began to roll. Like droplets of mercury being drawn to thousands of tiny magnets scattered across the ground, they reunited and formed perfectly unscathed centipedes, which also joined in the retreat. Scurrying single file back to the grave, millions of tiny feet pounded the ground, sounding like fine rain falling on dry leaves. Resembling army ants marching on a jungle floor, they followed each other up the piles of dirt, down the walls of the grave, then up and over the lip of the coffin before disappearing back under Rachel's hands.

The very last centipede stopped at the edge of the grave before going over, it turned and faced Thaddeus, as he gasped for air. For a few moments, maybe even a full minute, it just stood there with its antennas waving in the air. Thaddeus felt it staring at him. The loathsome and stinky insect kept waving its antennae slowly, menacingly back and forth. Then it quickly turned and also disappeared into the grave.

Thaddeus heard a loud whack, as the lid slammed down on the coffin.

The boy felt as though the intimidating little bastard had just issued a warning. Furthermore, and oddly enough, the young, unsuccessful archaeologist understood exactly what that message was — "Summon us again, Boy... And there will be *no* retreat!"

He shoveled the half ton of dirt back into the grave as fast as humanly possible. Then he grabbed the scythe and beat a hasty departure for home; his feet barely touched the ground as he raced like the wind.

Not until Thaddeus reached the lane, did he stop running. Hoping and praying nobody was watching, he returned the shovel and scythe; then entered the house, still gasping for breath.

His mother, serving Seth lunch, looked at the panting boy and could not help but to notice the disheveled, frazzled state her eldest son was in. "Thaddeus! What in the world happened to you?"

During his sprint home, the boy came up with an alibi just in case he would be questioned on his appearance and state of mind. He thought it was a good one, "I was uh, lookin' for huckleberries up on the ridge, an' I musta gotten myself positioned between a mama bear an' her cubs, because she chased me, an' I, uh, had to climb up a tree to get away from her. I thought I was a goner; I tell ya."

Pale and still slightly panting from his ordeal, he plopped into his chair at the table, opposite his brother.

Seth suspiciously eyed the storyteller as their mother said, "My stars, Thaddy! You'd better be more careful next time. At least you were smart enough to climb a tree."

Then she asked him, "Hungry? I made chicken soup with those alphabet macaronis you like so much."

"Yes, please. I'm starved."

His mother served him a bowl, then told him, "Wash your filthy hands before you eat, you boys can clean up after yourselves; I have laundry to hang on the line."

"Yes, Mom," both boys answered in unison.

Seth didn't say a word until Thaddeus returned from the sink and sat; the younger boy chortled, then sarcastically asked, "Huh! A mama Black bear?"

"That's right, an' she was a big one," Thaddeus answered, but sheepishly avoided Seth's gaze by sprinkling salt and pepper into his soup.

Over the years, Seth came to recognize his brother's idiosyncrasies, especially when he was lying, as he was obviously doing right now.

"An' of course, she even had cubs, huh?"

"That's right, Little Brother."

"Everybody in the whole world, except for Mom, I suppose, knows that there is no way in hell that a person can outrun a bear... out swim a bear... an' especially... out *climb* a bear," Seth stated as a matter of fact.

"Maybe she just wanted to uh, uh, scare me off," Thaddeus rebutted. He stirred the salt and pepper in his chicken and alphabet macaroni soup and took a spoonful. Then he put the spoon down and picked up his butter knife and a slice of bread. He continued to avert eye contact with his interrogative little brother.

"Maybe you can bullshit Mom, but you ain't foolin' me, Thaddy. How did you get so much dirt under your fingernails then? Musta been one helluva dirty tree that bear put you up," Seth said sarcastically.

Then he went on, in a parental scolding tone of voice, he said, "I know what you were doin' up on the ridge... You went up there an' dug up Rachel Petersen's grave. Didn't ya? Don't lie to me, Thaddeus!"

"Did no such thing, Seth," Thaddeus answered rather defensively as he was about to plunge his spoon back into the soup but froze. His eyes widened and his jaw fell open. Floating on top of the broth were the words... '*help me*'... spelled out with the alphabet macaroni! Thaddeus quickly stirred his soup and watched in awe as the words reappeared amongst the chunks of chicken, chopped celery, and diced carrots — '*help me.*'

"Quit playing with your soup, Thaddy, and answer me," Seth demanded.

Ignoring his little brother's request, Thaddeus stirred his soup one more time, but with much more vigor. All the letters scattered and swirled about in the tiny whirlpool. However, as before, the letters began to surface one by one, spelling out the request for assistance.

By now, Seth was intrigued by his brother's fixation on the soup, and a look of terror he had never seen on his brother's face before. He stood up and peered into the bowl. Those all too familiar icy shivers ran down the smaller boy's spine as he watched the letters continue to line up. He read the words aloud, "Help, me."

Seth then brought both hands to the sides of his head and raked his fingers through his hair. With disgust in his voice, he snapped quietly at his older brother, "You couldn't leave well enough alone, could ya Thaddy? Could ya? No! Not you, ya stupid ass. You had to go an' let her out!"

Seth slowly sunk back into his chair, frowning, he told his brother, "In case you don't live to see your birthday tomorrow, I better tell ya now. Happy Birthday, Moron."

Chapter Ten

Chapter Six

Looking at Thaddeus while slowly shaking his head in utter disgust, Seth absolutely could not believe how stupid and thoughtless his older brother could be at times. He wondered what consequences Thaddeus's mindless act of insanity would produce this time. Probably fatal ones, he reasoned. Could his dream have been a premonition? Was his entire family in jeopardy thanks to his idiotic brother?

Everybody knew how twisted that girl was. To think she was able to kill her family and then hang herself. To make matters worse, she was now an invisible foe. Seth's head was swimming. *We're all gonna die! Stabbed to our deaths while we sleep.*

Thaddeus stared at the words floating on top of the soup, and then he glanced at Seth who was still glaring back with an irritated look. Thaddeus simply shrugged his shoulders and nonchalantly said, "Oh well."

Seth then began to doubt if those letters actually did have assistance from the spiritual world, or could it be that his brother was up to his shenanigans again? His sudden devil-may-care-attitude just did not sit quite right with Seth. Didn't their mother comment on how much his brother liked those macaroni letters? Why were they one of his favorite foods? Because the prankster would always spell out swear words to make his little brother giggle at the supper table. Seth remembered the last time his mother made soup and added them — Thaddeus spelled out the word *fart*! He got Seth's attention and pointed to his bowl, causing them both to chuckle, which in turn made their mother scold her oldest son, "Quit being a clown, Thaddeus. Can't you just eat your soup without making a game out of it first?" However, her doing so only made the whole episode that much funnier to the two boys.

Curiosity and doubt finally got the best of Seth. Acting on an involuntary impulse, he reached over and stirred the soup with his own spoon. When the letters stopped swirling, nothing appeared except for scattered letters, no words. Convinced he was the butt of his brother's practical joke, a feeling of great relief descended over him. He laughed and said, "Ha ha, Thaddy. You almost had me. Very funny."

Then, thinking how he was once again duped by his big brother, he viciously added, "You're an ass!"

Now, Thaddeus was curious. Three times in a row for him could not have been a mere coincidence. He told Seth to watch closely, then swirled the soup, put the spoon down, crossed his arms, and waited.

Seth kept an eye on him, looking for any trickery, then he glanced back and forth from his brother to the soup. Thaddeus did not move a muscle.

One by one, the letters resurfaced, spelling '*help me!*'

Seth's eyes bulged out of his head, "It's you! It's you she's after, Thaddy!"

He then pointed a finger at his brother and laughed, "Haha, I'm in the clear."

Next, he danced a little jig around the table, stopped by his brother's side, picked up his spoon, and stirred the soup once again. Nothing but scrambled letters, he sang, "Happy Birthday to you! Happy Birthday to you! Happy Birthday Dear Thaddy. I'm going to live, not you!"

Overly melodramatic, Seth wiped his brow with the back of his hand, saying, "Whew boy! I sure am glad that psycho bitch ain't after *me*."

His jig intensified, and then in a musical *eat your own words* tone, he gloated and said, "Better check under your bed tonight, Thaddy!"

With a cupped hand to his ear, he teased his brother yet more! "Listen! Hear Rachel sharpening her knife?"

Seth's little jig came to a screeching halt, however, when he skipped through an icy cold spot in the kitchen, causing him to shiver violently for a split second. His eyes widened as he gasped, and in a profoundly serious tone he whispered to Thaddeus, "She, *is*... Here!"

"What're you talkin' about?" Thaddeus asked with a scrunched-up face, irritated that his younger brother was getting the best of him. He was not accustomed to Seth getting *his* goat, and he was hating every second of it.

"I think I just walked through her ghost," Seth whispered, shivering once more.

"Ain't no such things as ghosts," Thaddeus said as he picked up his full bowl of soup and started to walk towards the stove. Then he abruptly stopped, as if he walked into an invisible brick wall; his upper shoulders and neck shivered, then he quickly turned and looked behind himself.

"You felt her too, didn't ya, Thaddy?"

Thaddeus did not answer. Verbally, anyhow. He simply dumped his soup back into the stockpot and walked speedily out of the room. Seth scanned the kitchen but saw nothing; he then ran from there and caught up to his brother on the porch.

They both sat on the swing in the warmth of the sunshine; the brightness gave the boys a sense of being safe.

"What do we do now, Thaddy? Do you think we oughta tell Mom an' Pa?"

"I ain't sure what to do. I reckon they'll find out sooner or later, even if we don't tell them."

"I can't believe you went an' dug up her grave!"

"I figgered there would be some kind of artifacts buried with her."

"Well, was there?"

The smaller brother then squinted and stared at his brother directly in his eyes; seriously, he demanded, "Thaddy, tell me the truth! Did you steal anything from her? Tell me honest."

"No, I swear. The only thing in there was a rosary, you know — prayer beads on a chain, but there was a silver cross on it. When I touched it, all these stinky *hunnerd leggers* came out from under it and attacked me. Then they all went back into the coffin. It was like they were guarding it."

"You either have balls as big as cantaloupes, or your brain is as big as a pea. I can't imagine diggin' up a dead person."

After a moment's thought, Seth was compelled to ask, "What'd she look like?"

"Like a prune with red hair. She wasn't just a skeleton yet. She still had skin, but it was awful wrinkled in some places, and tight in others."

"Were you scared?"

"No. Of course not."

"I know you felt her ghost in the kitchen. Don't tell me that didn't spook ya."

"Maybe a little, okay?"

"I wonder what she meant by, '*help me?*'"

"I dunno, but I did cover her coffin back up. What could she want from me? I just want her to leave me alone. Maybe if I can tell her I'm sorry somehow, she'll..."

Thaddeus stopped talking when he noticed one of the two old hickory rocking chairs begin to rock back and forth. However, nobody could be seen sitting in it, and there was no breeze whatsoever!

For a few moments, both boys watched in awe as the chair continued rocking. Thaddeus eventually rose from the swing and cautiously walked towards the rocker. He stopped three feet from it, bent down, and spoke as if someone was actually sitting in it, rocking back and forth, "I'm sorry. I shouldn't have dug up your grave. I wanted your rosary, but I did not take it." He tried to sound both sincere and apologetic.

Thaddeus continued talking to the empty chair, "You are dead. Shouldn't you be somewhere? Like in Heaven?"

He used hand gestures as if he were waiting for a reply, "I'm really sorry, I tell ya."

The rocking abruptly stopped. Both boys were so mesmerized on the empty, but rocking rocker, that they did not notice or hear when their mother came up the steps behind them, carrying an empty laundry basket.

Both boys jumped out of their skin when she spoke, "Thaddeus! What in the world are you doing? Talking to a rocking chair? Did you fall out of that tree this morning and hit your head?"

She could not help but notice how peculiar both of her sons were acting. She glanced at Seth; her younger son looked pale, worried.

Thaddeus thought astonishingly fast and replied, "I was uh, practicin' my lines for a school play, Mom."

Seth, amazed at how quick his sibling was able to concoct a lie, rolled his eyes and offered a suggestion, "Maybe you should tell her the truth, Thaddy. Don't you think she'll find out sooner or later? When it might be too late?"

Mary set the basket down, put her hands on her hips, and said, "I have to agree with Seth. Now tell me what is really going on, Thaddeus. Just what might be too late?"

Thaddeus threw an angered look at his big-mouthed brother, hung his head, then shamefully came clean, "I wasn't pickin' any berries up on the ridge this mornin', an' there weren't no bears either. I was diggin' for treasure."

He nervously scratched at the back of his neck and said, "That's all, I tell ya."

"Well, if *that's all*... Then why were you talking to that rocker? And you still did not explain why it's too late." Her tone had reflections of her patience wearing thin, and Thaddeus knew all too well what the repercussions of her becoming mad would bring.

"When I was diggin' for buried treasure, I might have, uh, freed Rachel Petersen's ghost," he sheepishly admitted.

A look of incredible disbelief slowly etched itself onto her face as she tilted her head to one side. Then she spoke very slowly and clearly so he would definitely understand the question, "Are you telling me that you dug up Rachel Petersen's... *Grave*, Thaddeus? You look me in the eye when you answer!"

Then a look of self-disgust came across her son's face as he slowly looked at his mother. "Yes," he blurted out, as if even he himself could not believe he could actually be capable of such a stupid, horrendous act.

"Oh my God, Thaddeus. That was so, so... sacrilegious!"

She shook her head in total disbelief. "And what? You were talking to her just now? She's sitting in the rocking chair because you *freed* her?" She looked at her son as if he was a flaming lunatic.

Thaddeus nodded yes; Seth spoke up, "She *was* there, Mom. We couldn't see her, but the chair *was* rocking."

"Both of you are off *your* rockers. Rachel Petersen's ghost! Good Lord. Now I've heard everything," she said, still shaking her head. "Such nonsense."

Thaddeus argued, "She *was* here, I tell ya. Rockin' in that chair. There ain't no wind, Mom, look."

Her son pointed to the clothesline and said, "The pants and shirts aren't blowin'. Oh, an' another thing, she went an' spelt out the words '*help me*' in my soup. Her ghost *is* here, I'm tellin ya!"

Seth spoke very quickly, hoping his mother would not interrupt as he backed up his brother's story, "Her ghost is definitely here, Mom! An' I seen everything, too, with my very own eyes. I saw the rocking chair rock and I saw when she spelled, '*help me*', in his soup. But the message wouldn't appear when, *I*, stirred the soup, only when *Thaddy* stirred it! I'm guessin' she's after him because he's the one that went an' dug her up. We're tryin' to figger out how she wants Thaddy to help her."

"I've heard enough of this hogwash. If you boys keep talking like this, they're going to take you away and lock you up in a mental institution. I wish you two would have never found that grave. See now why we didn't want to tell you?"

Then she pointed a finger at Thaddeus, and warned him, "You just wait, Young Man, till your father finds out what you did."

She picked up the clothesbasket and stormed into the house.

Once the screen door slammed shut behind her, Thaddeus threw a menacing look toward Seth and bitched, "I told you we shouldn't have told her. Now I'm gonna be in big trouble with Pa."

He spit on the ground.

"I dunno, Thaddy. I still think it was best we told, instead of them findin' out on their own," Seth argued. "What would've happened if Mom walked into the kitchen an' a knife flew at her or somethin' like that? At least now, she can be ready."

Thaddeus argued back, "She doesn't believe us, Seth. It didn't do any good in tellin' her. The only thing it accomplished was probably gettin' me grounded and gettin' extra chores. Thanks to you and your big mouth."

Seth frowned. He saw there was no point in arguing his reasons for being honest any further, so he changed the subject, "I wonder why she stopped rockin' when Mom came on the porch. Almost like she didn't want Mom to know she was here."

"Dunno. Can't figger that one out. Maybe she's afraid of grownups or somethin'. I imagine she's just a little girl ghost. Her body weren't no bigger than this." He held his hand three and a half feet from the ground.

"She might be little, but she's big enough to kill people," Seth pointed out.

Then a terrible thought flashed through his head, and he whispered, "She's probably listenin' to every word we're sayin' right now, too, Thaddy." Seth had been keeping an eye on the rocker ever since his mother went back inside, but now he was scanning the entire porch. Then he clammed up. He didn't want to accidentally say anything that would piss off Rachel.

Seth did not sleep well that night. But at least he did not have any nightmares.

Chapter Eleven

Chapter Seven

"**R**eal nice birthday present, Little Brother, let me tell ya," Thaddeus complained sarcastically as he tossed a heaping shovel load of Dolly's manure into the cart. He had correctly predicted what punishment his father would dish out. He was grounded for the next two weeks, and cleaning the mule's stall, which was normally one of Seth's chores, was added to his list.

When Mary informed Ralph that his eldest son dug up the Petersen girl's grave, he was not the least bit surprised. He knew Thaddeus was the more adventurous of his two boys, whereas Seth was levelheaded and more of a bookworm than an explorer. What was done was done, and Ralph reprimanded his son mainly to appease his wife. However, he could not help saying to her, "Maybe we can forget the dollar bill and get him a pick and shovel from Agway for his birthday instead."

His wife responded with a frown and a disgusted look.

Seth grabbed a spade, threw a shovel load of manure into the cart, then told his brother, "You don't hafta do my chore, Thaddy. Go an' clean your own stall."

"You won't tell on me for *that*, will ya?" Thaddeus said in an attempt to make his brother feel worse than he already did.

"No," Seth replied, slightly irritated with his brother's attitude.

The old barn owl sat perched on the highest timber and kept an eye on the two boys as they cleaned the stalls. When they finished, Seth looked around the barn and said, "I wonder which beam she hung herself from."

"Probably that one," Thaddeus said, pointing to the lowest beam in the barn, which ran across the mule's stall.

"Maybe. It is low enough for her to throw a rope over," Seth noted.

"She probably tied it off to that railing," he said, pointing to the top rail of the stall.

Both boys cowered from fluttering wings as the owl took flight. The bird landed on one of two main support beams running down the center of the barn, which was a good twenty feet off the ground. Then it proceeded to use its beak to pick at something stuck on the crudely sawn beam.

"The old hooter musta gotten himself a mouse," Thaddeus said. They watched as the huge owl tore at something between its feet, but then drop it over the beam. It looked like long strands of golden hair slowly flitting down. Then the owl flew back to his usual perch.

The brothers walked over to where the tassel had landed; Thaddeus picked it up and smelled it, "It's pieces of rope, I tell ya."

He handed it to Seth for his opinion, "Yeah, it is. I think Rachel somehow just made that old owl show us which beam she used. These fibers musta got shredded off the rope and got stuck up there when she pulled the rope over."

Thaddeus looked up at the beam and brought up a good point, "That beam is way up there. I can't imagine a little girl bein' strong enough to toss a rope that high in the air. Somebody musta helped her."

Seth's eyes widened, he said, "I don't think somebody helped her, Thaddy, and I don't think she hung herself. I think somebody *murdered* her!"

"Hoot! Hoot!" The night raptor asserted his two cents into their conversation while bobbing his head like owls do.

They both looked quizzically at the clichéd *wise old owl,* Seth said, "It's almost like Rachel's spirit is in that bird."

Thaddeus asked, "I'll say! But why would somebody want to murder a little girl?"

"For killing the Tremonts. Maybe before it went to court, family members lynched her. That's what she wants you to help her with; she probably wants you to find her killer."

"If somebody did do her in, Seth, he would be dead by now himself, anyways. Mom said this all happened, when? Almost ninety years ago?"

"Yeah, but I still say that it was no coincidence that the owl showed us which beam it was. She's probably listenin' to us talkin' an' somehow she got inside that owl an' made him do that. The ghost of Rachel Petersen is tryin' to tell us, or you, somethin'. I can feel it. If she wanted us dead, Thaddy, she would've killed us last night when we were sleeping."

"Dunno, but I betcha we ain't heard the last from her," Thaddeus said, as they walked out of the barn and headed for the house. Then he added, "Thanks for helpin' with my chores."

"That's okay, Thaddy. Sorry Pa punished you, but I still think it's best they know."

"You're probably right, Seth. Even if they don't believe us."

The sweet aroma of a cake baking greeted them as they came into the house on that Sunday morning. "Smells good," Seth told his mother as he walked into the kitchen, while Thaddeus trudged upstairs to his room, beginning his two week-long grounding.

"Did you boys get your chores done?" she asked.

Seth nodded his head yes then said, "Mom, I know you don't believe us about Rachel Petersen's ghost, but the owl that lives in the barn? He showed us what beam she was hung from."

With patience in her voice she said, "Seth, when are you going to stop believing in your brother's nonsense? Just how did the owl show you?" she asked after opening the oven and sticking a toothpick into the center of the cake.

"Look!" He pulled the yellow strands from his pocket, then explained, "He flew to the beam an' pulled pieces of rope from it that musta been stuck there all these years. Then he dropped them down for me an' Thaddy to look at," Seth said, trying to be convincing with his words.

"Now why would the owl do that?" she asked while pulling the cake out of the oven since the toothpick came out clean.

"He wanted us to see that the beam was too high for a little girl to throw a rope over. Me an' Thaddy don't think she committed suicide. We think somebody murdered her."

"Seth, everybody knows she hanged herself. Nobody in this town would've killed a little girl. Not then, and certainly not now. These are good, God-fearing folk that live around here."

"I dunno, Mom. I think she wants us, or Thaddy, to find her killer an' bring him to justice."

"Oh please, Seth. You read too much. And if someone hanged her, they'd be dead now, anyhow."

Her patience was wearing thin, she told him nicely to get lost, "I have a hind quarter to baste, scalloped potatoes to put in the oven, and a cake to frost, why don't you run along now?"

Defeated, Seth shrugged his shoulders and left with his head hanging low, he thought, "*Why don't grownups ever listen?*" He hoped she would not be sorry for not believing the facts.

The boy wandered into the living room and absent-mindedly stopped to admire Bocephus, as he did daily since his Dad hung the buck above the mantle last month. Professionally mounted, the taxidermist did a magnificent job; it looked as though it was alive and looking directly at you.

Mesmerized by those glass eyes, Seth fell into a daydream and relived the hunt.

The taxidermist also researched the records and discovered that Seth's buck was the second largest deer ever taken in Pennsylvania. However, it did break the record for being the largest one ever bagged in Westmoreland County, which delighted the proud, young hunter to no end.

Thirty seconds passed before Seth bounced back into reality and interrupted his dad, who was reading the Sunday paper. He told his father exactly what he had told his mother, but received the same negative response from his father as he had gotten from his mother.

Disappointed that neither of his parents would believe in him, he moseyed on upstairs to Thaddeus's room.

From sheer boredom, his brother was stretched out on his bed, staring at the ceiling.

"Wanna play a game of Scrabble, Thaddy?"

"No! I ain't gonna play any game that has letters in it, but I will beat you in a game of Monopoly."

"You're on," Seth said. They set up the board. Thaddeus picked the shoe for his marker, and Seth picked the dog. Then they rolled the dice to determine who went first.

Thaddeus rolled a nine and smiled. "Beat that, Little Brother."

Seth rolled an eleven. "Ha ha," he rejoiced. Then he rolled a five to start the game; he naturally bought the Reading Railroad for two hundred dollars.

His brother tossed the dice next; boxcars came up. Seth moved the tiny shoe twelve spaces.

Just as Thaddeus reached for the one-hundred and fifty dollars to purchase The Electric Company, he felt that icy breeze pass by him. The deed for the utility company flew from the box lid and landed in front of Thaddeus before Seth, the banker, had a chance to pull it from the stack of available properties!

Then one of the dice flipped, then again, and once more until it had a one showing. The other die did the exact same thing. The original roll of Boxcars turned into Snake eyes. Two.

The brothers stared at each other. Finally, Seth said, "Two. Two what?"

He made a face as if he were deep in thought, then his eyes widened and he blurted out, "Two killers! I betcha that's what she means, Thaddy! Two people hung her after she killed her family. Maybe the Tremonts' kin did it, but I'm sure she did not hang herself as the story goes. Didn't the owl hoot twice?"

Wide eyed and staring at The Electric Company deed, Thaddeus nodded in agreement.

After more thought, Seth arrived at another hypothetical conclusion, "Or maybe the same people who killed her, killed everybody else in this house, an' then pinned the blame on her. Like I told ya out in the barn, she could've done us in last night, Thaddy, but she didn't because that little girl ain't a killer."

"I dunno, Seth. That's not what Mom an' everybody else says about her. I hope you're right, an' now she'll let me be for lettin' the truth be known," he said and quickly grabbed the dice and tossed them in the box, followed by the fake money, markers, and deeds. They both sat on Thaddeus's bed looking around, wondering what was going to happen next. However, nothing did, which did not upset, nor disappoint them.

The time dragged on for the two restless boys. The only other board games they had were chess and checkers, but Thaddeus refused to play them; he could not win at either against his younger brother.

Finally, their mother called up the stairs, "Dinner's ready." They flew down, famished.

"I really like the spuds this way, Mom," Seth said, using his bread to sop up the remaining cream sauce left on his plate. He had devoured his second helping of the scalloped potatoes.

Living on a potato farm, Mary knew every recipe out there for preparing taters; she told her son, "Well, I'm glad you like them that way, Seth."

"Time for birthday cake!" Ralph, with his sweet tooth, announced once the casserole dish had been scraped clean, and only half of the venison hindquarter, compliments of Ol'

Bocephus, remained for another meal; more than likely, stew. (Undoubtedly served over mashed potatoes!)

"I thought that this big ol' buck was going to be tough, but he was nice and tender, Mom," Seth made supper conversation, proud he provided the meat.

"Cook venison low and slow with a sliced onion and bacon strips on top. Every now and then, baste it like it's a turkey; that's the trick to cooking deer," his mother informed him, clearing the dishes.

"Memorize that recipe so you can give it to Tammy Wilson when you marry her, an' she can cook your venison good like Mom does," Seth teased his brother.

"Yuk! Tammy Wilson! I don't like her."

"Yeah, you do! I see the way you look at her on the bus."

"Shut up! I do not."

"Do too. Your eyes are all dreamy, like this," Seth then made an overly dramatic lovestruck face.

"I do not! You're cruisin' for a bruisin', I tell ya!"

"Boys! Stop it right now! And you, Thaddeus, start acting your age!" Mary griped, then placed the cake, which had sixteen candles sticking out of the peanut butter icing, on the table.

While lighting them, Ralph said, "Happy Sweet Sixteen, Son! Enjoy this time of your life, it flies right on by all too soon."

After they all sung happy birthday, Ralph, in his deep singing voice, added his usual last line to the song, "And... many... more."

"Make a wish," Mary told her son.

Thaddeus closed his eyes; he made his wish out loud, and aimed it at Rachel, "I wish that... *Rachel Petersen would leave me alone!*"

He took a deep inhale, but before he exhaled, the candles began to blow out on their own! One after another, each candle individually blew out! Except for the last two!

Everybody, including Ralph and Mary, watched in awe.

"See Mom. What'd I tell ya? The ghost of Rachel Petersen *is* here!" Thaddeus exclaimed.

"Yeah, Mom. *Now...* Do you believe me an' Thaddy that she's tellin' us there was two killers?" Seth asked.

Thaddeus inhaled again; as he started to blow out the two lit candles, however, Rachel beat him to it. As the smoke rose from the two extinguished candles, Mary answered Seth, "I don't know what to believe, anymore."

Mary then nervously asked her husband, "What do you think, Ralph?"

"I told y'all I hadn't seen her for a while, but ghost or no ghost, I'm having a piece of that cake."

"Here, Son." Ralph handed Thaddeus an envelope; the boy immediately tore it open; inside was a crisp dollar bill.

"Wow! Thanks, Pa. A brand-new, one-dollar bill!" (In 1951, a dollar was a lot of money to a young farm boy.)

The four of them then ate their cake in silence while glancing around the room.

Rachel did not bother them anymore that evening, even while they enjoyed The Grand Ole Opry Show on the large Zenith tube radio. Grandpa Jones's voice crackled through the speaker, "You folks just listened to some mighty fine banjo pickin' by the youngest person ever to win the National Banjo

Contest. Seventeen-year-old Roy Clark, ladies and gentlemen. I'm sure we'll be hearing an awful lot from this young man in the years to come. Thanks again, folks, for tuning in to the Grand Ole Opry."

THE NEXT MORNING WHILE waiting for the bus, the two boys were sneaking their morning smoke. Thaddeus took the last toke from his cigarette, while exhaling, he said, "I betcha they believe us now."

"Yeah. I think so. She didn't do anything else after blowin' out the candles, though. Maybe that was her way of sayin' goodbye and showin' Mom an' Pa that we weren't just makin' it all up," Seth said and then flicked his butt.

"I sure hope so," Thaddeus said to the sound of brakes squealing when their bus pulled up.

They both said, "Good morning, Mr. Fisher," as they boarded the old Ford rattletrap. Then they sat in the very last two seats on the bus, each one having a seat to themselves. Thaddeus and Seth were the first students to get on the bus; they had a lengthy ride to and from school each day.

Scanning for deer as they always did on the morning bus ride, Thaddeus saw a little girl standing by Old Man Woodley's mailbox up ahead.

"Who the heck is that?" he asked Seth while pointing.

"Where? I don't see anybody."

"Right there! By the mailbox. A little girl," he said anxiously, getting louder as they passed by the mailbox. Both boys had their faces pressed up against the side windows.

Thaddeus was able to read, '*Woodley,*' on the box... Right through the girl's body!

"I still don't see anybody, Thaddy."

Both boys had their faces plastered to the rear window now. "Look! Right there, Seth. She has red hair an'..." he knew immediately who the girl was "... She's wearing a flowered dress!"

"Ain't nobody there."

"It's Rachel, I'm tellin you. Or her ghost! That's why you can't see her. Maybe I'm the only one who can see her."

"Are you sure you saw something?" Seth asked as the bus went around a turn and the mailbox left their sight.

"Now *you* sound like Mom an' Pa. She was there, I tell ya. I could see right through her. Like she was nothin' more than... a puff of smoke from a cigarette!"

The next morning was a repeat of Rachel standing by Woodley's mailbox. Again, Seth could not see her. However, this time, she was pointing down Woodley's Lane.

"She must be tryin' to tell you somethin'. I can't see her, but if you're tellin' me she is standin' there, an' she's pointin' to Old Man Woodley's house, she must want you to go there."

"I ain't goin' there; no way. I hate it when Mom sends me over for apples. That old man gives me the creeps; he always has his one eye closed, an' squints through the other one. I wonder how old he is?"

His brother informed him, "When me an' Pa went to pick my deer up at Mr. Custer's, they were talkin' about Old Man Woodley and how many deer were shot in his orchards. The taxidermist is pretty old himself; he knows Woodley from buyin' his apples there. He said Mr. Woodley was a boy when the Civil War was bein' fought, an' that he turned one hundred years old last month."

"Sonna bitch!" Thaddeus reacted, then said, "I knew he was old, but not a hunnerd."

"It's 1951 now, that means he was born in 1851," Seth said, doing the math in his head. Unlike his brother, Seth could remember names and dates. Another difference — he was good at math.

He then realized, "Holy Hell! That's the exact same year when Rachel Petersen was born!"

Thaddeus deducted, "If he lived here all his life... that means he might've known her."

"Exactly, Thaddy. He was twelve-years old when she was twelve-years old an' died. That's why she wants you to talk to him. I betcha he knows everything there is to know about Rachel's legend," Seth insisted. "He might even know who hung her."

"I would go see him, but I can't. I'm grounded."

Seth victoriously squashed his brother's lame statement, "Well then, that gives you two weeks to figger out what you and Samuel Woodley are goin' talk about, don't it?"

However, since a boy, the old man liked everybody to just call him... Sam.

Chapter Twelve

C hristian's next chapter also stayed focus on the Yoder boys; his words still flowed elegantly, effortlessly...

Chapter Eight

Thursday morning, the mercury had dipped below freezing.

Western Pennsylvania, especially the higher ridges of the Appalachian Mountains, has always been infamous for its drastic weather changes; snow had been known to fall well beyond the first days of May; causing fishing lines to freeze on the opening day of trout.

Although it was not snowing now, it certainly was cold enough. The Yoder boys shivered as they enjoyed their first smoke of the day while waiting for the bus. They both sighed in relief when the old Ford finally pulled up to their lane, getting them out of the frigid cold, into what little heat the old clunker did have to offer.

As the bus neared Woodley's mailbox, both boys had their faces pressed to the windows in anticipation of seeing Rachel Petersen again. Seth had even cleaned his glasses that morning before leaving the house. He so desperately wanted to see this apparition, or whatever it was that his older brother swore he saw every morning of the week so far.

Three days in a row now, he had insisted she was there. The last two days, according to Thaddeus, she was pointing down Woodley's Lane towards his house.

"Is she there?" Seth excitedly asked, even before the mailbox came into their view.

"I'll let you know in a minute, Seth, when we get to the mailbox," Thaddeus replied, upset over his brother's anticipation, and doubting him.

"Yeah, she's there! She's pointin' down the lane again," Thaddeus exclaimed as the box came into view, which again, he could see through her.

Seth strained his eyes hoping to see something, but as it had been every morning, so far he saw nothing but a dilapidated mailbox with the name, 'Woodley,' hand-painted on it.

A visible puff of exhaust smoke belched from the exhaust pipe when the driver double clutched from second to third gear as they passed Woodley's Lane. The small hazy cloud of exhaust fumes passed over top of the little girl's image, and Thaddeus watched as she then rose up in the air below the puff of smoke. As the vapors disappeared, she did not; rather, she *levitated* and followed behind the bus.

"She's followin' the God damned bus, I tell ya, Seth!" he excitedly told his brother, who was still looking ridiculously hard to see something.

"I wish I could see her too, damn it. You're not just toyin' with me?"

"No. Swear to God, Little Brother; she's taggin' along."

The bus squealed to a stop for the Wilson twins to board; Rachel stayed hovering twenty feet off the ground, thirty feet behind the bus.

"Is she still there?" Seth wanted to know.

"Yeah. She's floatin' in midair, I tell ya."

The bus pulled out; she followed. The exhaust passed right through her when Mr. Fisher shifted gears, outlining her completely in a shadowy, watery silhouette. For a moment, Seth's wish came true. Well, at least halfway. He did get to see her blurry resemblance briefly, until the exhaust fumes dissipated.

"I saw her, Thaddy! I actually seen her. You weren't lying." Seth became so excited he had to go to the bathroom.

The Wilson twins, Tommy and Tammy, who were the same age as Thaddeus, watched the Yoder brothers, wondering what could possibly be keeping them so mesmerized and excited this early in the morning.

Obviously, it was more than a deer following the bus.

Finally, the boy asked, "What are you two looking at, Seth?"

"The ghost of Rachel Petersen is followin' the bus," Seth answered.

"Very funny," the twin said. "She ain't for real. My mom says she's just a myth."

"Wanna bet? Watch when the driver shifts gears, Tommy. You'll see her shadow in the exhaust fumes," Seth told him and his sister.

However, he did not let on that Thaddeus could see her the whole time. He was not about to go into detail on how and why. Also, Thaddeus made Seth swear he would not tell anybody about him digging up her grave.

Anxiously, they waited for Mr. Fisher to shift to the next gear. When he finally did, and the bus coughed out the cloud of exhaust fumes, the twins' eyes widened when they saw her form in the vapors.

"There! Did you see her?" Seth asked.

Both twins nodded their heads, their eyes as big as hubcaps, their mouths hung wide open.

Six bus stops later, fifteen wide-eyed faces were now plastered to the back windows, gasping every time the old driver shifted gears. They all made comments such as, "There she is. Did you see her?"

Tammy Wilson exclaimed, "I did see her! I'm pretty sure she's holding a knife."

A little first grade girl couldn't believe her eyes, she cried out, "I want to go home!"

And finally, Tommy Wilson added his two cents worth, "I knew she was more than just a myth! I heard my dog barking at her last night!"

A half mile from the tiny schoolhouse, Thaddeus watched as she drifted backwards, then upwards until she simply... Vanished! All the children remained packed at the back of the bus, staring out the rear windows when the tired old bus pulled up in front of the school.

Seth and Thaddeus chuckled when Mr. Fisher had to coax half of the students from the bus. Especially four petrified girls who absolutely flat out refused to get off. They told the driver why they would not get off, "Rachel Petersen is waiting for us, and she has a really big butcher knife in her hand."

The quick-witted old driver thought up a good one, "I think it's this bus that is haunted, and sometimes I see her sitting in the last seat when I'm driving back to the garage. Are you sure you want to stay on? You can if you want, but I have to pull out." His comment caused the four girls to climb over one another to get out. On his way back to the bus garage, Mr. Fisher had to chuckle to himself when he thought of how he tricked those girls. Then he wondered how he was going to coax them back on the bus for the return trip home.

Since the school only had six classrooms and roughly seventy-five students, the sighting of Rachel Petersen's ghost spread like wildfire through the tiny Jonesboro School. By second period, the news was over the entire school. Moreover, rumor had it she was spotted in the girl's latrine between classes. Even the teachers caught wind of the exciting bus ride. They had their hands full trying to contain the worked-up students. None of the kids could, or wanted to, concentrate on their lessons.

Mr. Altemus, the squirrely little eighth grade math teacher who was no taller than some of his students, finally managed to get his third period algebra class under control after a minute of his yelling. Once his students calmed down, the teacher explained Pythagoras's theory on the blackboard when moaning and banging sounds wailed from the closet in the back of his room. The noises interrupted, "A squared plus B squared equals C squared."

He immediately set the chalk in the tray and picked up his yardstick before finishing the theory, "Only if C is the hypotenuse in a right triangle."

The children sitting closest to the broom closet jumped out of their seats and ran to the front of the room. Slowly, Mr. Altemus approached the closet with his *weapon* held high over his head as one student whispered to his classmate, "It's her, she's going to stab him."

The moans and thumping got louder as he neared. Cautiously, he grabbed the doorknob as complete silence fell over the classroom. Every wide-eyed student, including Seth, held their breath and watched as Altemus slowly turned the knob then quickly yanked the door open.

Then, little Jimmy Kirby, with a mop on his head, jumped out and screamed, "Boo!"

In a case of mistaken identity, Mr. Altemus automatically whacked the kid on his head, but luckily for the boy, the mop took all the force. Everybody laughed with relief and pointed at Jimmy. Altemus grabbed the class clown by his ear and marched him straight to the principal's office, lecturing him on heart attacks the whole way. All of the students laughed harder. The other classrooms wondered what could possibly be going on, as the ruckus echoed out of the room and through the halls of the tiny schoolhouse.

One half hour later, fourth period found Thaddeus in English class with Mrs. Monahan as his teacher, the seventy-four-year-old chain smoker had a sandpaper voice and a nasty cough thanks to her two pack a day habit. For today's extremely boring lesson, she was explaining transitive verbs; she wrote two sentences on the blackboard: "The dog *lays* on the sunny porch." And, "The dog *lies* on the sunny porch."

"One sentence is correct, one is not. Who can tell me which verb is used correctly?" she asked in her gravel-coated voice.

Of course, no hands shot up. Scanning the room for a designated volunteer, she spotted Thaddeus looking out the window, daydreaming, paying only half attention.

Her loud voice instantly brought him back to reality, "Thaddeus Yoder! What is your answer to my question, Young Man?"

Quickly, he mentally read the two sentences, trying to decide which one to guess at.

As he looked at her and was about to incorrectly say, "The dog *lays* on the sunny porch," he watched in total amazement as his teacher's old, wrinkly, face... *morphed*, into the youthful face of a young girl, having a beautiful, flawless complexion. At the same time, the old lady's permed grayish blue hair changed to curly red locks. While the old woman's transformation was taking place, a dim, glowing *halo* encircled her. Her aura grew brighter, then light reflected from her tiny silver cross on the white beaded rosary she held in her hands.

She stared directly at Thaddeus with her piercing green eyes. Everybody and everything else in the room faded away into a fuzzy darkness, leaving just an image of Rachel, and the young adventurous boy who released her tormented soul. The boy felt *connected* to her on the same mental plane.

Then she spoke! In the voice of a small, naïve little girl, she told him, "Lies... It's *all*... Lies! Thaddeus Yoder! Everybody is telling lies about me!"

For a few seconds, she stared at him with pleading eyes.

Then the halo waned, and her innocent and ever so young face slowly turned back into Mrs. Monahan's weathered, haggish smoker's face. The room grew bright once again, everything returned to normal.

"Lies!" Thaddeus hollered out, all wrapped up, lost in the moment. "It's lies, I tell ya. Lies!"

His teacher's gruff voice also returned, she congratulated her pupil, "Lucky guess, Thaddeus, but you don't have to be so dramatic and scream as such. My hearing is not that bad yet," she said, as the dinner bell clanged and echoed through the halls of the tiny school, announcing lunchtime.

"*Thank God*," Mrs. Monahan thought, "*I need a God damned Marlboro. These kids today!*"

WEATHER PERMITTING, the students were allowed to eat their lunch outdoors; the playground became an oasis for the brothers who'd always sit and eat lunch together, then take turns standing sentry while the other one puffed on their hand-rolled dessert.

Seth explained to Thaddeus how Jimmy Kirby jumped out of the closet in Algebra class, scaring the shit out of everybody, and Mr. Altemus bopping him on his head.

Then Thaddeus told Seth, "In English class, Mrs. Monahan's face changed from her old prunish self to a pretty little redheaded girl, and then she told me that everybody was telling lies about her."

"That proves it, Thaddy! The story about her hackin' up her family an' then hangin' herself ain't true. An' I still say she ain't gonna rest until you talk to Old Man Woodley," Seth insisted, then took a bite of his jelly sandwich; talking through a mouthful, he said, "He's gotta know somethin'. An' I think you should talk to him. Tonight. Right after school."

"I would, but I'm grounded. Remember?" the older brother said with a shrug of his shoulders, then shoved the last bite of sandwich into his mouth.

"How could I possibly ever forget? You reminded me plenty of times. I figgered you would use that as an excuse, too. That's why I came up with a plan. Tonight, after school when we're out in the barn doin' our chores, we're gonna take Dolly an'..."

Chapter Thirteen

Halfway through this next chapter of his book, Christian returns to The Civil War era, but for now, he's still with the Yoder Boys. And Rachel...

Chapter Nine

"That old Mr. Fisher sure is a sly fox, I tell ya," Thaddeus mentioned to Seth as they were walking down the lane after jumping off the school bus.

"Yeah, he is," Seth agreed, "Telling those girls he saw Rachel Petersen followin' a different bus, just to get them on his, was pretty slick."

Then he asked his brother, "Speakin' of Rachel, what are you gonna say to Mr. Woodley?"

"I dunno yet. Probably ask him if he knew her or heard of her legend, I guess. We're just assumin' that he did, maybe he didn't," Thaddeus replied as he tossed his jacket over his shoulder. The mercury had risen; the afternoon had warmed to a normal seasonal temperature once the Sun rose high in the sky.

"I'm sure he knows something, the way Rachel pointed for you to go to his house. She won't leave you alone till her soul rests; you better tell him that," Seth wisely offered encouragement.

After the boys said hello to their mother and changed into their old blue jeans, they went to the barn just like any other day to start their chores and put the gears to Seth's masterminded scheme in motion.

The initial step of Seth's ingenious plan was simply leaving the barn doors wide open.

Step two, they let Dolly out of her stall, walked her to the doors, then whacked her butt with a leather strap.

Thus, initiating step three: send the mule racing in the direction of Woodley's Apple Orchard with Thaddeus chasing after her, giving an occasional smack to keep her going.

Next, Seth ran to the house and informed his mother of Dolly's taking off; he gave a good reason why the mule would suddenly bolt like that, "Sam Woodley musta gotten a shipment of apples in, an' she smelled them, but don't worry; Thaddy and I will chase her down."

Before his McIntosh trees bore apples for customers to come and pick their own, the old man bought them wholesale which he would then resale for a profit. The money from the fruit, and the rent he received from leasing his hay fields to neighboring farmers, were his only sources of income.

Tennessee Walkers were no longer bred and sold on this farm once his father had passed forty years earlier.

Seth jumped on his bicycle and tore down the lane to meet up with his brother, who already had the mule out of sight from the house when Seth caught up to them.

The final step was for Thaddeus to ride the bike to Woodley's house, which was now only three fourths of a mile away, five minutes by bicycle, and have a conversation with their neighbor.

"Good luck! Don't chicken out because he's spooky lookin'," Seth told his brother before he pedaled off.

The younger brother sat and kept an eye on Dolly. The mule was elated that her little run was over, and even happier to be munching grass on this side of the fence, *where the grass is always greener!*

Mr. Samuel Woodley, lightly snoring away the afternoon in a rocking chair on his front porch while his cane rested against his leg, woke up from his daily catnap when he heard gravel crunching under the bike tires as Thaddeus pedaled down the lane. Extremely thin, the century old man may have looked and felt his age; however, he still had a fairly sharp mind. Yawning, he exposed two bare gums as Thaddeus pulled up to a stop at the porch; the neighbor boy straddled the bike.

Keeping his right eye closed and squinting through the left one, the old man instantly recognized the boy from the few times he was sent here by his mother to fetch apples. In his low, gruff voice, he informed the neighbor boy, "Tell your Ma I ain't got no apples till Thursday, Thaddeus."

"I ain't here for apples, Mr. Woodley."

The old man's boney hand shook when he raised his liver spotted arm to scratch his nearly bald head; he had just a few long strands of reddish blond hair left around the backside of his head.

"Well, what do you want then? I ain't got nothin' else," he asked, still squinting through only one eye. He tilted his head backwards to get a better look at Thaddeus, his good eye showed signs of cataracts.

"I'm hopin' you can answer a question for me. You did live here all your life. Ain't that right?" Thaddeus inquired of the centenarian.

"Sure did. Each and every day for a hundred years."

From being considered a historian in this part of Westmoreland County, people were always asking him about occurrences that happened decades ago, he asked the boy, "What is it *you* want to know?"

"Well, Mr. Woodley, Sir, uh, I was wonderin'... if you knew... uh, Rachel Petersen?" Thaddeus finally asked.

Upon hearing that name, an angered, hurt look crossed the old man's face as he leaned forward a bit; in a mean, defensive tone, he ordered the kid, "I don't know nothin' about Rachel Petersen! So, you just run along on home now, and leave this old man alone! You hear me, Boy? Now git! Git on outta here!"

Thaddeus apologized, but insisted, "I didn't mean to upset you none, Mr. Woodley, but I... uh, I did somethin' really stupid an' I... uh..."

He finally quit stuttering and blurted out what he had come here to tell the man, "I, uh, went an' dug up her grave, an' now she won't let me alone. I was only looking for..."

"What? You did... What? Boy?" he hollered, looking at Thaddeus with such great disbelief on his face. The right eye that had remained closed until now also popped wide open. The boy could not help but to stare at the repulsive, light lime green eyeball, completely covered in cataracts. Mr. Woodley was only able to distinguish between light and dark with that eye, seeing only extremely obscured grayish shadows.

A very hostile tone resonated in his voice as he chastised Thaddeus, "Did I just hear you say you went... And dug up that little girl's grave?"

The old man brought both shaking hands to the sides of his head, he questioned the boy, "What in Hell ever possessed you do something like that, Boy? Are you insane? For Christ Sakes! You don't go messin' around with dead people when they're in eternal rest. Good God Almighty!"

"I dunno why I did it, Sir. Maybe because we were studying King Tut in school, an' I thought I'd find some buried treasure. Then I..."

Mr. Woodley grabbed his cane, pointed it in Thaddeus's face, and loudly threatened him, interrupting the boy once again, "If you tell me you stole that rosary from that pretty little girl... I will beat you to every square inch of your body with this walking stick, Thaddeus Yoder. That was my mother's holy rosary! Damn you!"

The boy leaned backwards, teetering on the bicycle while pleading his case, "Oh no, Sir. I did see it, but I did not take it, or *anything* from her. I admit I wanted that rosary in the worst way, I did, I tell ya. But I swear, Mr. Woodley, Rachel is still holding on to it. But I think I let her spirit out. She's been givin' me signs to come see you. Just today, she told me everybody is telling lies about her, I think she..."

"She's been... *Talkin'* to you?" he once again interrupted, unable to mentally grasp this revelation.

He looked at Thaddeus as if the boy were certified mentally ill, he told him, "No, Boy. *She* ain't talkin' to you. That's your *conscious*, tellin' you that you did something really awful. Your *conscious*, won't let you sleep at night; will it, Boy? Every time you close your eyes, you see her beautiful little face... with those big green eyes, an' you can see the sunlight reflecting off her red hair... Don't ya?"

A tear ran from his bad eye when he said, "And you can still remember how she giggled when the horses took apples from her... It's your conscious talking, telling you that you were a fool!"

"Please hear me out, Mr. Woodley. It is not my conscious talking to me. It's her! Rachel!" Thaddeus did the interrupting this time when he noticed the elderly man becoming a bit confused. The boy had become intrigued, though, that the old man not only appeared to know Rachel! But now, he had remorse feelings for the girl!

He continued talking fast with hopes the old man would not interrupt him anymore, allowing him to explain fully why he was there, "She spelt out the words, '*help me*', in my vegetable soup. Then me an' my brother Seth were playin' Monopoly, an' she turned the dice over from a twelve to a two. We figger it was two people that hung her an' she didn't hang herself like everybody says. Then an owl showed Seth an' me pieces of rope on a beam in my Pa's barn that is too high for a little girl to throw a rope over. I even seen her, Mr. Woodley... She was standin' by your mailbox an' pointin' to your house three days this week goin' to school."

The old man leaned forward and buried his face in his hands, slowly shaking his head from side to side, quietly asking himself over and over, "Why? Why?"

Thaddeus continued, "It's not in my head, I tell ya. My brother seen all what she did too. My Mom an' Pa seen when she blew the candles out on my birthday cake, all of them, except for two. She *ain't* restin', Mr. Woodley. I'm tellin' ya, she *won't* rest in eternal peace until the truth is spoken. She kinda told me in school today that everything said about her has all been lies. I think she knows that *you* know the truth. If you didn't know her like you say, Mr. Woodley... Then how come you know she was buried with a rosary?"

The old man leaned forward as far as he could, right into Thaddeus's face; with those hideous eyes he glared at the boy, then hollered at him, "Because my mother put it in her hands before my Daddy an' me buried her!"

Then Mr. Woodley slumped back in his rocker and closed his bad eye but resumed squinting through the other one; he spoke in a lowered voice, as if confessing to a priest while lying on his deathbed, "Ain't a day goes by... that I don't think of that poor girl. Pretty little Rachel Petersen."

He raised his hand and wiped a tear, then continued, "I was maybe twelve, an' so was she. Her Daddy sent her here to live with her aunt when her mother died. It musta been pure hell for that little girl. Rachel wouldn't talk to anybody, except for me, that is. My daddy said it was cause I reminded her of her brother back in Ohio, but it made me feel special like anyways."

Thaddeus leaned closer so he could hear better.

"I would go to her house, your house now, just about every day. We would play hide an' seek in the barn or catch frogs by the pond. Some days we would just sit an' talk. But I always brought a couple of apples, an' we'd feed the horses. She really liked this one big black stallion in particular that Josef Tremont owned. It was a magnificent horse; I think his name was Midnight. Rachel would giggle when the horse took the apples from her."

Thaddeus sensed the old man had softened up a bit, so he laid the bike down and sat on the top step. He also sensed that this was the first time Mr. Woodley ever spoke about Rachel. To anyone!

The old man closed both his eyes and laid his head on the back of his rocking chair; he spoke as if reminiscing, "I went over there one day... an' the place was... quiet. Too quiet! The men folk weren't workin' the fields... Her aunt weren't hangin' clothes, or making soap outside. I didn't see Rachel anywhere either; she always sat in a rocker on the porch, but she wasn't there, so I went in the barn."

He choked up and tears came to his eyes. He needed a moment before continuing; he swallowed really hard; between sobs, he cried out, "I found her! Dear God! Yes, I did!"

He pulled a hanky from his rear pocket, wiped his eyes and blew his nose.

Nothing could have made Thaddeus feel worse at that moment; he never dreamed he'd make the old man cry.

"What I saw was the most God-awful sight. Especially for a boy of twelve to see."

He had to stop again to regain his composure, but then he continued on as hard as it was for him, he said, "She was... Hangin' from that real high beam like you say, and her bloomers were tossed on the ground."

Mr. Woodley stopped momentarily, fought back the tears and took another hard swallow before continuing, "Even though I knew it was too late, and she was already gone, I tried to get her down, but I couldn't."

Again, he blew his nose and wiped his eyes.

"Damn," Thaddeus murmured, his own eyes beginning to water.

"Oh, an' then, Dear Lord! What I found when I ran to the house for help. Every one of the Tremonts was murdered in their beds where they slept. I took a knife an' ran back out to the barn an' cut Rachel down. I knowed she wouldn't want anybody to see her like that. She was so prim an' proper, very ladylike for a young girl. So, I put her bloomers back on without lookin' at... you know... her private parts. But I did see she was holdin' something in her hand."

Old Man Woodley pointed into the house, "On top of the buffet, there's a little wooden box. Go fetch it."

Thaddeus jumped to his feet, went inside, and found the small container. Once he blew the layer of dust off the top of it, he saw the name, '*Shiloh*' had been scratched into the wood, probably with a pocketknife.

He handed the tiny, wooden box to Mr. Woodley, who rested it on his thin boney leg, opened it, then pulled out a piece of tattered cloth. The name *Gatlin* was scribbled on the cloth in blue ink.

The man handed it to Thaddeus, "I ain't sure what this is, but I imagine she snatched it from the bastard that raped her an' hung her; she was holding it in her hand when I found her."

The boy looked at both sides of the faded material and quickly said, "I think I know what this is! We learned about this in history class; this is a homemade dog tag that the Civil War soldiers made so people would know who they were if they got killed in battle."

Young Thaddeus must have been paying attention in History class that day, probably in fear of failing, for he was one hundred percent correct about it being a cloth dog tag; predecessor to the military issued, stamped metal ones used today.

ROUGHLY EIGHTY-EIGHT years ago, when the Confederate army was camped fifteen miles south of the Mason Dixon Line, a twenty-year-old Confederate soldier had constructed this cloth dog tag, and one for his brother. The Rebel ripped two pockets off a dead Yankee's uniform, took the Lieutenant's fountain pen and scribbled the name, "Gatlin" on them. Then, using the dead officer's bootlaces, he fashioned *necklaces* with the pockets, put one around his neck, and gave the second one to his two years older brother. These bearded scoundrels, Todd and Roy Gatlin, were from the hills of Georgia; they unwillingly marched with General Robert E. Lee into battle at Gettysburg, Pennsylvania, on that historical first day of July, 1863.

Late afternoon on the third day of July, amidst cannon balls flying, and bullets whizzing past within inches of the brothers fighting side by side, Todd ultimately took one in his left thigh. The led ball lodged in his femur; luckily for him, the projectile not only barely missed vital arteries, but the Yank that shot him was rationing his gun powder, hence why the ball did not have enough force to shatter bone.

However, he immediately collapsed to the ground and applied pressure to the puncture wound.

"I had enough of this God damned shit!" Todd screamed out to Roy through clenched teeth.

Wincing from the intense pain, he bitched, "I might not be so lucky on the next one. God, Roy! This hurts... really fuckin' bad!"

"Yeah, I'm fed up too. I've been itchin' to get on back home," Roy agreed as he reached over and pulled a belt from a dead comrade's trousers lying beside him.

He no sooner tugged the belt off the man, and the brothers rolled into fetal positions and covered their heads when they heard the telltale whistling sound of an incoming mortar. The deafening impact exploded the ground into a crater, showering the two with dirt, rocks, and shrapnel.

The forty-pound cannonball left a hole three feet deep, fifteen feet away.

Once the dirt shower stopped, Roy had severe ringing in his ears as he used the belt to fashion a tourniquet around his brother's leg while telling him in a southern drawl, "Here's the plan! I'm going to get us situated in that pit, and we're going to pretend we're dead. Then come dusk, we're outta here. Georgia bound, Brother!"

Todd quit wincing long enough to nod in agreement, and produce a weak smile.

Roy then hurriedly pulled his brother into the crater which the mortar had just created; he positioned Todd's leg upon his own chest which allowed his brother's blood to soak into his shirt.

Once satisfied with the pretense that he took one to the chest, he told his brother, "Try to keep an eye open, and your rifle close by in case you have to shoot somebody. Try to keep pressure on that leg, and keep it propped up on the side of the pit."

Then for the ensuing three hours, the gutless Gatlin brothers feigned death as hundreds of their fellow Confederate soldiers around them valiantly took a bullet. Lying opposite each other so they could see behind each other, the pit offered some protection from the battle that raged on all around the brothers. Chaos, confusion, and carnage on a massive scale!

During Todd's bouts of passing out and regaining consciousness, Roy kept a vigilant watch through squinted eyes as soldiers from both sides fell.

He knifed a Yankee when the teenager, who hadn't shaved once in his life yet, reached for Todd's canteen; then he shot a Union soldier who was about to bayonet him — a common practice used on hundreds of battlefields over the centuries to ensure your enemy was indeed dead.

While the horizon slowly devoured the last of the Sun's rays, allowing dusk to settle in over the bloody war-torn countryside, the two cowardly deserters crept past hundreds of deceased, and soon to be dead, soldiers from both sides. The acrid smell of gunpowder hung heavily in the air as never-ending bullets whizzed overhead and mortars continually destroyed the countryside. Countless mutilated men were moaning, slowly bleeding to death while woefully calling out the names of loved ones back home. Hail Marys and The Lord's Prayer were heard being uttered from the men as they prayed to their Creator for forgiveness with their last dying breaths.

The fighting took an easterly course as the two Gatlins snuck off in a westerly direction. Todd used his rifle as a cane. Roy ransacked dozens of knapsacks belonging to his dead comrades and fallen foes. He stuffed his own bag with jerky, tobacco, hardtack biscuits, salt pork, and any other food items he could find. The younger Gatlin brother also conjured up two canteens of water; all the while ignoring the numerous, pitiful pleas for help from the wounded as he robbed them of their food and drink.

A badly injured Northern soldier grabbed Todd's hand when he had reached down for the boy's jerky protruding from his shirt pocket. Blood had soaked through the soldier's blue uniform where a visibly splintered rib bone pierced through.

He pleaded mercifully to Todd, "Help me, Brother. Please, help me."

Todd easily broke free of the Union soldier's weak grasp. He looked directly into the nineteen-year old's eyes while snatching the jerky, then kicked the projecting rib and sneered while saying, "I ain't your brother, but I'll put that rib back in for ya, you no good Yankee Fuck."

THREE WEEKS AND ONE hundred and sixty-five miles later, the starving, foul stinking brothers sat atop the utmost ridge in the tree line overlooking the sprawling Tremont farm. The pair had to travel slowly over the mountainous terrain because of Todd's severely injured leg, averaging only eight miles a day. Roy had been stealing food from farms along the way, such as eggs or an occasional chicken. Once, he even made off with a whole ham from a farmer's smokehouse, while his wounded brother waited safely in the woods for him to return with the bounty.

Twice, Roy had to outrun buckshot from an irate farmer. If Todd had been stealing the farmer's eggs alongside his brother, the limping chicken thief would have been shot for sure.

Now, the thin, scraggly brothers were beyond hungry; they were dangerously desperate for food. The Tremont farm was the first opportunity these two low life rebel rats had in six days to pilfer a meal.

"My belly feels like it's on fire," Todd bitched as they stayed out of sight in the tree line, watching the Tremont men folk put the plow horses in the barn for the night. "An' my leg's hurtin' real bad, it needs some serious doctorin.'"

"I know exactly how your belly feels. Don't you think I didn't have any chow in the last four days, either?" his quickly agitated and miserable brother shot back.

Roy had been fed up with his older brother's constant whining since the day they went AWOL, he grumbled at him, "Just shut your God damned mouth already, you complain worse than my old lady does, even when the bitch is on the rag. We are going to have chow tonight. There's only one man an' two boys on this farm; an' I ain't seen a woman, but I imagine there is one."

Todd squinted in an attempt to see the farm better, he pointed out a key element for a successful raid, "I ain't seen or heard no dogs; that's a big plus."

Then he sat alongside his brother and informed him, "You're comin' along tonight, an' we're gonna feast like kings. Hell, Roy, we might even have the missus for dessert."

"Yeah! I can taste that already," Todd said, smacking his lips and rubbing his crotch, knowing damn well what his little brother had in mind.

Todd assured Roy, "After dessert, we'll doctor your leg. I'm sure they have gauze and alcohol; maybe they even have that new snake oil I heard about, Tincture of Iodine."

After watching the three Tremont males enter the farmhouse for the evening, a crazed look settled in Todd's eyes as he stroked his beard and gazed into the future; he giggled with excitement while telling his brother, "Hehe! We're gonna kill us some God damned Yankees tonight, Private Gatlin!"

He smiled, showing that all eight of his front teeth were gone; he spouted off, "Yessiree, Roy! General Robert E. Lee drafted us to kill Yankees, an' that's exactly what we are gonna do, God damnit! We're gonna raise that Confederate Flag high in the sky!"

Mildly hallucinating from starvation, the demented idiot then saluted an imaginary Robert E. Lee. "General! We will do Old Dixie proud tonight, Sir! We won't stop killing them Yankee bastards until they are stone, cold, dead!"

Chapter Fourteen

Chapter Ten

Taking cover in the shadows cast from a full moon that had risen high in the sky, the crusty pair slipped down to the darkened farmhouse. To the Gatlin brothers, it seemed like an eternity had passed from the time they sat in the tree line picking ticks off each other to kill time, until now, standing in the murky darkness of the mudroom!

They gave their eyes time to adjust. Then, very quietly, Roy opened the kitchen door, and both men tiptoed inside. Todd winced, gritted his teeth, and held back the moans.

Delicious aromas of freshly baked goods caused Roy's mouth to water as he picked up two butcher knives from the sink area; he handed one to his brother. Todd smiled the same repulsive, toothless grin as his brother's; he nodded and lightly ran his thumb over the knife's edge; his stomach rumbled.

Heading up the stairs, a step creaked under Todd's foot; they both froze for a full minute. No sounds from any of the family members stirring were to be heard.

Roy, following, avoided the squeaky stairstep as they continued up.

Todd limped to the first bedroom. Roy stealthily crept past him to the next room.

In the hallway, dimly lit by moonlight, Todd watched his brother hold up his hand and count with his fingers. One. Two. On three, Roy pointed in; both brothers simultaneously went into a bedroom.

Roy had entered Clara and Josef's room; he slowly inched his way to the sleeping husband and wife, reached across the bed with knife in hand and lowered it to Josef's throat. In one swift, sudden motion, Roy sliced deep through the farmer's throat, across the bed sheet, pillow, and across his wife's throat just as she woke and looked up at him. Blood squirted as far as to the wall and onto Roy with every beat of their hearts. Awful gurgling sounds escaped their throats as they gasped their last breaths, quickly bleeding to death.

Todd was to deliver the same fate to Jeremiah; then Jacob was to be the last victim as he also lay sleeping in his room. However, the seventeen-year-old Jacob awoke when he heard his brother scream. Apparently the knife that Todd used on Jeremiah was either dull, or Todd was weak from hunger, for Jeremiah screamed out in pain and terror when Todd sliced only halfway through his throat on the first attempt; he had to take a second swipe across the boy's throat to finish the gruesome task.

When Jacob ran into the hall to investigate his brother's screams, Roy jumped from the parents' room and drove his knife deep into Jacob's abdomen, pushing him back into his own room. The boy stumbled backwards and fell onto his bed. Roy, on top, pulled the knife out of Jacob's liver, then delivered the final slash across his throat; Jacob Tremont was dead in seconds, his lifeless eyes stared at the ceiling.

Rachel, also awakened from the terrible sounds and screams, ran to her door and peeked out. She saw, and smelled, an ugly, filthy, strange man standing in the hallway!

Todd, ready to help if need be, watched Roy finish Jacob as the boy lay in his bed.

In a split-second decision, Rachel had reasoned they were going to find her in her room and kill her too, so she decided it was best to make a run for it.

However, she had to make it past the older Gatlin!

Todd turned when he heard her coming; he grabbed her as she tried to run past him. He held her tight to his body with one arm around her neck and proclaimed, "Lookie what we got here!"

He smiled that disgusting toothless grin and giggled; with that southern drawl, he told Roy, "Hehehe! We got us... A God damn *virgin*!"

Just as Roy came out of Jacob's room, Rachel bit down on Todd's wrist as hard as she possibly could, breaking free of her captor. She then tore down the stairs. Roy took off after her with Todd following, limping down the stairs as fast as his bum leg would allow. Rachel ran through the parlor and out the front door. Roy tripped over the coffee table when he gave chase through the darkened room, he cursed when his head smacked off Clara's sewing basket, "God damnit! You're going to pay for that!"

Rachel knew the table was there, she safely maneuvered around it, distancing her from her pursuer.

The terrorized twelve-year old nearly made it to the barn when Roy stumbled out onto the porch; he saw the barndoor closing and took off as his brother came hobbling out of the house; he hollered over his shoulder to Todd, "She took cover in the barn!"

Rachel imagined she would be able to conceal herself in one of her hiding spots she used when she and young Sam Woodley played hide and seek.

Just as she closed Midnight's stall door behind her, Roy came into the barn. He shouted, "Come on out, ya little bitch. I got somethin' for ya. Somethin' you probably ain't never had before!"

He scanned the area for Rachel while waiting by the door for his brother to catch up.

Every horse became skittish in their stalls, snorting, stomping with an occasional whinny; the animals sensed something was out of the ordinary. Rachel stayed alongside Midnight, moving in synch with the stallion's movements, trying to stay out of Roy's view.

"Post sentry on the door while I pull a recon, Todd," Roy quietly instructed his brother when he finally made it to the barn. The younger Gatlin brother enjoyed talking in the new military jargon he learned, even more so now since they had deserted.

He listened for any noises she might make, but the stirring animals were all he heard. Then he proudly stated to the hiding girl, "You're gonna like me! All the Southern Belles like me. They all call me their, 'Southern Stallion'!"

Roy picked up a pitchfork and began searching stalls for the little girl hiding in any; he would open a stall door, squat, and look all around. Then he poked the animal with the handle so it would move, enabling him to see all around inside the stall. Any piles of straw in the stalls received a jab from the business end of the pitchfork.

Midnight nervously jerked his head up and down when Roy opened his stall and went in.

When he squatted and looked under the horse, he saw Rachel's bare feet covered in horse manure. "I found where the enemy is camping, Todd," he victoriously relayed back to his brother.

He then attempted to guide the horse around so he would not have to walk behind the stallion and those two powerful legs, which could very well deliver a lethal kick. However, the Tennessee Walker would not cooperate for the strange, foul-smelling man; the stud horse tried positioning his rump to do exactly that. Rachel used this opportunity and ran from Midnight's stall to the barn door, but unfortunately, when she turned to look back at Roy, she ran right into Todd's waiting arms!

This time he clamped his hand over her mouth so she could not bite him and flee again.

Rachel squirmed and kicked at him with her bare feet; she punched him with her tiny fists.

"I captured the enemy, Roy," Todd hollered to his brother, who finally managed to move away from the horse and exit the stall unscathed.

"She's a wild cat, she is," Todd said as Roy came over to them; Rachel continued struggling.

"Good. I likes them frisky," Roy said.

The brothers carried the squirming, twisting girl to the center of the barn where the moonbeams pierced a dusty window like a spotlight illuminating a stage.

They forced the young girl to the ground.

Rachel clawed at Roy's face, pulled his beard, and tore at his clothing as he positioned himself on top of her. Just as she pulled his dog tag off, the older brother pinned both her arms to the ground above her head. Roy used his body weight to keep her flat on the ground.

He then reached down, pulled her nightgown up, and her bloomers off!

He undid the button fly on his pants while the little girl used every bit of energy and strength she could muster, twisting and turning beneath him to no avail. Roy kissed her and licked her face as she turned her head from side to side, trying to bite him as he did so.

He taunted her, "You look like, *and* taste, just like cherry pie!"

Todd's eyes bulged, "Jesus Christ! I see why the bitches back home *do* call you their Southern Stallion! Maybe you should let me go first."

"Fuck you! This cherry is mine!"

Roy stuck his hand between her legs; the twelve-year-old girl felt something touch her where *nobody* had ever touched her before!

She fought even harder now and kept trying to bite him; he simply arched his back, avoiding her teeth.

He positioned himself between her legs, then pushed down, her eyes widened. In intense pain, the girl screamed at her tormentor, begging, "No, Mister! Please stop. No! Please!"

Midnight thrashed about in his stall, reared up and whinnied, then he continually slammed his body into the walls, neighing, snorting.

Roy screamed at Rachel, "Quit your God damned whining, already! Look at what you're doing to the horses."

Panicked with terror as the pain intensified, Rachel's eyes widened even more; she screamed from the excruciating pain when he violently penetrated her, tearing through virgin tissue, "Noo!"

She screamed louder and turned her head, unable to look her abuser in his eye as his grunts, and her pain, intensified with every forward thrust he made.

Immediately, her tiny body lapsed into shock, both mentally and physically; she fought no longer, and went totally limp... Roy had his unbridled way with her.

"The bitch lays there just like my God damned wife," he laughingly told Todd once he was done with her.

The brothers traded places...

Todd's grunting lasted less than two minutes.

Joking, he told his brother, "You're right! She does just lay there like your wife does!"

"Fuck you. Did you bring a knife with ya?"

"No, I didn't; I dropped it when the little bitch bit me," Todd replied, buttoning his fly.

"Damn it. I didn't either. You know we can't leave any witnesses," Roy said, looking about the barn for a means that would permanently silence the little girl who was now lying curled up on the dirt floor in a fetal position. Her hair was strewn with straw, dirt, and specks of manure. She sobbed quietly, trembling.

Roy spotted a coiled rope lying by the stallion's stall door.

Todd smiled when he saw his brother pick it up; he said, "Once, I hanged a stray mutt that knocked-up my full-blooded

Bluetick Coonhound, but I ain't never seen a *person* be hanged before. I reckon I'm gonna love this."

Ironically, his leg did not seem to be hurting as much now.

Roy tossed the rope over the beam; hastily, he concocted a makeshift noose on one end, tied the other end to a plank on Midnight's stall, then positioned a hay bale directly beneath the noose.

Rachel had no more fight in her as Roy stood her on it. The bloodied, battered girl had a blank stare on her face; while gazing at her undergarment, she took short, quick sips of air.

He positioned the knotted rope around her neck.

Todd hurriedly stepped forward to the bale. "This is what you get for biting me, you no good little Yankee Bitch!" he exclaimed before forcefully shoving her backwards!

The noose tightened up as she swung back and forth. Rachel kicked wildly; frantically tugging at the rough fibered rope as it burned and dug into her skin.

She used all the fingers of her left hand, but only her thumb and two fingers on her right hand, keeping the dog tag securely clutched to her palm.

The tiny girl struggled hopelessly against the rope, which, obviously, was stopping the blood and oxygen supply to her brain. However! Every time she swung back over the bale, she was able to drag her toes across it, which slowed down the swinging motion until she finally stopped and stood back up on it!

She was able to loosen the rope just barely enough to take a deep inhale.

But then Rachel watched in terror as Todd hobbled back; he pushed her off the bale again, much harder this time; then he sarcastically scolded Rachel, "No! No! No! You naughty little bitch! Now you just be a nice girl, an'... Hang proper like!"

That statement caused Roy to roar with laughter and enjoy the event that much more; he complimented his brother, "Hang proper like! Now, that's fuckin' funny!"

Rachel's eyes widened even more as the rope dug in again, and she watched Todd drag the bundled hay backwards a scant three inches, just out of her toes' reach. Now, as she swung back and forth over the bale, her big toe touched only a few stems protruding from it.

Satisfied she wouldn't talk, the murderous pedophiles left the barn; they laughed on their way back to the house when Roy reiterated, "Hang proper like!"

Once in the kitchen, Roy lit a kerosene lamp, and then the pair proceeded to gorge themselves.

They ate as if they were two obese Roman Statesmen feasting on exotic delicacies while enjoying the enslaved gladiators fight to their deaths inside the Coliseum on a sunny Sunday afternoon. The brothers ate everything and anything they could find in the warm house, while the bloodied bodies of four dead people lie upon their beds upstairs; and out in the cold dark barn, a frail, fragile girl's body swung like a pendulum winding down, twitching a few times from occasional muscle spasms as her precious young life slowly drained from her abused, battered, child's body.

"This pumpkin pie is way better than what my fat assed wife could ever bake," Todd said, sitting in Josef Tremont's chair at the head of the table.

"Ain't no wonder, ya back ass country hick. This ain't no pumpkin pie. This is God damned sweet tater pie. But you sure are right about it being good, though. Why, it's just a cryin' shame that our women folk can't get together with the woman who baked this one an' exchange recipes, now ain't it?" Roy asked, laughing.

He then shoved the last slice of pie into his mouth, licked the pan clean, and downed it with freshly brewed coffee.

When they eventually could not force in another morsel, Roy poured bromine, an early antiseptic, on and into Roy's punctured leg; he had found this germicide in a cupboard while searching for coffee beans to go along with dessert. Finding no tobacco though disappointed them both.

However! A different cupboard rewarded him with three fourths of a bottle of moonshine!

"That ain't lookin' so good; the bullet never came out, that's what's causing the infection," Roy informed his brother while watching large globs of yellow and green streaked pus bubble out of the seriously infected, sickening smelly hole in Todd's leg; the bromine foamed like peroxide.

Todd took a seriously deep breath, shoved a balled up dirty dish towel in his mouth, bit down on it, then squeezed his thigh under and around the bullet hole. Intense pain caused him to wince and grunt out one long, screaming groan when he used all his might to compress his leg and feel for the bullet, which only forced more nauseating chunks of excretion to squirt out; not the led ball he had hoped for!

"I ain't sure what gangrene looks like, but I suspect that's what this is," Roy speculated, correctly.

Once the last drop of bromine dripped from the brown bottle, Roy poured just a little bit of the moonshine into the infected hole.

Todd grimaced immensely and painfully moaned while nearly passing out.

Roy then tossed a roll of gauze to his brother. "Here, you can field dress that nasty thing yourself. I sure as hell ain't touchin' it!"

Once Todd had cleaned and bandaged his leg, they finished the rotgut whiskey, then traded their military garb for Josef's overalls and clean shirts, which were two sizes too big on these skinny brothers whose family tree did not branch off very much. They tried Jacob's and Jeremiah's clothes on as well, but the boys' clothes were either too small, or too short.

The derelicts then stuffed their knapsacks with as much food as possible; Todd tossed the remaining gauze into his.

The outhouse offered a comfortable bowel movement for both.

Lastly, the filthy, murderous brothers gathered up all incriminating evidence, which they then hid under rocks in the woods as they started their trek back to the Georgia hills beneath a waning full moon as it slipped behind the trees on the horizon, giving way to a gorgeous sunrise.

The Sun's rays pierced the early morning's rising fog, then reflected off countless tiny dew droplets that had formed on every blade of grass and on every leaf in every tree. The countryside looked as though, during the night, forest nymphs had lit millions of minuscule candles, illuminating the way for Rachel, as she bid farewell from this world.

But perhaps Rachel's soul did not depart the Earthly bonds immediately upon her death!

It could not possibly have been just sheer coincidence when one of her killers got slapped in the face with irony at its ultimate that very afternoon.

Only four miles from the Tremont farm into their southbound trek, Roy stopped at a downed tree and rested his foot atop it. He turned around and hollered back to Todd, who was hobbling fifty feet behind, "If you don't hurry your goat smellin' ass up... we ain't never gonna make it back to Georgia."

He made faces and rolled his eyes, patiently waiting for his limping brother to catch up.

"I'm doing the best I can. My leg is hurtin' like a sonna bitch," Todd said as he hobbled up to his brother; grimacing, groaning with every step.

Although he was using tree branches fashioned into a pair of crutches to aid his walking, the man still had a miserable time stepping over downed trees and rocks, especially the slippery ones in all the creeks and streams.

"Well, you'd best be tryin' a bit harder, cause I'm about ready to forget you're back there and just keep on a walkin'. I would like to get home in *this* God damned lifetime," the younger brother threatened.

Todd made a face of disgust and very bitterly struck back, "I'll fuckin' try, okay? Christ Almighty!"

"Okay then. Let's move out. You'd better keep up, Private," Roy said and stepped over the log.

His foot landed square on the back of an unusually large Timber Rattlesnake, which had not given the usual tell-tale rattling warning! Rather, the Rattler remained camouflaged by concealing itself under dead leaves, staying in a coiled position... silently waiting.

Quicker than lightning, the stealthy snake lunged. Its two sharp fangs easily pierced through Roy's trousers and continued deep into his calf, delivering a quick, large, lethal dose of venom.

Roy shrieked out in pain as he fell backwards over the log onto his buttocks, smacking his head off a rock in the process. Then he quickly sat and rolled up his pant leg, revealing two puncture holes.

He hysterically ordered his brother, "Hurry! Cut it right here with your knife an' suck out the poison."

His older brother shook his head, "Nope! No can do. Not with the holes I got in my teeth. Sorry, Brother. An' for your information, since you think you're so fuckin' smart, it ain't '*poison*', it's... *Venom*!"

Then, watching the serpent slither into the undergrowth, Todd calmly commented, "I ain't never seen a God damned rattler that big in my whole entire life before. How about you, Roy? Have you ever seen one that big? That bastard's gotta be all of ten feet long! "

His brother, sweating like a man on the gallows with a noose around his neck, grimaced, and frantically squeezed his leg with one hand while pulling his belt off for a tourniquet with his other hand. He looked at Todd with pure hatred in his eyes and grunted, "Fuck you, ya Prick!"

As unreligious as Roy was, he begged and pleaded with the Good Lord in Heaven to please have mercy and take his soul every day for the next six days. Those final days of his life were filled with fever, then chills and convulsions. The deserter also suffered unstoppable bouts of throwing up disgusting, black bile; accompanied with uncontrollable bloody diarrhea caused from his internal organs dissolving. The rattler's toxic *venom* reduced his liver, pancreas, and spleen to jelly. All the while, his swollen, aching leg turned black and began rotting before his eyes; he now was limping as slowly as Todd, who stood by, eating every scrap of their precious pilfered food, helplessly watching him die.

Roy Gatlin's famous last words were, "I'll be waiting for you in Hell, Todd. I promise you that!"

And the other Gatlin bastard's fate? Without having his brother's sense of direction to guide him, that brilliantly ignorant hillbilly ended up lost. He limped in circles throughout the Appalachians for the final seven days of his undeserving life. He also suffered a well-deserved, but wretched and miserable death.

The morning after Roy died, Todd awakened to delirium setting in from the gangrene. It eventually drove him insane in the end, but the onset was slow and gradual. Perhaps, deliberately so?

His morning began with occasional hallucinations, all of which were hazy images of Rachel peeking at him from behind the maple trees and oaks as he walked by, occasionally giggling at him.

As starvation complicated the gangrene, his hallucinations intensified, the girl became clearer in his focus. She would step out from behind the trees now and point in which direction he was to walk; her giggling had now turned to laughter.

Todd couldn't help noticing the purple and red bruises encircling her neck.

The next morning greeted him with a half-hour long, bone-chilling downpour, along with Rachel's laughter. Constant, insidious laughter.

Todd kept telling himself, "She's not there; she's just in your head. Keep walking with the Sun on your left side, and you'll be heading south. Don't pay any attention to her, or where she's pointing."

Less than a full minute later of her unbearable laughter, he would scream at her, "Would you just shut the fuck up already?!"

Was it also in his mind that now, every time he disobeyed her instructions and attempted to go a different route... She would push him? Causing him to stumble and fall? Then she would laugh so hard at him that her laughter echoed throughout the valleys. Louder yet was the laughter resonating inside his head.

"Quit laughing at me, you little Yankee bitch. You're dead!" He would scream at her. "I saw you swinging in a noose. You, are... Dead! Fuckin' die already!"

But she would only smile, then run, push him down again and laugh louder. Even though he held his hands tightly over his ears, her laughter seared through to his brain, never letting up. Her snickering grew louder, and it would awaken him when he finally ignored both the pain in his leg, and the burn of starvation in his gut, allowing him to nod off for a much-needed rest.

On the seventh day, *atop the utmost ridge in the tree line overlooking the sprawling Tremont farm*, the stumbling man finally reached the point of total exhaustion where he could not lift his foot to take one more step. He flat out stopped, wobbled.

With arms so weak, they simply dangled at his sides when the delirious man fell to his knees.

When his body, along with his head, teetered fairly far backwards, he used the last scrap of energy he had left to jerk himself back into an upright position; but with no more muscle control whatsoever, his body continued falling forward, which caused the Confederate soldier's head to also jerk violently forward upon impact; his face smacked the ground, and bounced off it.

As fate would have it, Todd fell less than twenty feet from Roy's maggot infested, foul stinking body! A feast for carnivores and insects alike, his brother's half-eaten corpse glared hatefully back at him!

The murderous pedophile's breathing became practically non-existent as the petite, barefooted, girl in a bloodied nightgown walked over to him. She looked over at Roy; then she looked down at Todd as his eyelids fluttered shut and he took his last breath. With pure terror in his cracking voice, he was barely able to whisper through his bleeding lips, "Roy? Is that... You? Oh, God! It is!... No!"

The red-haired girl then smiled with satisfaction.

Rachel Petersen's laughter and snickering gradually faded to silence inside Todd Gatlin's head.

However! Her cackling had merely been replaced with the beginning of his own eternal screams, mixing in with thousands more, in Hell!

Even more unbelievable was that Roy Gatlin fulfilled his final words. 'Twas, undoubtedly, the only promise ever kept by that despicable inbred!

Chapter Fifteen

Christian brought his story back to present day 1950, he ties up the loose ends to The Legend of Rachel Petersen...

Chapter Eleven

Thaddeus handed the cloth dog tag back to Mr. Woodley while saying, "Yes, Sir, I betcha Rachel kept this as evidence so the police could track down her killer."

The old man informed the youth, "There wasn't much of a police force back in 1863, especially with the war going on."

Mr. Woodley squinted into the box and pulled the only other remaining item from it, then placed the ID tag back inside. He handed Thaddeus a photograph of Rachel; she was standing in front of the four Tremont family members; Aunt Clara posed directly behind her with her hands resting on Rachel's shoulders.

This old snapshot was taken by a young entrepreneur who invested his money in photography equipment and traveled the country. He sold pictures to people who had never seen this new technology before, and were very willing to pay for a family portrait that wasn't painted by an artist while they sat motionless for hours.

"Ain't that new-fangled camera something else! What will they think of next?" Josef had exclaimed to Clara when he saw the freshly developed photograph of himself and his family, taken roughly three weeks before Robert E. Lee and his Southern Army stormed across the Mason Dixon Line into Pennsylvania.

Mr. Woodley handed the faded picture to Thaddeus and informed him, "I took this from her house when me an' my Daddy went there lookin' for a clean dress to bury her in. The little girl is Rachel. It's black an' white, so you can't really tell, but she had the prettiest red hair you ever did see."

A puzzled look flashed across Thaddeus's face when he looked at the individuals.

"All these people look awful familiar to me; who are they, Mr. Woodley?" he asked as his mind raced; the boy knew he had seen them before. But where? When?

"Those people are the Tremonts, the uncle and aunt that Rachel came to live with when her mother died. That's the family who was murdered in your house!"

"*Aha*!" The young boy's eyes widened when the memory of where he saw these people finally flashed into his mind. They were posed exactly then, as in this photograph. He brought the old-time photo closer to his eyes and scrutinized it — they had the same clothes, same hair, same... *Everything*! It was as though they walked out of his dream and into this photo, or vice versa! But they were the five people who were not clapping, rather, just standing soberly in the crowd when he exited Rachel's Tomb!

"I had a dream, an' every one of these people were in it, I tell ya!" Thaddeus excitedly told the old man.

"Perhaps, like Rachel... they are not restin' either," Mr. Woodley said. "I am to blame for the whole mess. I never should have disturbed anything that day. Why I didn't just run home an' tell my Daddy... I'll never understand myself. Maybe I was scared. I was so young, an' confused. I never showed that name tag to anybody, except for you right now. It's all my fault that the town folk started that ugly rumor about Rachel killing her family before taking her own life. They thought she used the knife that I took out to the barn to cut her down."

A wide-eyed Thaddeus sat in silence, not knowing what to say.

Mr. Woodley lowered his head into shaky hands; he stayed like that for few long seconds before looking to the clouds. In a broken-up voice, he spoke apologetically, "Oh, Rachel!... Rachel! God, I am so sorry! I beg of you to forgive me. I only wanted you to be thought of as... being... *pure*."

After another pause to wipe his eyes with severely shaking hands, he looked back at Thaddeus and tried to continue, but ended up blurting out, "The *good* people of Jonesboro wanted to *burn* her!"

Thaddeus's eyes really popped when he heard that. Apparently, another historical fact flashed through his mind which caused him to ask, "You mean they wanted to burn her at the stake? Like they did to the women they thought were witches in Salem, Massachusetts?"

"Yes! But my daddy stood right here on this porch an' fought an' argued with them all; he told them she was not a witch, but just a sad and lonely, little mixed-up girl who didn't talk much. So, they finally told him to just go an' bury her out in the woods somewhere — the town folk said she was not to be buried in the church cemetery alongside the Tremonts."

Woodley closed his eyes and took a few deep breaths before continuing.

"My Daddy built her coffin, an' my mother washed an' combed her hair. She also put the clean dress on Rachel before placing a pillow under her head. Then the three of us said a prayer for her soul, an' my mother put her rosary in Rachel's hands. With tears in my eyes, Boy... an' a painful secret deep in my heart... I helped my daddy dig her grave. It was hot that day; July 26, 1863, when we lowered her little pine box into the ground up on the ridge."

Thaddeus looked up to the blue skies, "Maybe her an' the Tremonts will rest now since you finally spoke the truth after all these years, Mr. Woodley. We know that it was Civil War soldiers who actually murdered the Tremonts as they slept. Most likely they were Rebel Sons of Bitches. Rachel Petersen did not kill anybody and then hang herself as the legend says."

"Yes, I think you are right!"

The old man also looked upwards through his tightly squinted good eye. "Perhaps I'll be able to sleep at night now, too. Maybe that's why I lived to be one hundred years old. I was afraid of the day coming when I would meet Rachel again, an' she would hate me, an' she'd holler at me for what I did."

"I think when you meet Rachel, she will understand why you did what you did, Mr. Woodley, an' she won't be mad an' holler like you think."

After reassuring the old man, Thaddeus spotted a small dust devil dancing amongst the apple trees, picking up dry leaves as it neared.

He pointed toward it and told Mr. Wilson, "Look at that!"

The tiny eddy then veered to the left and headed straight for them; it swirled up the porch steps and lingered next to Mr. Woodley for a few seconds before skipping off the porch, spinning back into the orchard, where the tiny whirlwind rose skyward.

After watching the dust devil rise upwards till it vanished from sight, Thaddeus excitedly told the old man, "I think that was Rachel saying goodbye, an' she's on her way to Heaven right now!"

"That may be! I feel as though a weight has just been lifted off me!" Mr. Woodley stated, also looking up, smiling.

The boy climbed back onto the old Schwinn. "I better be runnin' along now, Mr. Woodley. I'll see you later; more than likely when my Pa gets hungry for some apple pie."

Thaddeus pedaled as fast as he could back to Seth. He couldn't wait to tell his brother what Old Man Woodley showed him, and more importantly, what he confessed. Thaddeus would never admit it to Seth, but he knew his little brother was right for insisting he visit the old man.

While listening to The Grand Ole Opry later that night and studying Lee's surrender at The Appomattox Courthouse, Thaddeus owned up about his visit with Mr. Woodley; he explained to his parents why he went to see the old man, and told them the secret the old man had kept to himself for all these years.

"It's a good thing that our mule just all of a sudden got hungry for apples when Thaddeus was grounded. Ain't that right, Seth?" his mother asked while giving her younger son the hairy eyeball.

"It sure is. Coincidences do happen, ya know, Mom," he sheepishly agreed, shrugging his shoulders.

Once again, Grandpa Jones praised Roy Clark for some mighty fine fiddle playing, and then he thanked all of his listeners out there in Radioland for tuning in.

Mary Yoder instructed her boys to hit the hay.

Upon entering his room, Thaddeus saw a small flash of light reflecting from his bed. He walked over and could not believe his own two eyes. Lying on his pillow was a white beaded rosary with a tiny silver cross attached to it!

Confused, he was not sure if he should thank Rachel, or tell her he was sorry; so he expressed his gratitude after he dropped to his knees, then he apologized to her, and said a prayer.

TIME MARCHES ON, AND children grow into adults. Only to be true, that is, if they are fortunate enough not to be destined for an untimely fate during their treasured childhoods. Moreover, most of us have high unspoken hopes of when the day arrives for each of us to leave our worldly material things behind, and pass over to greener pastures, also hoping to be granted the privilege of resting comfortably, undisturbed, in our own peaceful eternal slumber. Perhaps that is the basis of our Faith, optimistically having dreams of being joyfully reunited with loved ones who went before us; to have bestowed upon us the euphoric pleasures of frolicking in a *Garden of Eden*, an exhilarating haven where we and everything surrounding us will be absolutely perfect as prophesized, delivered to us mortals from a supreme being.

Two weeks after the old man bared his soul to the young boy in their open discussion, a sad day was to be had in

Jonesboro, Pennsylvania. Mr. Samuel Woodley, their oldest resident who was known county wide for his delicious McIntosh apples, passed away peacefully in his sleep. Having never married, he was the last surviving member of the Woodley clan of Westmoreland County.

Forty years down the path of life finds Seth living comfortably in the big city of Pittsburgh, earning his way as a computer programmer with a large insurance company. In his spare time, he enjoys doing research on the Internet. The subject which he devotes more time to than any other item of interest is the Civil War, and in particular, the name Gatlin. He finally came across an archived Georgia newspaper article, dated July 30, 1863, which stated: *"Brothers Todd and Roy Gatlin, soldiers proudly serving with the Georgian Sixty-Second Infantry Division, are reported missing in action and are presumed to be dead and buried in Gettysburg, Pennsylvania. Devoted husbands, our courageous heroes both leave behind a loving wife and one daughter each."*

Thaddeus also matured into a caring, responsible adult. After attending Mr. Woodley's funeral services, he once again visited Rachel Petersen's grave with shovel and scythe in hand; not to dig up the grave, but rather to dig up the massive amounts of briars surrounding her tombstone, then plant grass seed. He then constructed a small, but pretty, white picket fence around her grave, offering the little girl, *with the prettiest red hair you ever did see,* the dignity of the final resting spot she deserved. He also straightened the tombstone that a good-hearted neighbor and his young, well-meaning son who deeply loved this little girl, chiseled from a large flat fieldstone, eighty-seven years in the past.

Black-Eyed Susans, which Thaddeus also planted by her stone, bloom every spring, the time of year when he visits her grave for its annual manicure and upkeep.

Thaddeus eventually inherited his Daddy's farm and married Tammy Wilson, who gave birth to a set of her own twin boys, who, after growing up, entertained dreams of bagging a trophy buck like the one hanging above their fireplace. To this day, that massive buck still holds the record in Westmoreland County. *Bocephus*, the giant buck their Uncle Seth bagged when he was but a thirteen-year-old boy.

Was it more than just fate how that whitetail deer led those two young boys to that lone grave in the middle of the woods? That shall remain another one of life's many unanswered questions.

Respectfully displayed on the fireplace mantle in Thaddeus's home directly under that record setting whitetail, sets a priceless vintage photograph, now enshrined in a frame. Encapsulated in time are the four family members who once referred to this farmhouse as their home. Also in the photograph, there stands a beautiful, petite red-haired girl in a flowered dress, whose precious innocence was maliciously stolen. Perhaps mother and child have been reunited, and are singing joyfully alongside all the other angels in Heaven's Choir.

For the last fifty years, there has been a tiny silver cross adorning Thaddeus's neck... as he happily, and contentedly, digs up potatoes for a living, I tell ya!

The End

I would like to dedicate this book to my lovely, loving wife, Shelby.

THE LEGEND OF RACHEL PETERSEN

Without her words of inspiration, my words would have never been.

Christian Kane

Chapter Sixteen

Only two days shy of three months was all the time Christian Kane needed to write The Legend of Rachel Petersen from start to finish. Of course, the ex-sports journalist now sported a seriously bushy beard, while his hair covered his ears.

Several times, he did not return home from the grave till past dark; Shelby would ask, "Were you at the tombstone all this time?"

And he'd reply, "Yes! Once I had the storyline for this chapter in my head, I couldn't stop typing till I finished it. I was afraid if I did stop, my train of thought would derail, and I wouldn't get it back on track."

"Weren't you scared out there, all by yourself, in the dark?"

"No! Scared of what?"

"Her ghost. I feel her presence when I'm out there."

Early on, Christian had asked his wife to read Chapter One after he completed it; again, he requested her honest opinion, knowing quite well she would be straightforward with her criticism, good or bad.

"It's really, really good!" she said, then further encouraged him, "I think you are on to something here. Keep writing. I can't wait to see how it turns out and what direction you are going to take it. I'm glad Igor crashed his truck," she chuckled.

"What part did you like best?"

"I liked the whole chapter, Christian. Your very first paragraph was beautiful. I could visualize gigantic snowflakes pirouetting to the ground. It was clever how you had the two boys tracking a deer through the woods, leading them to that grave."

"Do you think any parts need to be worked on?"

"No, Baby. It's perfect just the way it is."

"You're not just saying this because you love me, are you?"

"No, *Igor Wazleski*, I would tell you if I did not like it. I knew you'd write a good story once you focused and, *wrote from your heart*. I can't wait to read Chapter Two and find out why Seth is so scared."

Weather permitting, Christian would sit under the evergreen tree by Rachel's tombstone and pound away at his laptop for hours on end while writing her story. Strange, but he felt so inspired and compelled to compile her bio when he visited her grave nestled among the Black-Eyed Susans. He was beginning to feel as if he actually knew Rachel Petersen as his story about her *matured*.

Stranger yet was the manner he would *interview* her.

He'd ask, "In what part of Ohio did you live?" Then he would write about Prosser's Hollow, simply because it popped into his head.

Not once did he suffer from every writer's most feared enemy — the dreaded writer's block. For the most part, the words flooded his brain faster than he was able to type.

At times, his tired hands were the only reason he would take a mini break, just to stretch and flex his cramping fingers.

THE LEGEND OF RACHEL PETERSEN

A person would have considered this man looney if they witnessed him interrogating a one-hundred and sixty-year-old tombstone. One such question he asked, "So, Rachel, I understand Midnight is your favorite horse on the Tremont Farm. Why would that be, may I ask?"

Then as previously stated, the words fell into place so gracefully, and he would type, "As they were driving down the lane, a beautiful black stallion came charging through the pasture. His mane flowed elegantly, as did his tail, which he held upright. The majestic steed charged up to the fence, reared up on his back legs, and whinnied a loud greeting."

Although his wife wanted to read every chapter as Christian finished it, he would not allow it.

"Not until I am done with the whole story," he told her; even going as far as to actually putting a password on his laptop so she could not hack into it and read his tale while he slept. His reasoning was she might influence him to change a part of the story, and then it would not be his words. He feared his wife's input might change the concept he had for how life was for the girl lying four feet beneath the badly weathered tombstone.

Shelby's reaction, after reading the first chapter, turned out to be that *shot of encouragement* he needed from her.

Totally amazed after reading his story in its entirety, she gave a five-star review critique, not a one star like she graded The Vampire's Feast, "My God, Christian, your words flow so beautifully. But how did you ever fantasize such a life for this girl? You gave her such an awful childhood; you uprooted her from her home in Ohio, sent her to Pennsylvania where she was brutally raped and murdered by those cowardly bastards. That part was so hard to read; I actually cried, but I liked the karma twist."

"I don't know. Where *do* our thoughts originate? Her story, or my story rather, just... came to me... out of nowhere! I swear, at times, I heard her *talking* in my head, telling me what to write. I did want to write a thriller after all."

"You're scaring me. I hope you don't go and pull a Jack Nicholson on me! Some parts were a bit gory like a slasher movie," she looked at him, curiously.

Her husband did his best deranged look and said, "Here's... Johnny!"

"Stop that! But don't take me wrong. I liked your story. You did an excellent job writing it. It held my attention to the very end, and... haha," she chuckled, then continued with her book review, "You had a plot in this one with no tackling. I really enjoyed the bittersweet, happy ever after ending."

Christian did not realize he had accomplished the easy part of being an unpublished, unknown author, which was simply writing a novel; now he was faced with what to do with his completed story. With the help of the librarian, he spent hours at the Latrobe Library researching the Internet on their free computers. The Kane's new penny-pinching budget did not allow for home Internet, or an up to date, faster computer having more and better features.

He soon found out that tons of information was available, both excellent advice, along with wrong, misleading information. And how many slick people wanting his money! Sharks! Scammers! The man learned to read the reviews. Then, should he self-publish? Hire an agent? Or deal directly with the publishers himself? These were only a few of the decisions he was faced with making; all of which could affect the overall outcome of his book.

After discussing his dilemma with Shelby over fish sticks and value brand mac and cheese, he opted to take her advice, which she very well spelled out for him, "Well! McKelvey did not give you the promotion because of your *'computer expertise'*, am I not correct?"

He nodded.

"So, we can cross the option of self-publishing off your list."

She continued, "Your name might be well known in the world of sports writing, but this is fiction, and those people who publish these kinds of stories probably never heard of Christian Kane, Sports Journalist. They won't give you the time of day, am I correct again?"

Once more, he nodded.

"Did we buy this house on our own? No, we hired a real estate agent who oversaw everything. Therefore, in my opinion, that is your best option. Hire an agent; a writer's agent, but find a good one."

"And all these years you thought I married you for your looks," he teased his wife while drizzling hot Chinese mustard onto his leftover eggroll.

After taking a bite, he exclaimed, "Damn, is that hot, but I like it!"

Nevertheless, he knew his wife had once again spoken words of wisdom. *"Maybe there is something to that, 'women's intuition,'"* he thought. *"Maybe my next novel will revolve around that."*

So, it was back to the library for Christian. He compiled a list of agents from the World Wide Web and wrote a clever query letter to send out. He thanked God when he stumbled across examples that he embellished with his own story plot and character's names. His query read as follows:

"A legend of a twelve-year-old girl viciously killing her foster family before hanging herself has been passed down for generations in the small town of Jonesboro, Pennsylvania. Then, two young hunters accidentally stumble upon her grave while tracking a wounded buck. Thaddeus Yoder, being young and adventurous, digs up the grave when the spring thaw arrives, releasing the tormented spirit of Rachel Petersen. This sets in motion a series of events, which, with the confession of a one-hundred-year-old man who knew the girl, provides evidence that she was actually a murder victim of Civil War deserters who raped and hanged her after they had slain the girl's family. Thaddeus proves she was innocent of her accused heinous crime, allowing her, and the centenarian to finally rest in eternal peace."

Being the Neanderthal that McKelvey had correctly labeled Christian, the man did not have an email address or have any idea how to correctly format and attach files to send in an email. He discovered most of the publishers today were going green and doing business only by electronically generated files as Shelby warned him at the onset.

Therefore, he was only able to submit to publishers still accepting paper, which dwindled his list down considerably. Following the agents' guidelines for submissions, he shot-gunned two dozen queries, or the synopsis and requested number of sample chapters, or full manuscripts, to the larger publishing houses. All by snail mail. Whatever and however they wanted it, he did it. They were all different in their demands.

Then, he impatiently waited.

Every day brought disappointment after he opened an empty mailbox at the end of his driveway. Until one day, a month later; a letter from New York City! He tore it open where he stood; it read: *"Mr. Kane, Thank you for your interest in publishing with Aldrich House, however, we feel your work is not suitable for our present needs. Feel free to submit any future works. Thank you."*

After tearing the rejection form letter in two, he scoffed when Shelby's words echoed in his brain, *"I thought you recluses developed a tough skin for rejection."*

Disappointed, but not defeated, he sent out another dozen queries, synopses, partials, and full manuscripts, and then waited again. Keeping a running log of the publishers he submitted to, and any responses received, he totaled forty-eight outgoing pieces of mail versus fifteen rejection letters and three publishers asking for full manuscripts. The latter really had his hopes up, until they finally all wrote back saying, *"Thank you, however... we're sorry... No!"*

Miriam Watson, a retired English teacher working as a part-time librarian where Christian has been spending an awful lot of time lately, the Latrobe Library, had a love for literature and books in general, hence why she worked where she did, not for the mere pittance she received. This spry seventy-four-year-old, gray-haired woman regarded Christian as an optimistic, young writer with potential; she offered her help.

"This is an exceptionally well written story you've compiled, Christian," she told him after reading his manuscript the night before. "I did not find one grammatical error in the whole story, except for one tiny oxymoron that I underlined on page one, 'the roaring silence'; but sometimes, a play on words or clever oxymorons fit right in, which can spark the story. You must have paid attention in English Lit class; even your adverbs and adjectives are all correctly used. I am impressed!"

"Thanks for the words of praise, Miriam. But why can't I find an agent to represent me then?" Christian asked one morning as he brought two cups of coffee with him to the library. One with cream for her, and one black for himself.

"Perhaps you did not send it to the right person yet. The Internet is a great tool, but it is also a feeding ground for sharks. Look behind you. What do you see?"

Christian looked over his shoulder at the numerous rows of shelves holding thousands of books, he answered, "Books of course. We *are* in a library."

"Exactly. Books! Published novels that have tucked within their pages, the names of the people and publishers who brought a writer's words to fruition."

The proverbial light bulb clicked on above his head. Two hours later, he had a list of fiction publishers, and he even found four agents' names. The next afternoon, Christian had six more pieces of outgoing mail. Once again, he hoped and waited for any replies.

THREE WEEKS WENT BY until he received the first rejection form letter. One week after that, another *no go* was in the mail along with a request for a full manuscript from Margo Duvall, an agent with a medium sized, but old and very well-respected publishing house in New York City!

Christian ran the box containing the freshly printed two hundred and thirty-three pages of his manuscript to the post office the next morning, then he stopped at the store on the way home for another ink cartridge for his printer. He learned not to be overly optimistic just because an agent requested a full script. So far, he has mailed out five of them and received five rejections in return.

"May as well have another one ready to go," he figured as he replaced the printer's ink cartridge, complaining to himself, "These damn things cost almost as much as a new printer."

On a Thursday morning two weeks later, Christian was printing out two more queries; the printer jammed and kept sucking in sheets of paper; then the phone joined the pandemonium. The man was tugging the crumpled sheets out as fast as the machine was eating them.

On the second ring, he muttered, "Of course!"

Frustrated, he reached under the desk and yanked the plug from the wall, which knocked the trashcan over, releasing a half-full Styrofoam cup of coffee onto the rug. However! The logjam stopped.

"Hello?" he answered gruffly.

"Good morning. My name is Margo Duvall with Brownstone Literature in New York," a friendly female voice with a heavily laden New York accent on the other end of the line said, "I'm trying to reach Christian Kane. I hope I am not calling at a bad time?"

His demeanor and tone changed in a heartbeat. "This is Christian Kane, and no, you are not calling at a bad time."

"Great. As I said, I'm Margo Duvall with Brownstone Lit, and I read your manuscript last night, Mr. Kane. I must say it is one of the best pieces of writing I have seen in years. I absolutely love your style. I felt as though I was back in fifth grade reading Tom Sawyer for the first time, and I couldn't put it down. You actually told an entertaining story like Mark Twain does; not like the majority of writers today who write just to impress people with their vocabulary. Big deal! They have a thesaurus, but no story. Well anyhow, I would love to represent you and your book, unless of course, you have signed on with another agent."

"No, I have not signed with anybody." Naturally, the excitement was evident in his voice. "I'm glad you enjoyed my work, Mrs. Duvall."

"That's Miss Duvall, I never found Mr. Right, but please call me Margo. I like being on a first name basis with my clients. Is that fine with you... Christian?"

"That is great with me, Margo. So, you must feel my book has potential?" he asked, trying not to come across as overly anxious, or the newbie that he was.

"Absolutely, Christian! Your protagonist, Thaddeus Yoder, is wonderful; he has faults like the main character is supposed to. The story itself is believable, and although Rachel has a tragic death, you wrapped it up very well with a bittersweet, happy ever after ending."

He thought, *"Where did I hear that before?"*

She continued, "Readers love that. So? Should I fax you a contract?"

Christian could barely operate a printer, let alone a fax machine. He never considered buying one. "Uh, no, my *fax machine* just bit the dust this morning. Could you snail mail them to me?" Christian said, smiling while looking at the wrinkled and smeared papers stuck all through his printer.

"Sure, no problem. It will be in today's mail, and you should receive it on Monday. You read them over and take them to an attorney if you wish. I can assure you we are a reputable firm. Without writers like you, we would not be here. We take pride in nurturing and developing our writers."

"Great! Hopefully, this is the start of a long and rewarding relationship."

"I hope so, too. It's been a pleasure talking with you, Christian. I have an extremely hectic schedule today, and I apologize for not being able to spend more time with you. I wanted to call you first thing this morning to hopefully bring you onboard before a different publisher snagged you. Get that contract back to me as soon as you can so we can get your book on Amazon and other websites."

"I'll be sure to do that."

"Oh, I will also need a photo of you for the back flap, a recent one if you have one. Better yet, our layout team likes it when they can get the memory chip from a digital camera with the author's image. It makes it easy for them to pop it in their computer and crop it, add text, or whatever else needs done. *Quick, efficient*! Don't forget to send that with the contract."

"I will definitely do that, too. It was my pleasure talking with *you*, Margo."

"Same here. I will keep in touch. Ciao!"

"Thank you, bye!"

Christian hung up the phone, sat back in his chair, stroked his beard and absorbed what just transpired. When it sunk in, he jumped up and threw his arms in the air, "Hallelujah! I can't wait to get a shave and a haircut, then tell Shelby!" he said out loud while running down the hall to grab a much-needed shower, but turned right around, came back, and cleaned up the coffee.

Chapter Seventeen

Shelby, sitting behind her receptionist's desk at work, looked up from her pile of court documents when she heard that distinctive elevator ding.

The door opened to the top floor of the Goldberg Building, and out walked Christian, looking like he did one year ago — a fresh, barbershop shave, and a nice, tight haircut that was slightly outdated, but looked good on this man.

Sporting a nice peach colored polo shirt, docker cargo shorts, and his good sneakers, his outfit looked like it came off a handsomely dressed mannequin in a Versace's window display. No longer was he the disheveled, long-haired, bearded bum in his favorite faded Steelers tee shirt and torn jeans who kissed Shelby goodbye only three hours ago.

That unique, manly scent of the men's perfumed talc, Clubman Pinaud, which his elderly old-school barber used to feather dust any fine hairs from his ears, cheeks, and in the folds of his neck, still clung to him and his shirt.

His wife did a double take. "Okay, Mister, what did you do with my husband?" she teased as he strolled to her desk with a smile plastered from ear to ear.

Nancy Whittaker, the Kelly Girl sitting behind her desk, stopped stapling papers to look at this handsome, delicious smelling man strutting from the elevator.

Inaudibly, she moaned out, "Whoa! Lunch!"

Christian told Shelby, "I dragged your husband's lazy butt to Gino's barber shop!"

A puzzled look etched its way across her face. "Why? Did you finally get tired of that mangy look, too?"

The words were no sooner out of her mouth, and she recalled his 'hermit's pledge', "*After my novel gets published, I'll shave. I promise.*"

Her eyes lit up with a matching smile, "Does this mean... You are getting published?"

His smile grew wider yet, "Yes! It! Does!" he triumphantly exclaimed; then stated, "The Legend of Rachel Petersen will soon be available on Amazon and other websites!"

Shelby rose, ran around her desk, and hugged him. "Oh, Christian, I am so happy for you!" she said as he picked her off the ground and twirled her around.

The elated man spun his wife in two circles before putting her back down, he explained, "I got the call from New York about an hour after you left for work. An agent with Brownstone Lit read my manuscript last night; she loves it. She called first thing this morning before I had a chance to sign with a different publisher."

"This is absolutely fantastic; I knew somebody would realize the potential in your story sooner or later. See? I told you to keep plugging away and learn to accept rejection."

"I was beginning to have my doubts, you had more faith in me than *I* did."

Bleached blond Nancy, much younger and wilder than Shelby, but equally attractive, had obviously been eavesdropping. She interrupted, "I couldn't help but to overhear, Christian, congratulations! I have a friend who has been trying for years to get his book published but with no luck. You must have written a really good story."

"It's a fantastic story, Nancy," Shelby interjected.

She always felt Nancy took more than just a friendly interest in her husband. It seemed the little sexpot could not hold onto a man longer than two months. Five was her record. Also, Shelby heard through the Secretarial Pool grapevine that her co-worker had a fetish for *conquering* married men. Therefore, Shelby would not allow any circumstances to arise between Christian and Nancy that would put her marriage in jeopardy. Although she felt she could trust her husband, Shelby also knew how tempting the forbidden fruit could be. Especially a peach as ripe and juicy as, '*Hot to Trot Nancy*'.

"Maybe I can give my friend the name of the publisher who signed you?" Nancy asked with hungry puppy eyes aimed at Christian.

"I didn't even get the contract yet, Nancy. After I get to know my publisher, I'll put a plug in for your friend," he said, not realizing he was being hit on.

"Wow! You would do that for me?" she asked, pointing her fingers at her now puffed out chest, hoping he would notice her scrumptious cleavage bulging from her skintight black cashmere sweater.

"Sure," he replied, caring none about her young firm bosom, which would have crippled most men, reducing them to slobbering fools. He was too excited about the call. The call he never would have received if not for his loving wife's sacrifices, understanding, and guidance.

He then faced his wife directly, who was sitting back at her desk now, and said, "I need to stop and buy a digital camera. That agent said she'd like my picture on one of those memory chips that cameras take, so the layout guys can edit it for the book's backflap."

Before Shelby could answer, Nancy jumped in, "Oh Christian, you don't have to run out and buy one, I'd be more than happy to lend you mine."

"That's quite all right, Nancy. I've been meaning to buy one for quite some time, and now, I have a good reason to get one," Shelby shot back, her husband still not picking up on the overly anxious implications.

"Thanks, Shell. I'll pick one up and learn how to use it by the time you get home, and then we'll snap a few photos. I'd better let you two get back to work."

He then leaned his lanky body over Shelby's desk and kissed his wife goodbye. His eyes widened when her tongue quickly darted in and out of his mouth.

"Bye, Christian," Nancy, waving, said in a very friendly tone as Christian stepped on to the elevator. He simply nodded goodbye to her; then he winked at his wife as the elevator door closed.

"You can put your tits away now, Nancy!" Shelby said to the temp. "My *husband* has left."

"Well!" The Kelly Girl refuted in a huff, pulling her sweater up, but then added, "He *is* cute; too bad there's a ring on his finger!"

As Christian walked to his beat-up pickup, which he had parked with one tire halfway on the sidewalk in all his excitement, he glanced at a row of newspaper boxes and stopped dead in his tracks.

On the front page of the Post Gazette — a picture of Robert J. McKelvey; the headline stated, *"Senior Editor Dies."*

Struck with mixed emotions, sadness intertwined with bitterness, Christian bent over and read what was visible through the glass door. The article said his ex-boss had died from a sudden heart attack while working at his desk.

Furthermore! The paper promoted David Campbell to Senior Editor!

Christian mumbled under his breath while staring at a smaller inset photo of Campbell, "I don't believe it! You! The Post's *Top Dog*! Ha! And McKelvey will never know I got published. Son of a bitch!"

"IT IS AMAZING WHAT forty-nine dollars will buy," Christian told his wife that evening while helping her carry in a few groceries from her car, "I got this camera all figured out. I knew it couldn't be all that hard if Campbell can operate one."

Then he shook his head and asked, "That reminds me, did you see where McKelvey died, and now Campbell is the paper's Senior Editor? The youngest ever."

"No, I did not know that. It's kinda sad that McKelvey died, but Campbell just seemed to be in the right place at the right time," Shelby said, using her butt to close her car door.

Christian said, "Yeah. I don't like talking badly about the dead, but it was probably one of Campbell's columns that stopped The Old Geezer's heart! The article said he died at his desk."

Walking up to the door, she changed the subject, "Just show me how to point and click; after supper, we'll get those poses. I was thinking maybe one of you outdoors by a tree or the flower garden. Then one by the fireplace, you know... to show off your, *sophisticated side*."

They shuffled in through the front door with the groceries in hand.

"I thought of those exact places too, but then I thought of an even better place. I want my picture taken right where it all began," he said, placing the bags on the countertop.

Shelby looked at him with her *I hope you are not serious look.*

He nodded, "Yep. Right by her tombstone."

"That place is... spooky," she argued, not wanting to go back to the little girl's grave, which she had not been to, since the day the two of them stumbled across it.

"Well, yeah. It *is* a spooky tale, Shelby," Christian argued back, knowing he had made a good point, and he would eventually get his way.

"Seeing the author by the tombstone on the backflap of the book just might entice more people to buy it," he added fuel to his fire.

"Okay, I'll do it, but it will be quick," she buckled. "Saturday, in the bright sunlight. Though I imagine the publishing house will decide which picture they want to use in the end anyways."

"Fair enough. Thank you for believing in me and helping me write this book." He pulled her to him and thanked her with a kiss.

"You did it all on your own, Baby." She returned the kiss.

"You contributed a lot more than you'll ever know, Honey."

He hugged her tighter, his kiss lingered a bit longer that time because her tiny tongue tickled his.

She batted her seductive eyes at him, cooing, "My long-haired hippie husband will be gone for a while, what do you say we, uh... take advantage of that fact, you good looking stud?"

Her eyes pointed up stairs.

He wondered, *"Did Nancy spark this?"*

As Klondike ice cream sandwiches melted over the countertop downstairs... a young, virgin cheerleader was shaking her pompoms upstairs. *"Yeah, Christian, he's my man, he makes me..."*

"COME LIKE THREE FEET closer and get one more shot of me kneeling by the stone; and try to center the stone in the picture," Christian suggested to Shelby, who was wanting to leave already because she had kept her promise and snapped a photo of him posing next to the headstone, and another one with him standing behind it, on that sunny Saturday afternoon.

Trying her best to keep a respectable distance between herself and the grave, his wife cringed when he asked her to come closer for that shot.

After taking three steps nearer to the grave, she quickly focused and clicked the camera, then told him, "There! Now let's get out of here; I always feel like someone is watching me when I'm out here."

"See you later, Rachel," Christian teased Shelby by patting the tombstone.

"That's it, go ahead and piss her off! Let's get out of here, Christian! This place gives me the heebie jeebies. C'mon! Let's go!" she somewhat ordered, then turned and began walking away without him.

He caught up to her, "Aw, come on. Don't tell me you're afraid. You watch too many scary movies."

"It's just so eerie back here in the woods; I'm a city girl," Shelby said, picking up her pace back to the tram road.

Feeling safe once back inside the house, she prepared a late lunch of tuna fish sandwiches while her husband fiddled with the new camera.

"It's too bad we couldn't afford to get a better laptop when we bought this one. We could have put the memory card in it and looked at the pictures on the screen instead of looking at them on this tiny view finder," Christian said as he flipped through the pictures of him standing beside a tree, sitting in a chair by the fireplace, and of course his favorites, by the grave.

Shelby set their sandwiches on the table and told him, "Maybe later on, when your writing career takes off, we'll buy a better home computer and get it hooked up to the Internet."

"Boy! Wouldn't that be something? To become a successful and well-known author?" Christian fantasized.

He then handed the camera to Shelby and explained, "Here, push this tiny button, and you can flip through the pictures you took today."

"You sure did master this thing," she said while squinting at the tiny pictures, surprised at how well he is now able to operate a new electronic gadget, an item which he normally avoided in the past.

However, Shelby did not know that Heather, Best Buy's electronics clerk, was once again more than happy to assist Christian, who on this particular day, smelled like her daddy! She spent as much time as possible with her handsome customer, teaching him how to operate his new digital camera.

"Anything is easy if you want to learn. Yeah, it would be nice to have a better computer and Internet access here at home, then I won't have to use the one at the library," Christian said while opening his diet cola. "I hate to admit it, but McKelvey was right about me being a caveman."

After Shelby flipped through all the pictures, she said, "I like the one of you by the fireplace; you look like a sophisticated writer in that one. Too bad you weren't holding a pipe."

"My favorite one is me on one knee beside the tombstone," he said, talking through a mouthful of tuna.

"I think it will give the book a feeling of uh, what's the word? Poltergeist? Just like you feel when you're out there in the woods, close to Rachel Petersen's grave — you say someone, or something, is watching you. But it's actually all in your mind because of the *macabre* sense of death, and a lone grave in the middle of the woods. People like scary, spooky stuff. I bet Margo's team will probably pick that one, since you took an excellent picture, and you're able to see her name, and the dates somewhat."

"I knew you would like those ones, and yeah, you're probably right," Shelby remarked.

Monday, as Miss Duvall promised, the mail carrier delivered a manila envelope from New York City containing Brownstone's standard publisher/writer agreement. Christian so desperately wanted to sign it then and there, and immediately get it back in the mail; but he took his wife's advice and let her take the legal papers into work for Mr. Goldberg to scrutinize the fine print. Her boss okayed them, and the agreement went back out in Wednesday's mail with the memory card, and a cover letter explaining that the tombstone in the pictures was the actual tombstone that inspired his book.

Margo Duvall telephoned two weeks later. "Christian! You are not going to believe this! If you are not sitting, sit! The layout team called me first thing this morning and said, 'Margo, you have to see these photos from Kane for yourself,' so I went down there. After I looked at them, I called my boss down to inspect them, too. You did not view these pictures on your computer before sending them, did you?"

"No, why? Is there a problem that's going to delay publishing?"

"No! The exact opposite! In every one of the photos of you by the grave, about a foot away from you... *There's a freaking orb*!"

Chapter Eighteen

"Orbs?" A dumbfounded Christian asked.

"Yes! There's an orb beside you in every picture of you by the headstone! I just called to tell you about them, and let you know the progress. My boss wants to get your book on the market as soon as possible since vampires, werewolves, and other supernatural thrillers are so hot right now. Your manuscript has been edited, my boss read it, and he's as excited about it as I am. We are going to start off with the print-on-demand option, and, of course, we'll make the epub version available on all the websites. You'd be surprised how many readers would rather read a story on their phones than turn pages in a physical book bought at a brick-and-mortar bookstore these days. I guess I'm old school, and this is called Progress! But hey! Revenue is revenue, no matter where it comes from. Right?"

Once the buzz hit the Internet concerning an orb being present in photos of an author standing next to the tombstone that inspired his supernatural novel, the news item immediately went viral, and the paperbacks flew from the shelves. As with many current events, the media blew it out of proportion.

The luminescent globes proved to be highly visible, authentic, and not photoshopped! Skeptics analyzed the photos, dissected them, trying to disprove them, but were unable to do so.

Margo wisely arranged an interview for her new novelist with a highly respected UK based Sci-Fi magazine; in which Christian explained how he knew nothing of the orbs until the photos were developed, however, his wife sensed a presence each time she went near the grave.

Consequently, Brownstone Lit was gearing up to print one million hardbacks with the last three pages being full size glossies of each snapshot Shelby took of her husband by Rachel's headstone.

How ironic! For the second time since her death, the location of the Petersen girl's grave had to be kept secret to keep people away!

Within six months, *The Legend of Rachel Petersen* hit number one on the New York Times Bestseller list, and Margo arranged a book signing in the Big Apple for her... protégé.

After the three-hour long event, which turned out to be a huge success, the new writer was ravenous, "This is totally phenomenal!" his agent, a middle-aged very classy and down to earth black woman, told Christian and Shelby over dinner at one of New York's ritzier restaurants — Sanford's Flame and Ale. The eatery reeked of delicious ethnic aromas, and money!

"I totally agree, Margo, this really is, uh... *Phenomenal*! I never would've imagined I'd pen a bestseller, especially being my first, *serious*, attempt at writing a novel," Christian concurred, pouring the remaining bubbly into everybody's elegant champagne glasses.

The ice-cold sparkling wine caused the name, Sanford's, which was etched into the flutes, (fancy, long-stemmed champagne glassware), be pronounced, which was a nice, subtle touch adding to the ambience, and overall dining experience in this five-star restaurant.

Christian raised his drink, "A toast! To my lovely, beautiful wife; my main source of inspiration!"

Their glasses clinked; Shelby blushed as they sipped their bubbly.

"You did not need me, Christian," his wife protested.

"I most certainly did!"

He turned to Margo, "I never would have penned that story except for this little woman."

Then he chuckled, "My very first attempt at writing a novel was titled *The Vampire's Feast*. I only wrote one chapter!"

He chuckled harder, "And my villain's name was..."

The new author then started laughing so hard he could not finish his sentence. His euphoria was not from the tiny amount of alcohol he had consumed, but rather, from being high on life. And lately, it has been an extremely good life.

"Igor Wazleski!" Shelby finished his sentence for him, and then the three of them laughed until they all had tears in their eyes.

In between his laughing, Christian told Margo, "She told me Igor Wazleski sounded more like a hunchbacked Polish truck driver than a bloodsucker."

The patrons were gawking at the three of them now because they were howling with laughter and not giving a shit what the other diners thought.

The waiter hurried to their table, "Pardon the interruption, but does anybody care for dessert? Our specials today are

Cherry Cheesecake and Baked Alaska," he asked as though it was a bother.

"Yes," Christian said, his laughter dying down to a chuckle, trying to regain composure, "I would like a slice of cheesecake, with cherries, please."

"And for you, Ladies?" the snobbish waiter with slicked back hair, beady eyes, and an unusually long pointy nose asked, looking down that beak at them.

"I think I also will have the cheesecake," Shelby said, wiping her eyes with her cloth napkin.

"Make it unanimous," Margo added, throwing her hands in the air. "And don't you dare forget my cherries!"

"Excellent choices, I assure you," their waiter said rather boringly, and left.

"Margo, would you believe three dozen agents rejected me before you signed me?" Christian asked, just to kill the awkward silence. "I imagine they are all sorry now! Most of them said no after reading the synopsis."

"That happens in this business. I am also guilty of letting a few top sellers get past me. If you are in this profession as long as I've been, and you read at least two full manuscripts a week, that's bound to happen. I felt the raw emotion you put in your story, and I knew it was a great tale. I had confidence it would be a good seller. Even the title is catchy; maybe it's the archaic word, *Legend*, or that Victorian name, *Rachel*. But my God, I was not expecting eighty million copies in six months!"

The professionally arrogant waiter returned and served their desserts; after he left, Margo asked, "So how long are you two going to be in New York?"

Christian had just taken a bite of cheesecake, but tucked it in his cheek to answer, "We're not in a hurry to get home; we packed for a week. We'd like to take in a show, do some sight-seeing, and shop."

"If I need to get a hold of you, I'll call your cell. Give me your number."

"That's one of the things we'll be shopping for, my old phone suffered water damage. I'll call you when I get one." Christian smiled, remembering how he gave his phone back to McKelvey.

"Get one like mine. This phone does way more than make calls and... *take pictures*!"

Christian recalled McKelvey's nearly identical comment as Margo showed him Apple's latest phone to hit the market.

She further advised him, "Don't get an Android, they are tricky to use. And don't forget to call when you get one!"

"I'll call you from the Apple store."

Just as the waiter brought the check, Margo commented, "Well then! Looks like the party's over. I certainly had a fun lunch for once. I'll deny ever saying it, but some of my clients are rather stuffy, which reminds me, I have another meeting to go to."

Christian snatched the bill from the waiter's hand, "My treat, Margo. I also enjoyed lunch; you're a really fun person. And that had to have been the best Lobster Newberg I ever had!"

He glanced at the check; keeping a poker face, he realized that those three meals cost as much as they spent for groceries in two months when the times were lean.

Shelby pointed out, "You can't compare your meal to something you never had before!"

They laughed some more as they walked to their cars.

"Well, I thank you again for such a good time, good food; Christian, Shelby. The next one is on me. It was a huge pleasure meeting the two of you. I will keep in touch," Margo told the Kanes, shaking hands before getting in her Porsche, which was parked next to Christian's brand-new BMW twin turbo coupe. Shelby snapped her seatbelt every time she got in it; her husband loved the torque the beast had.

Margo hit the window down button, smiled, "Ciao!"

The Kanes got in their car. "Keep your eyes open for an Apple store," he told Shelby.

Then he asked her, "Who does Margo remind you of?"

"She's beautiful! She reminds me of Tamron Hall, but with Roseanne Barr's disposition on life."

"I was thinking Dianna Ross, but your description is better. She is down to Earth, very classy!"

"Yeah, she is, I like her."

AFTER THEIR FUN-FILLED week of living it up in New York City, the successful young writer and his wife were ready to get home, relax, and start his new book. However, it was not the same home where Christian had written his bestseller. They bought a very nice, and much newer, comfortable split level log home on three acres, twenty miles from their old place.

On the day they found out about the orbs, Shelby wanted to move far away from Rachel's grave.

She also chastised her husband, "See! I told you it wasn't in my head when I told you I felt like somebody was watching me when I was out there by her grave. Maybe she *is* lost, or confused where to go, like in your book, after the Gatlins killed her."

Once the royalty checks started pouring in, they relocated. Shelby was able to tell Mr. Goldberg, "Goodbye," since her husband was financially secure now; they also made a nice profit when they sold their house thanks to Shelby's perfection in painting. Her choice of contrasting colors proved exceptional.

A month went by until they heard from Margo Duvall again, "Hello, Christian?"

"Yes, oh hello, Margo. Are we doing lunch again? I'm getting a craving for Lobster," he teased.

"Better than that! You are not going to believe this. I just got off the phone with some big shit CEO from Warner Brothers; he told me a twelve-year old granddaughter of one of the owners wants to break into the movie industry. The studio wants to put 'The Legend of Rachel Petersen' on the big screen with the granddaughter, of course, playing Rachel!"

"Wow!" was all dumbfounded Christian could say, with Shelby straining to hear the other end of the conversation; her husband hadn't found the speaker button yet, so he twisted the phone from his ear so she could hear.

"That's pretty much what my reaction was, too. You know what this means, don't you, Christian?"

"Yes. No. I'm not sure. For Pete's sakes, just tell me already, Margo!"

"This means Warners will spare no cost in making sure the movie is a chartbuster. They will probably spend more in hype than it costs to make the flick, ensuring the girl is an overnight sensation!"

"This is totally mind-blowing," a surprised Christian responded.

"I've never had one of my client's books made into a movie! I am as excited about this as you are. There is some serious coin to be made. Should I tell them you're interested and will sell the movie rights?"

"Who said there's no such thing as a stupid question? Hell yeah!"

"I kind of figured you would say that, but only with a few more expletives. I will let you know when we have to sit down and hash out the legal bullshit."

"Great! I'll be waiting. I am available anytime you set it up."

"Terrific. Ciao!"

Since she only heard half the conversation, Shelby impatiently asked before he had the phone back in its cradle, "What Christian? What's going on now? Another reprint?"

With the dumbfounded look still attached to his face, he said, "No! Way better than that. Warner Brothers Studio wants to make a movie based on my book. Apparently one of the big wig's granddaughters wants to be a movie star, so they're going to cast her in the role of Rachel!"

"Wow is right! This is unbelievable! Fantastic," she said all aglow, hugging her husband, "See? Just like I told you; those famous writers are no smarter, or better than you."

MARGO WAS CORRECT IN her assumption of the millions spent on advertising the movie, which they wisely scheduled to hit the theaters one week before Christmas. The studio also made sure to cast quite a few big stars in supporting roles, paying dearly for their appearances.

No doubt, Rebecca Warner would be a star.

The only *demand* Christian asked for was that he would like a part in the movie, even if it was just a fleeting shot of him standing in the crowd.

Stunned, he couldn't believe it when the movie producer asked him if he would be happy to play the part of Mr. Wolford, the school principal. Of course, Christian said yes; it was a much bigger part than he had ever hoped for, and he even had one line to memorize!

Premier night of '*The Legend of Rachel Petersen*' at the famous Grauman's Chinese Theatre on Hollywood Boulevard had onlookers standing in line for hours. Thousands of fans strained behind the velvet ropes to get a peek at the stars, or maybe even snag an autograph from their favorite actor.

High intensity floodlights crisscrossed the evening sky as dozens of stretch limos arrived, dropping the rich and famous off at the red carpet. The paparazzi came out in full force snapping pictures of the stars, directors, producers, and celebrities, like Christian, walking with his arm around his lovely, smiling wife on the red carpet. He wore a tailored tuxedo, she was in a very expensive evening gown, the Kanes resembled the rich, young celebs that they now were.

Numerous famous people were invited who had no connection to the movie, but were simply family, or actor friends, which also added to the hype.

Since the famous rock band, Aerosmith, had debuted a new ballad titled, "Stolen Innocence", which was written solely for the rape scene, they were on the 'A-list'. Their new song soared to number one on the music charts, and Shelby nearly peed her pants when Steven Tyler shook her hand, flashed his famous, huge, toothy smile at her, then complimented her, "Love your hair, Babe!"

Christian had two favorite parts of the movie. The first one was when the audience screamed with fright during Seth's dream, when he turned back around from sharpening the knife in the barn, and an unsuspecting wild Rachel was in the noose, madly swinging her knife.

The second part was when they all called the Gatlin brothers *filthy bastards* during the rape scene, but then they all cheered when the brothers met their fates.

Christian was a natural; he played a fantastic principal, even if all he had to do was roll his eyes when little Jimmy Kirby was dragged by his ear to his office, then say his line with a bit of annoyance in his tone, "What did the class clown do... *this* time, Mr. Altemus?"

The movie pretty much followed his book, which thrilled Christian; Shelby was ecstatic about her husband being in the movie.

"Look, Baby! Your name is up there as Principal Wolford," she excitedly whispered when the movie started, and they watched the credits scrolling up against a background of *gigantic* snowflakes falling gently over the Appalachian Mountains.

Once the credits finished, the opening scene then slowly zoomed through the falling snow, and singled out a huge

Pinetree in the forest from a mile away as the Sun peeked over the horizon; then the camera descended from the top of the tree, down through the limbs and branches to the Yoder boys hunkered down under the giant Hemlock, clutching flintlock rifles, slightly shivering.

Naturally, Christian, Shelby, and Margo had already watched the movie when invited to the director's Santa Monica home for the private viewing two weeks prior to the well-publicized premier.

Vincent Malcotti's home theater was spectacular to say the least. He had an auditorium in his mansion's basement that seated one hundred people in luxurious comfort. The *screen* was actually a one hundred and fifty-two-inch, high-definition flat panel TV, custom ordered from Sony at a cost of one hundred and twenty grand.

Acoustically, a state-of-the-art Bose surround sound system brought the movie to life. The privileged viewers were right there, amongst the Civil War soldiers on the battlefield in Gettysburg with bullets ricocheting and whizzing by, men praying or screaming in agony, and the cannonballs exploding the ground from every direction could be felt in their chests from the powerful bass.

No popcorn was served from Malcotti's fully restored, antique popcorn cart that adorned the entrance to his theater along with numerous vintage movie posters, such as 'Gone with the Wind,' and 'Psycho.' However, a catered chef set up a buffet table that offered lobster tail, shrimp, crab cakes, and an assortment of finger sandwiches and desserts for his guests.

Of course, there was an endless supply of the finest imported French champagne, as well as an open bar.

All of the VIPs gathered in the ballroom for drinks and mingling when the movie was over. Mr. Malcotti, a man of average height with a thin build, looked like a movie star himself right out of the Thirties with a pencil-thin moustache and his thinning, jet-black hair slicked straight back.

The director, with a Dirty Martini in hand, approached Christian and Shelby.

"Christian!" he exclaimed with an Italian European accent, "Please do tell me you have started the follow up," he said with a serious smile, raised eyebrows, then a kiss on Shelby's hand.

In an attempted sophisticated tone, Christian answered, "I have yet to hit upon the right angle for the sequel. However, I have a few chapters started on my next novel, which revolves around a pregnant woman who has psychic abilities. Her son inherits those powers, but of course he is evil and uses his gift to seek his fortune at the expense of others. Starting from when he is in her womb!"

"Ooh! That sounds devious and deceitful. Just my style! Now you *will* make certain that I get *that* screenplay in my hands before anybody else. Understand?" he stated to Christian more so than asking, then sipped his Martini.

"Absolutely, Vincent. I'm quite certain we'll have another box office hit if *you* direct it!"

"Flattery, *will*, get you to the top in this business, Christian. Now if you will excuse me, I absolutely *must* congratulate our newest star, little Miss Rebecca Warner herself."

Malcotti ate the olive from his drink then raised his glass; the Kanes tapped theirs to his.

"Cheers," the director toasted them then flashed a quick smile before chasing down the spoiled rotten little brat. They heard Malcotti muttering to himself when he left, "Now where is that contemptible little snot?"

He tracked her down to his veranda — the twelve-year-old Warner girl and the seventeen-year-old boy who played Thaddeus were seated at a table under a palm tree, snorting earthworm-sized lines of coke!

The Kanes were living, and loving, the good life, which was expected to get even better if the movie's projected gross income by Warner Brother's bean counters becomes a reality.

The accountants projected this movie would break Avatar's two point eight billion record box office take by four hundred million; their predictions usually came in close, give or take fifty million.

After the premier, Christian and Shelby returned to their hotel suite, somewhat tired, but too pumped up to sleep. Christian peeled off his tux and tossed it on a chair; the pants and shirt followed, then he plopped onto the king-sized bed while Shelby slipped out of her gown and hung it on a hanger.

Wearing a lacey black bra, matching thong, and her pearls, she cuddled up to her husband and told him, "What a night! This evening was probably boring and a run of the mill event to these people we were rubbing elbows with at Grauman's, but it was the best night of my life. Especially when Steven Tyler called me Babe; he even told me he likes my hair!"

"Yeah! I heard him hitting on you. I agree though, what a life, huh? I think I could learn to adjust to this," he said while absentmindedly stroking her back. "You know what else?" he asked.

"He was *not* 'hitting on me', but what?" She threw him a suspicious look.

"You were the prettiest girl at the party, as usual."

"Oh yeah! Like I'm going to believe you this time. Every one of those women at the premier tonight paid a professional to put their makeup on for them."

"You were too the prettiest lady there, that's why the rock star flirted with you! Because you have natural beauty. And, I'll have you know... I even caught Tyler staring at your ass!" he said and began tickling her.

She scolded her husband, "I told you to quit talking about my derriere like that! He was not!"

"Yes he was! When I caught him, he shrugged his shoulders and nodded in approval!"

His wife laughed and tickled him back, "Feeling frisky, are we? You are such a bullshitter!"

Then she climbed on top of him, tickling him more. Her sexiness, exotic perfume, and the friction of their bodies rubbing together was obviously getting her husband aroused.

"Want to see my new outfit, Mr. Big Movie Star? Promise me an autograph, and I'll go put it on!" she teasingly cooed as she ground her satin covered bottom on him, teasing him to great lengths.

"Another new outfit! I'll sign whatever you want."

She slid off him; his desires for her grew even more so as he watched her do her sexy sashay the entire way to the bathroom, which adjoined the bedroom.

Christian heard the distinct clicks when Shelby opened the suitcase.

Then he heard the shower curtain hooks sliding on the track.

Next, he heard Shelby gasp, followed by a sickening thud; sounding like she fell and hit her head.

He looked overtop his toes into the bathroom; the only thing he was able to see was Shelby's arm as it slowly extended down onto the tiled floor, a puddle of blood began pooling at her elbow.

In her hand, his wife held onto a sequined hat, the style which Flappers glamorized during the Roaring Twenties; a long hatpin secured an ostrich feather to it.

Christian's mouth fell open, his eyes nearly popped from his head as four tiny, bloodied fingers reached around the door, then the evil face of Rachel Petersen slowly peered from behind it!

Smiling that hideous grin, she stepped from behind the door and looked exactly as Rebecca Warner had portrayed Rachel in the movie. She brought her hand up; Shelby's blood dripped from the knife she clutched, causing Christian's eyes to widened further yet; however, he was paralyzed, unable to move.

It was like Christian was rewatching the dream scene in the movie; this girl holding a butcher knife was identical to the psychotic little redhead that chased Seth from the barn.

The demonic girl then ran, *in slow motion*, from the bathroom and leapt up on to Christian's chest! Her momentum rocked him and the bed.

Before the man could react, she brought the knife's edge to his throat; he felt the coldness of the razor-sharp blade press against his skin when he gulped.

In a small girl's innocent voice, she calmly informed the man, "Do you know? That you are no better than those filthy Rebel deserters? How *dare* you, slander my name!"

She leaned forward; her blood splattered face and crazed green eyes but mere inches from his face, she calmly asked, "Who do you think you are, *Christian*? To also... *Use me*?"

Scowling now, "You exploited my name, my death! For what?"

She cocked her head and quizzed him further, becoming aggravated, infuriated, "Are you seeking fame? Fortune? Like Thaddeus Yoder? You too, like the Gatlins, must pay, with *your* life!"

She let go a sinister cackle.

In one swift motion, she brought the knife across his throat!

"Join those *bastards* in Hell, *Christian*!"

Chapter Nineteen

"Christian!"

Just as the demonic little girl sliced through the writer's jugular, Shelby reached down and shook her husband, who was fast asleep, snoring away in his recliner!

Again, she shook him and hollered, "Christian!"

Her husband instantly bolted his recliner to an upright position and immediately brought his hands to his throat, then looked at her; the man surveyed his surroundings as though this was his very first-time laying eyes on the living room in their townhouse.

"I couldn't wake you up! You were really zonked! We're going to be late for the banquet if you don't get a move on. I can't imagine you'd fall asleep, *tonight*! *Of all nights*! But that's what happens when you sit back in that beat-up recliner."

He continued looking about the room. ESPN was interviewing Sydney Crosby about his new three-year contract with the Penguins!

"I put it over here so it wouldn't get wrinkled. I can't believe you hung it like that on the lampshade, Christian. Really. Sometimes you act like a little boy," she said and picked the neatly folded rented dinner jacket from atop the sofa. "Let me help you put it on."

Thoughtlessly, he stood to wobbly legs and allowed her to guide his arms into the coat sleeves while assuring him, "We still have plenty of time. There's no need to go speeding."

Shelby had transferred her ID, keys, cellphone, and other odds and ends into a tiny clutch purse for the evening and had it sitting on the table. She heard her phone ringing through the purse; she grabbed for it; however, she did not notice when her compact slid out of the purse, ending up between the sports pages of The Post Gazette lying on the table.

"Hello? Oh! Okay, Dave. We were just leaving. I'll let him know. Oh, Dave, tell Debbie to save some stuffed mushrooms for me if they have them for appetizers again this year. Oh, they do! Great! Thanks, we'll see you in a bit."

"That was Dave Campbell, Baby. He called to let us know there was an accident just outside the tubes again, and the cops are detouring traffic onto Smithfield Street. I sure am glad Dave stopped over the other night and showed me how to use this new phone. I never would've figured out all these options. *He's a whiz with these new gadgets.*"

Her comment smacked Christian between his eyes with the force of a ballpeen hammer.

Like all caring wives do, Shelby stood facing her husband and straightened his tie and fixed his collar. She then stepped back to make certain his attire was in order. Christian noticed she was wearing her favorite angel necklace. He immediately patted his coat pocket and felt two De Roy's jewelry boxes still secretly tucked away.

He thought, "*I never surprised her with these! It was all a dream! Everything! We didn't even go to the awards banquet yet! Cosby's on the tube! But we moved out of this place a year ago, and I wrote a book about that little girl! They even made it into a movie!"*

He decided to wait to give her the pearls when another thought hit him, *"Am I? Or Campbell? Getting the promotion?"*

His head was swimming. *"This means McKelvey's not dead!"*

Shelby then gave him a wink, and in a sexy voice, asked, "Did you notice the bottle of Asti Spumante in the fridge? Mr. Goldberg said it's really good, and we'll like it. Did you ever try Spumante before?"

A look of indecision crossed his face. "What? Yes. No. I'm not sure anymore."

"Maybe you'd better grab a cup of coffee and splash cold water onto your face to wake up, you look like you saw a ghost!"

He thought, *"A ghost! Ha! I think I did!"*

Then she added in her sexy voice, "I'll have you come on up later, *Cowboy*, and we'll celebrate your promotion!"

Her husband remembered the Stetson and assless chaps.

When the couple were walking to the car, Christian heard and felt something crunch under his shoe. Looking down, he saw what was left of a huge centipede that he had squished the guts out of.

Shelby noticed it too, "I stepped on one of those ugly things when I left for work today. They're nasty, and they stink so bad! Try to wipe your shoe off in the grass."

Christian looked at the squashed bug while scraping his shoe on the lawn, waiting for it to congeal back into a whole centipede. However, it did not. He caught up to Shelby as she opened her car door, which he usually did for her.

Christian pulled out of the drive and started around the cul-de-sac; Shelby made small talk while rooting through her tiny accessory purse, "A Kelly Girl started at the office today. A blond bimbo named Nancy. Louis hired her because there's so many foreclosures and bankruptcies right now. We're swamped. She filed papers all day long; that's how busy we are."

Then she griped, "Oh crap, don't tell me I forgot my compact."

A petite girl in a floral print dress was riding her bicycle down the walk, but she stopped as they approached. She lowered her head to her chest and stared with piercing green eyes at Christian from under her curly red bangs. Staring back, he watched as the corners of her lips curled up one at a time into an evil little smile. He felt her icy stare burn down to his very soul. Then she slowly, deliberately, shook her finger at him, foreboding him... *Don't do it*!

"Who is that?" he hurriedly asked, his eyes the size of hockey pucks.

Shelby looked up from her purse and caught a glimpse of the girl. "Oh! I forgot to tell you. Yesterday, a family moved into the vacant town house right next door to us. A family from Ohio. The Petersens. That little girl is their twelve-year old daughter. *Doesn't she just have the prettiest red hair you ever did see?*"

"Her name is... Rachel!"

Chapter Twenty

The little redhead's index finger continually wavered that foreboding 'no, no, no' warning gesture in his rearview mirror, then disappeared as he rounded the cul-de-sac.

The thought, *"This can't be happening. This isn't real. I must still be dreaming!"* ran continually through his mind.

Nervously, he asked, "Rachel? Did you just say... *Rachel... Petersen*?"

Christian prayed he heard wrong; he desperately needed verification from his wife, who was still caught up in her frantic search for her missing compact, which she then finally deemed MIA.

"Yes, Baby. Rachel Petersen. I could have sworn I put my compact in my purse, but I cannot find it. Oh poop," she replied, snapping her purse shut and extinguishing the tiny light in the sun visor.

Confirming the little girl's name caused a lingering look of pure bewilderment to plaster his face, while no compact brought about a brief look of despair on hers.

Pittsburgh had been enjoying a rather unseasonably warm mild winter so far this year with very little snow accumulation as decades ago. Perhaps global warming had become the reality as predicted by meteorologists.

Understandably though, once the horizon devoured the last of the evening Sun's rays this time of year, the mercury could drastically drop fifteen or twenty degrees in a snap of a finger, dipping just low enough to tantalize the freezing point. Creeping in unannounced, the northerly breezes slowly sucked the day's heat from the concrete skyscrapers while etching their windowpanes in frosty ice patterns, as if leaving a sarcastic handwritten thank you note.

The stiff coldness radiating from Shelby's leathered bucket seat caused a brief shiver; she wrapped her shawl tightly over her thin arms in an attempt to capture any escaping body heat.

"Do we have heat, yet? My toes are frozen," she asked, wishing now she had worn a heavier wrap.

Her query about any possible warmth did not register.

"Christian?" She asked again, only much louder this time, "Do we have heat?

Christian jumped as if his wife had startled him, he mumbled, "Oh! I'll check."

Trying to focus, he turned the dial to defrost, then turned the fan to low and placed his hand over the defroster, "Just a little." He kept his hand there, waiting for warmer air.

All the while waiting, the impish face of the redheaded girl with her mischievous smile and warning finger, danced vividly in his tortured mind; along with her name, 'Rachel', continually echoing, as if it were resonating from a giant gong.

Mindless as a robot, Christian switched to the floor vent when he felt heat, then increased the fan to high.

"Your heater works way better than my Mazda's," Shelby said, shifting her feet closer to the vents, trying to thaw her exposed toes sticking out from her high heels. As fashionable and trendy as her stilettos by Missoni were, they offered very little protection from the cold; however, the pricey footwear definitely accented her shapely legs.

Thanks to the heater, an acrid odor wafted from under Christian's shoe.

"Ohh! There's that nasty smell again," Shelby blurted out, covering her nose, "You must not have gotten all that bug's guts off your shoes."

Christian, also grimacing, changed the heat from the floor to the dashboard vent, then he cracked his window, attempting to suck out the offensive odor. Shelby followed suit, opening her window a fraction of an inch; she then raised her nose to breathe in the cool, clean night air rushing in. Although the fresh coldness chilled her, she reasoned having a cold nose was better than smelling that foul stench.

After a few moments of the damp night air circulating throughout the interior of the car, most of the rank scent dissipated. "What an awful stink those creepy crawlers make," Shelby made note, closing her window, "They're worse than stinkbugs."

Christian, only half-aware of her comments, had his mind in overdrive, rewinding, searching for a minute shred of logic that could remotely explain why he dreamt of this girl and her grave.

Could the reason be, she just happens to be living next door to him? *Rachel Petersen!... The little girl who died in 1863, but she's here, in the flesh! How is this remotely possible?*

That question, along with many more unanswerable questions, swirled in his mind, only deepening this enigma. *The stinking centipedes! Did they come... From her grave? Why did I dream of her? Is she trying to warn me? If so, of what? Not to quit if I don't get the promotion?*

"Christian!" Shelby quietly hollered at her husband, as though scolding a little boy.

Startled back to reality, he glanced at her.

"You've been acting really weird since I woke you from your little catnap. I've never seen you like this before. You're pale white; you really do look like you've seen a ghost!"

He shot his hand up and raked his fingers through his hair; in a trembling voice, he told her, "I had a really bad dream when I dozed off."

Then he sheepishly added, "I didn't get the promotion, Shell, Campbell did."

"What? It's just your nerves, Christian. Come on now, you know you're more qualified than him to fill Max's position. Oh, Baby, it was just a dream."

To further reassure her husband, she confidently added, "You *are* the man for the job. How many times have you told me Campbell and Rogerson were too young and not experienced enough?"

"I'm not so sure anymore. Campbell is pretty slick with any new electronic gadget," Christian said, being interrupted by a multitude of blurred flashing lights coming into view through a layer of dense fog up ahead. Several police cars, ambulances, and a fire truck responding to an accident now sat idling; parked helter-skelter, their exhaust fumes adding to the surrealistic murkiness being dissected by the pulsating red, blue, and amber warning lights.

Traffic, directed by a policeman waving his flashlight, slowed to a turtle's pace. The two-lane road was reduced to a single lane. The eerie wail of sirens off in the distance pierced the darkness, nearing, as additional help raced to the scene. Every radio in the already present rescue vehicles belched out a female 911 dispatcher's voice, spewing forth co-ordinates for the scene of the wreck for the late responders.

Apparently, a minivan had spun out of control on a patch of treacherous black ice and slammed the passenger's side door into a utility pole, coming to rest half on and half off the road. Sparks crackled overhead, flying sporadically from an unhinged transformer now swinging precariously midway up the splintered pole. Firefighters swept broken window glass and tossed salt to the slippery pavement. Two paramedics were attempting to restrain and bandage a young mother's bleeding forehead as she fought them, mercifully screaming, "My baby! My baby! Where's my baby?"

The Kanes saw why the child's mother was frantic, driven to the point of hysterics; two more paramedics were performing CPR on a one-year-old child lying motionless on a stretcher. Blood oozed from the tiny baby's ears and nose.

"Oh, Dear God," Shelby said under her breath while watching the EMT perform chest compressions on the unresponsive little boy.

A second cop directed traffic on the backside of the accident. His face, from under the wide-brimmed hat, turned toward Christian's Bimmer as the cars crept slowly along the berm, crunching gravel under their tires.

The patrolman's eyes locked onto Christian's when the BMW was a mere ten feet away; Christian had his window down and the heater going full blast, trying to make the car smell better.

The officer snarled at Christian as he passed by, then barked out through the side of his mouth, "Buckle up, Kane!" The cop then smiled a self-satisfying sneer of sweet contempt.

Christian instantly recognized that unforgettable, lop-sided sneering face. *Fitzpatrick*!

Christian's heart skipped a beat as an icy chill thrashed his senses.

"What a terrible accident," Shelby said once they passed the scene, "I feel so bad for that poor mother, I hope her baby will be okay. What an awful thing to see."

Again, her comments had only half registered with her husband. Another piece of this nightmarish puzzle had just played into existence, pushing Christian under deeper still, furthering him from the reality he once knew.

"Huh? Yeah, right," Christian replied, wrestling with the demons gnawing away relentlessly at his mental stability. *"Buckle up, Kane!"*

"Just what in the Hell's going to be next?" He wondered as the chilling stranglehold of fear tightened in his guts.

Having just relived another fragmented portion of his dream, Christian became nauseated to the point of holding back a case of dry heaves.

First, there was centipedes, then a redheaded girl appears, named Rachel Petersen, nonetheless! Then, that smart-assed cop with an unforgettable obnoxious sneer and his remark echoing from the past.

Too many circumstances, Christian surmised, to be merely coincidental.

Just like a dog that viciously chases its own tail madly in never ending circles, this man's head was spinning when he wheeled his Bimmer into Sheraton's lot, as though his car was on autopilot.

Walking hand in hand to the door, a Bavarian version of the Chicken Dance Polka blared up and down The Monongahela River while a man could be seen throwing up fuzzy navels over the railing on The Gateway Princess.

Over the din of the crowd, Christian knowingly led Shelby to their reserved seats in the huge, packed banquet hall; they were to sit with Campbell, Rogerson, and their wives. Dave Campbell stood when Christian and Shelby walked up to the table. The two men shook hands; Campbell said, "God, Christian, I was beginning to wonder if you were going to show up for your big night."

An uneasy feeling cascaded over Christian as the chain of events unfolded exactly as he had dreamt, along with the conversation being damn near, *but not quite*, one hundred percent verbatim.

Campbell continued, "I like the tux. Nice touch."

Then he addressed Shelby before Christian had a chance to reply, "Wow! You're looking extra good tonight, Mrs. Kane. New hairdo? Losing weight are we?"

She gave Campbell a weak smile, "Thank you, Dave. Nope, same old cut," she said while watching in her peripheral vision Dave's wife Debbie, who was rather plain looking and fighting a losing battle of the bulge, give her slinky figure a quick once over from her blond curls all the way down to her high heels.

"Just like you warned us, they detoured us on to Smithfield Street," Christian interrupted Campbell to get his eyes off Shelby, "Did we miss anything?" he asked, pulling a chair out for his wife, seating her and then himself, facing the Campbells; then realizing he too, had just quoted himself!

"Not a damn thing, Christian. It's actually been boring as shit. You know how stuffy these Old Farts are. At least the drinks are free. And the appetizers are good."

"Yeah. They're excellent," Debbie interrupted in her nasal tone, as she popped a whole mushroom stuffed with crabmeat into her mouth.

Then with a muffled mouthful, "Try one, Shell; I saved these for you."

She pushed the plate towards Shelby. Only three were left. Moreover, they were ice cold.

"No thanks, maybe later. My stomach just started acting up. Probably just nervous about tonight."

"Well, uh, yeah. You two are like George and Weezy, ya know!"

Debbie then butchered the famous Jefferson's jingle while flailing her arms in the air and swaying her big ass, "Movin' on up... to the deluxe apartment in the sky... eye. Christian's got a piece of the pie... eye."

A tone of jealousy was just a bit too obvious in her voice. As was the fact she downed four Captain Morgan Spiced Rum and Cokes in thirty minutes, in between a plate and a half of appetizers.

Shelby didn't know what to make of her exhibition, however, Christian was expecting it, so they both forced a chuckle, along with her red-faced husband, who then shot a disgusted, warning glance at his wife.

The Senior Editor walked up to the podium; as he reached for the microphone, Christian said, "Cover your ears, everybody."

A high-pitched squeal blasted from the ceiling speakers when McKelvey turned on the microphone and began to emcee the party.

"He does that every year," Christian whispered, to answer the puzzled look plastered on the faces of everybody who had heard his remark.

"Good evening, everybody." All the guests cringed as his voice made the squelch louder, and rise an octave. He then tapped the mic a few times, which only added thumping noises to the cacophony; finally, he realized he was too close to the mic and backed his mouth away. To the delight of the partygoers, the shrieking stopped.

In an attempt to make light of the matter, McKelvey said, "Now that I have gotten everybody's attention. Good evening, Folks, and thank you all for being here tonight for The Post Gazette's annual dinner and awards banquet. On behalf of the stockholders, I am pleased to announce that 2022 was a banner year. Exceptional..."

Christian could not focus on McKelvey's rambling, monotone spiel because he had only one thought bouncing around inside his head, "*Who's getting the promotion?*"

Besides, he felt as though he had already sat through the Senior Editor's boring bullshit speech.

Christian's ears automatically perked up real quick when he heard the 'Old Geezer' say, "After forty-two years of continuous and dedicated service, it is with mixed emotions that I sadly, but joyfully, tell you all, that one of our beloved co-workers, and one of my dearest friends, has decided to retire. Please join me in giving a really big round of applause to... Max... Reynolds!"

"Max," McKelvey spoke into the mic once the crowd settled down, "Please. Come on up here to the podium." Max stood, then went front and center.

"My good friend, Max," McKelvey said as they shook hands, "I am advising everybody here tonight to dump their stock in the Gazette since you won't be working here anymore!"

After the dinner guests finished laughing, McKelvey continued, "Forty-two years. Forty-two... *Fine* years! Gosh, Max. How fast it goes, huh, buddy? Here's a little token of the Paper's appreciation." McKelvey handed the retiring gentleman a small box.

"I bet it's a trip to the Bahamas, and a check for five-thousand-dollars," Christian whispered in his wife's ear.

Max pulled the mic down to his level, "I really hope that it's not a gold watch. Because I already have two, but now that I said that... I think one doesn't work, and the other one is broken."

Again the crowd had a small bout of laughter while Max nervously fumbled to open the present.

He then pulled two cruise tickets to the Bahamas and a check for five thousand dollars from within the box.

A tear sprang from the old man's eye; the reality of retiring just smacked him in the face. He held the tickets and the check high in the air and spoke into the mic again, "Thank you, Bob, but I thought the Gazette had a banner year..."

Once Max finished his little speech about expecting to get a Tesla, then kissed his wife, and sat, McKelvey continued, "The Post has selected a fine young man to fill some pretty big shoes left by you, Max."

He then stopped and looked at Max, "They're about a size sixteen, aren't they, Max?"

Christian closed his eyes. He felt his heart pounding at two hundred beats per minute in his ears as he waited for McKelvey to make the announcement.

"Who's it going to be? Come on already, McKelvey! Spit it out!"

The hall fell completely silent.

Christian noticed Debbie popping the last stuffed mushroom into her mouth; he watched through tunnel vision as McKelvey's lips moved in slow motion.

Everything and everybody else in the hall faded away; only McKelvey's big fat face existed, his mouth slowly formed the words Christian was dying to hear.

"The Post has selected a very qualified, young, and aggressive writer to lead the sports team into the new year. He has been with us for quite some time now. Ladies and gentlemen, let's have another big round of applause; but this time for... The new Chief Sports Journalist of The Pittsburgh Post Gazette, Mister........"

The End

ABOUT THE AUTHOR:

LIVING IN WESTERN PENNSYLVANIA all his life, JT Baroni, now sixty-six, has been an avid Whitetail hunter since he was old enough to tote a rifle, which is also how long he has had an addiction to word games, and a fondness for literature.

When deer hunting one day, Jim actually did stumble upon this weathered tombstone in the middle of the woods one half mile from his house. While patiently waiting for that big buck to cross his path, he had plenty of time to think about that lone grave's inhabitant and ponder her story, which he then was driven to write. Eerily enough, this is the premise of The Legend of Rachel Petersen, his first novel.

Jim resides in Johnstown, Pennsylvania, a small town sixty miles east of Pittsburgh, where he and his wife, Becky, share their home with two Retrievers.

THE LEGEND OF RACHEL PETERSEN

[]